TIME SWITCH

Matt Chamings lives in Devon with his wife and four very noisy children. He studied archaeology at university and has had a variety of jobs, including being a hospital porter, genealogist, teacher and library assistant. He now divides his time evenly between writing, doing the housework and telling his kids to be quiet. He likes to write because it allows him to combine his love of stories with sitting around all day not doing much. His other interests include reading, going to church, watching films and supporting Leeds United.

MATT CHAMINGS

Time Switch

ff

faber and faber

First published in 2004
by Faber and Faber Limited
3 Queen Square London WC1N 3AU

Typeset by Faber and Faber Limited
Printed in England by Mackays of Chatham plc, Chatham, Kent

The right of Matt Chamings to be identified as author
of this work has been asserted in accordance with Section 77
of the Copyright, Designs and Patents Act 1988

A CIP record for this book
is available from the British Library

ISBN 0–571–22113–0

2 4 6 8 10 9 7 5 3 1

For Yvonne, who let me write
and didn't nag me to get a proper job – much

JULY 7TH, 1879

A small group of mourners stood around the open grave. The early morning mist had not yet cleared from the hillside graveyard of St Thomas's parish church and everything seemed unnaturally quiet – even the birds were still. A small white coffin had been lowered into its resting place and the bearers had retreated to a respectful distance. They stood with their heads bowed, their caps in their hands. Josiah Rawlings had insisted that the funeral should be private, so only he and his son Edward, the surviving members of the family, were there along with Wilkes the doctor and a few servants. Together they gathered to pay their last respects as William Rawlings was buried.

Quiet sobs could be heard from cook and nanny as the rector intoned the service but the menfolk were stony faced in their black morning suits. These were dangerous times and not even the rich could expect to escape personal tragedy. Even so, the loss of a wife and a son within five years seemed a cruel punishment to bear. Josiah stared straight ahead throughout the ceremony. His face showed no emotion except perhaps anger. Edward stared down at his feet and did not look up until the service was over and the mourners began to drift away. The gravediggers stepped forward to complete their task and soon the crunch of shovels in earth could be heard, breaking the morning peace.

Edward made a last attempt to speak to his father, but was immediately cut off.

'I have nothing more to say to you.' Josiah's voice was full of quiet fury. 'Your passage has been booked. You sail from Southampton on Tuesday morning.'

With that, the old man turned and walked back down the gravel path that led to the church gate. He and Edward never spoke again.

Jed Stokes was worried. The uneasiness had been nagging at him for weeks. Either something very strange was going on, or something was wrong with him and he did not know which he wanted it to be. He shifted the pile of books he was holding from one arm to the other as he turned the corner into his road and glanced nervously behind him. In his black trousers and white shirt, he looked just like any other schoolboy walking home with his tie loosened and his bag slung over his shoulder. But not many other boys had spent an hour after school at the library reading history books. It was not that Jed particularly liked history; he just had to find out what was going on behind his house.

Theirs had been one of the first houses built on the new Rawlings Estate. There were still JCBs and piles of bricks everywhere as he walked down his street. Dad said it was more like a building site than a housing estate. Mum was always grumbling that the windows were dirty again as soon as they had been cleaned. They joked as they said it but Jed knew they missed their old home. They all missed it. It had been a big, old, rambling house in the country called Little Moor. Surrounded by fields and woods with an enormous garden, it was completely different from the new estate with its rows of houses crammed in with barely any space between them. They would still be there now if it had not been so expensive to maintain. Jed scowled as he wished again that they had never moved. Strange things happened here.

Outside his home he turned again for a last anxious glance behind him. His nerves must be bad. He could not get it out of his mind that he was being followed. He shook

3

his head to clear his thoughts and pulling a key from his pocket he let himself in at the front door, slamming it behind him. As he disappeared inside a man in a brown overcoat stepped round the corner and walked up the street. He loitered for a few moments, leaning on a rubbish skip on the opposite pavement, his keen eyes watching the door Jed had just entered.

In the hall Jed threw his bag over the banister and dumped his pile of books at the foot of the stairs. Arthur, their red setter puppy, came bounding up to greet him, barking with excitement. 'Hello boy. Are you pleased to see me?' The affectionate dog cheered Jed up a little and he spent a few minutes playing with him. His sister, Lizzie, heard the noise and wandered out of the kitchen to see him. She had not been to school for a week because of a chest infection. Now that she was beginning to feel better she was bored at home.

'Where've you been?' she grumbled, coming straight to the point.

'Nowhere,' said Jed. He kept his head down as he stroked the dog and did not make eye contact with her.

'You're an hour and a half late. You can't have been nowhere.'

'Well it's none of your business where I've been, so leave me alone.'

Jed had spoken more fiercely than he meant to. He looked up at his sister. She looked hurt and he immediately regretted what he had said. 'Sorry,' he mumbled. 'Just don't ask. Please.'

He was quiet and distracted at teatime. The family of four sat around a huge pine table that nearly filled the room. It was too big for the new kitchen, but Mum had insisted on keeping it when they moved. Leaving Little Moor had been

4

hardest for her because she had grown up there. Dad as usual was providing most of the conversation, and Mum had to ask Jed three times if he wanted more mashed potato. When he finally said yes, she told him to help himself from the saucepan on the hob and he scraped back his chair. Dad was still speaking as Jed stood up.

'Did you know that nothing ever happens in this town? Nothing at all.' It was not the sort of question that needed an answer. Dad worked for the local newspaper and he often grumbled at some of the dull stories he had to cover.

'Don't wave your fork around while you're talking, dear,' said Mum. Dad lowered his fork and continued.

'No, seriously, I mean it. Last week the front page ran a story on increases in bus fares of all things. And do you know what this week's lead story is?'

'Finish your mouthful before you tell us,' said Mum. 'Lizzie, have you finished, dear? You ought to eat your beans if you can. You need to eat to get better.'

Lizzie pushed her plate away. 'I don't fancy them, Mum.'

Mum looked worried. She leaned over and put her hand to Lizzie's forehead. 'You ought to be shaking this infection off quicker than this. Are you sure you're taking your medicine properly?'

'Yeah, I think so,' Lizzie replied vaguely.

'Well, as you're all so clearly interested, I'll tell you,' Dad persisted. '"Ghost Sighting on Common".'

The entire family jumped with surprise – even Dad – and Mum gave a little cry.

'Oh Jed!' she said. 'It's all over the floor and on your uniform.' It was not the news story that had shocked them all. Jed had dropped the saucepan with a huge crash just as Dad had said the word ghost. Mum got up to clear the mashed potato off the floor. Jed mumbled an apology, saying the handle had been slippery. Lizzie looked at her brother thoughtfully.

'What sort of ghost?' Jed asked, when order had been restored to the kitchen.

'What?' asked Dad. 'Oh, I don't remember. Here, I've got the paper in my briefcase.' He pulled out his copy of the *Milford Gazette* and looked at the front page. 'A woman in a white dress. Well, that is original. Nearly as bad as the headless highwayman. I don't suppose anyone considered that there might simply have been a woman wearing a white dress on the common. Oh no, a ghost is a far more likely explanation.' Dad could be sarcastic sometimes.

After tea Jed went up to his bedroom. Like the kitchen it was much smaller than his old room, but he was getting used to it. Most of his things were unpacked and his posters were on the walls but it still smelt of new carpet. He threw the pile of books on to the bed and stood at the window, thinking about what he had found out. He was brooding minutes later when Lizzie entered. At thirteen she was a year younger than Jed, but she was tall for her age and many people mistook them for twins. They both had their father's dark hair and eyes, but it was Lizzie who had inherited his sharp wit.

'What *is* wrong with you, Jed?' she demanded. She stood in the doorway with her hands on her hips.

'Huh?' grunted Jed, coming out of his thoughts. 'Don't you ever knock?' he complained. 'I might have been changing.'

Lizzie waved this objection away. 'Seen it before. Now tell me, what is going on?'

'Nothing. Why?'

'Why?' asked Lizzie in disbelief. 'You've been acting weird for weeks. All grumpy and not answering questions. And today you start throwing mashed potato around the kitchen.'

6

Jed's eyes were fixed on the floor, so Lizzie crossed the room and tilted his chin up until she could look him in the eye. 'Jed, tell me straight. Are you in love?'

Despite his worries Jed couldn't help smiling. She was good at cheering him up. A glint appeared in his eye as he faced her. 'What does your girlie intuition tell you?' he teased.

'It tells me that someone is going to get a punch in the head unless he tells me what's been going on. Where were you after school?'

Jed thought for a minute. He badly wanted to tell someone what was on his mind, and he could normally talk to Lizzie about anything. The problem was that it was all so strange. He did not know how to tell her without sounding mad. He tried to work round to the subject gently.

'Do you know why this housing estate is called Rawlings?'

'Nope.'

'Nor did I until today. Griff mentioned the name in class and I asked him what it was. He said a couple of hundred years ago this town had a cotton mill and the owners were called Rawlings. They got really rich and owned a big house and a lot of land around here. I went to the library after school to find out more.'

'So that's where you were. I thought you were seeing some girl.'

Jed ignored the interruption. 'The house they lived in is that big one on the corner as you turn off the main road. The one with ivy growing on it. It's a nursing home now. Their grounds stretched all the way from there to the stream that runs down by the wood over there.' He pointed out of the window. 'I saw it on an old map. That's why the estate is called Rawlings. It's built on their land.'

'Well, that's interesting.' Lizzie could be sarcastic as well. 'Now get to the point.'

This was the part that was going to be difficult. Jed turned back to the window. Somehow what he had to say would be less embarrassing if he was not looking at his sister. 'I wanted to know what was here before the houses were built.'

'Why?'

'Because of something I saw.'

Lizzie was infuriated. 'Jed! You're still not making sense –' She broke off as her brother gripped her arm. 'Ow! That hurts. What is it?'

Jed had suddenly gone white, but he spoke quietly and urgently. 'Lizzie. This is really important. What do you see over there? Quick. Look.' He pointed to the area of wasteland between the end of their garden and the woods in the distance.

Lizzie looked. 'It's just a kid,' she said, turning back to Jed.

'No! Don't take your eyes off him,' pleaded Jed. 'Whatever you, do keep looking at him. Please.' Lizzie was about to argue but Jed sounded so anxious that she did as she was told. 'Now, do you notice anything odd about that kid?'

'Not as odd as the kid in this room,' muttered Lizzie, but after a few moments she said, 'He's dressed a bit strange. What's that white thing round his neck?'

Jed seemed a little relieved to hear Lizzie say this but he kept on. 'And what about where he's standing. What's different about that?'

Lizzie was beginning to catch some of Jed's panic now. The late afternoon sun had passed behind a cloud, throwing the view into gloom. But not where the boy stood. He remained bathed in a luminous glow. When Lizzie next spoke she sounded puzzled. 'It's lighter where he is, and the grass is a lot shorter. It's neat, just like a lawn. What's all this about? You're scaring me.'

'Just keep watching and you'll see.'

They stayed at the window for some minutes, never taking their eyes off the spot where the boy was standing. In the distance the small pale-faced boy stood still, staring straight ahead. He was dressed in a high, white collar and black jacket. His trousers reached just below his knees and he wore lace-up boots and long socks. Lizzie was beginning to fidget and was about to ask Jed again what it was all about when something happened that made her cry out in shock.

She turned to face her brother, white and shaking. The boy, who had been standing there so clearly moments before, had rippled slightly and then disappeared.

Will ran through the grounds of Rawlings House, his boots kicking up the gravel as he raced down paths and skidded around corners. Today was the first day of the summer holidays and he had ten whole weeks to fill, doing whatever he liked. There was boating and fishing and swimming in the lake. He could take the dogs rabbiting in the woods. Edward had promised to teach him photography this summer, and Father had promised him a bicycle. Today, though, he had different plans.

He slowed to a walk as he reached the vegetable gardens. Old George Harris was there as always, his cap pulled well down over his forehead. He was on his hands and knees thinning out the lettuces, but he quickly leaned back when he heard Will approaching.

'Morning, Master William. You'm up and about early today.'

'Can't waste time in bed, George. It's the holidays.'

n every day's a holiday for some,' teased George.
as indignant. 'That's not true. I'd far rather be dig-
garden like you than having to do Latin and arith-
d all that sort of rubbish.'

George laughed. 'I know you would, Master Will. I was only teasing. I expect you'd like something?' Will had only just finished breakfast but he quickly agreed. 'You'll find some strawberries over in that bed,' said George, waving his grimy hand to show where he meant. 'What are you up to today?'

'I'm off to the mill. I haven't been there for weeks.'

'Well, you can say hello to my Molly if you see her then, and you mind the machinery.' Will assured George he would be careful and thanking him for the strawberries he set off for the cotton mill.

He chose not to walk through town, but to follow the tow path along the canal. He stopped when he reached the waterway and lay on his stomach for a while swirling a stick through the weedy water, getting his jacket dusty as he did so. Some chub were feeding on the weed but soon scattered as Will churned up the surface. Before long he heard the approach of a barge and scrambled to his feet. The heavy shire horse strained at its harness as it pulled the boat along the canal. The horse's hoofs on the path, its heavy breathing and snorting, the creak of leather and the gentle splash of water were the only noises the huge vessel made. Will grinned. He knew the barge man and shouted to greet him.

'Morning, Jake. What have you got today?'

Jake's leathery face crinkled into a smile. 'Morning, Will. I got cotton bales for your father's place.'

'I'm going there. Can I ride with you?'

'You'd get there quicker walking, Will. There's the lock to do yet.'

'Oh please, Jake. I don't mind. I've got nothing to do today because I'm on holiday. I could help you.'

'All right then. Jump aboard. Mind, it's slippery.'

Will spent the next hour and a half helping the barge man. At the lock he leaped on to the bank and turned the great lever to swing the gates open. He waited as Jake slowly manoeuvred the barge through the gates, then he closed the gates after him. Next the sluice had to be opened and the barge slowly rose as the water bubbled and churned around it. Finally, when the water levels were even, the second set of gates could be opened and the barge was towed out into the final stretch of canal before Rawlings Mill. Will leaped back on board.

'Thank you, Will. I reckon that deserves a mug of tea.' The kettle was already boiling on an oil stove and soon Will and Jake were drinking tea out of tins. Will didn't really like tea, particularly not strong and black, but he drank it anyway because that was what barge men did.

'Where did you get the cotton from, Jake? Bristol?'

'Get on, Will. You know this canal don't go to Bristol. It's come from Liverpool. Taken me two weeks.'

'The train could do it in five hours.'

'Yes, but it would cost your father twice as much.'

The barge was approaching the mill now. The mill had its own channel which flowed through some huge wooden doors and into a big warehouse. Once through these doors the barge would be secured and the bales of creamy white, raw cotton would be unloaded. Jake would then make the return journey to Liverpool dock, where the great steel ships were forever unloading new cargoes from the Americas.

Rawlings Mill was huge. It was built of brick and was four storeys high. Two tall chimneys belched out black smoke as tons of coal each day were burned in the furnaces to make steam to drive the machinery. Will did not go to the engine room today though; he wanted to go into the workshop to see the great machines at work weaving the cotton into cloth. The noise was loud as he approached the building, but once through the doors it was deafening. Will had been terrified when he first went into the machine room but now he loved it even if he did come out with his ears ringing. His mother had never liked him visiting the mill. She had said it was too noisy and dirty and dangerous, which it was, but even aged seven he had loved to visit. Now he was twelve, he went where he liked, unless his father stopped him.

Great banks of looms filled the room, clanking like huge mechanical spiders spinning their webs. Huge leather belts were driving them, powered by the spinning shaft that was mounted along the ceiling, and oily cogs rumbled and groaned as they turned relentlessly. Before the safety guards had been fitted over them their constant grind had been the cause of some horrific accidents. More than one poor woman had been dragged into the machine when her loose hair or clothing became entangled. Even now it was not a safe place to work. Women could lose fingers if they were careless while untangling a twisted thread. And, as well as the scream of engine noise, a heavy cloud of dusty fibres constantly hung in the air. Many of the workers wore cloths over their mouths, but not all of them bothered and most suffered from weaver's cough.

Will wandered up and down the aisles for a while. The women smiled and waved to him as he passed. They could not talk because of the noise but they were always pleased to see him. He was a favourite with the mill workers because he visited them far more often than his father did. The twelve o'clock whistle sounded, the machinery ground to a halt and there was quiet for a brief spell. The women had half an hour for their lunch break. Will found George's daughter, Molly, and passed on her father's greeting and some of the strawberries. They were squashy by now but she was grateful.

Will was just thinking he ought to go home when a voice called to him from across the room.

'William, what on earth are you doing down there? Come here at once.'

It was his father.

It was some moments before either Jed or Lizzie spoke after the boy vanished. Lizzie was shocked and did not know what to say. Jed, though, felt more relieved than frightened. He had seen the boy disappear before and he was comforted to know that it really had happened – that he was not going mad. Lizzie sat down on Jed's bed before speaking.

'That kid just disappeared.' She could not keep the tremble out of her voice.

'I know,' agreed Jed. 'I've seen him before.'

'But people don't just disappear. Unless . . .' Lizzie was too embarrassed to say what she was thinking, so Jed finished for her.

' . . . they're a ghost?'

'Yeah,' she said with a weak smile. 'You haven't seen the woman in white, have you?'

'No. I'm not sure that boy is a ghost either. I know he disappears but he doesn't behave much like one.'

'I know what you mean.' Lizzie agreed. 'Ghosts are s'posed to drift about moaning, aren't they?'

'I dunno about that, but this one took a photo of me.'

'What? You're joking.'

'No, really. I've seen him twice before. First time was about two weeks ago and he just stood there like today. He only seems to stay about three or four minutes each time. But last week he had one of those old cameras with him. You know the big box on three legs where the photographer has to get under a black cloth to take the picture?' Lizzie nodded and Jed continued.

'I was doing some homework and I'd had enough so I got up and looked out the window. A minute later he was just there. He appears just like he disappears. I watched him the whole time. The grass around him was short and neat like a lawn. The camera was already set up and pointing this way. He took a cover off the front of the camera. Then he looked at a watch for about thirty seconds – one of those big watches on chains, not on his wrist. Then he put the cover back on and a couple of minutes later he was gone.'

'That *is* weird for a ghost,' Lizzie agreed. The shock was passing now and some of her sense of humour was returning. 'I don't s'pose you tried making a sign of the cross and saying "Begone unrestful spirit", did you?'

Jed laughed and it was his turn to look embarrassed. 'Well, I might have.'

Lizzie noticed the books on Jed's bed. One was called *A History of Milford*. Another was called *Milford through the Ages*. The rest had similar titles. 'So that's why you wanted to know what went on here before,' she said. 'You've been ghost hunting. And that's why you jumped when Dad said the word ghost. Have you discovered anything?'

'Not much more than I've already told you,' said Jed. 'The books all talk about the Rawlings family, but there's no ghost story or murders or anything. The last person who owned the house was called Josiah Rawlings. He died about 1900 and then the house was sold. There's a picture of the family in this book.' He flicked through the pages and showed his sister the old brown and white photograph. Josiah looked about fifty years old, with grey hair and enormous sideburns. He wore a long jacket over a waistcoat, similar to the clothes bridegrooms often wear at their weddings nowadays. He was pictured with his wife, who had fair hair and looked about ten years younger than her husband. There was also a boy of about twelve or thirteen. A baby about a year old sat on the mother's knee. Lizzie read the caption.

'"Josiah Rawlings, nineteenth-century industrialist. Pictured here with wife Sophia and sons Edward and William."' She studied their faces. 'He had two sons.'

'Well?'

'Well, why did you say Josiah was the last and that the house was sold when he died?'

'I dunno. I only told you what I read. Perhaps the boys died. Nearly everyone died young then of plague or dirty water or something.'

'Well, if they died,' said Lizzie cautiously, 'perhaps one of them is our ghost boy.' They both studied the picture.

'He's wearing clothes that look about right, but it's not that one,' said Jed at last, pointing at the older boy. 'He's got dark curly hair. The boy we saw had straighter, lighter hair.'

'Maybe it's the other then. How are we going to find out?'

'I don't think these books are going to tell us any more,' said Jed. 'The woman at the library said if I wanted to find out anything else, I would have to go to the records office. They've got old newspapers and stuff. I was going to try there tomorrow.'

'I'll come with you,' said Lizzie. Jed smiled. It was good to have someone to share the secret with.

*

Next day was Saturday. Jed and Lizzie often went into town with their friends although not usually so early. If Mum was curious about what they were up to, she didn't say anything. She took Lizzie's temperature and listened to her breathing. When everything seemed normal she let them go.

'It'll do you good to get out,' she told Lizzie. 'Make sure you're back for lunch, or call me.' The two assured their mother they would and then they were gone.

At half-past nine they were standing on the pavement outside the old brick building that held the town records. Ivy hung on the walls and the sign over the heavy wooden doors read 'Milford Borough Archive'.

'Never been here before,' said Jed.

'No,' said Lizzie. 'Looks pretty crusty.' Jed nodded in agreement. He pushed open the tall, wrought-iron gate which creaked on its hinges as the two made their way into the old building.

Inside, the records office appeared even more intimidating. The ivy grew partly over the large windows, casting a greenish, eerie light across the room. Three or four old people sat in front of screens that were displaying old-fashioned writing. A few more sat at wooden desks, poring over ancient-looking volumes bound in crumbly leather. At least one old man was snoring and one of the women was definitely talking to herself. Many of them turned as the two children entered. They stared for a moment, frowning in disapproval, before returning to their reading. They grumbled a little to each other.

'What *are* these people?' whispered Lizzie in disbelief.

'Dunno,' muttered Jed. 'People doing history, I suppose.' Nervously they approached the woman behind the reception desk. 'Please, can you help us?' Jed asked quietly.

'What?' boomed the woman, making them both jump.

'You can speak up. There's no need to whisper.' She was dressed in a tweed skirt and horrible cardigan and smelt of cough medicine. 'Don't worry about waking Mr Jenkins. He always sleeps until lunch-time. Then they come and take him back to his nursing home. What can I do for you both?'

'We want to find out about a man called Rawlings, please. He died about a hundred years ago.'

The woman frowned over her glasses. 'You're a little young to be interested in family history, aren't you? Why aren't you outside playing football or writing on walls or something?' Jed was confused.

'I don't know. I mean I don't think I am interested in family history. I just want to find out about this man.'

'It's a school project,' Lizzie lied. The woman softened.

'Ah! That's all right then.' She clearly approved of school projects. 'It'll be nice to have some young faces around. Make a change from the usual mob doing their family research. Rawlings you say? Do you mean the ugly old fella who used to own the cotton mill?'

'Yes,' said Jed excitely, 'do you know something about him?'

'A little. He died about the turn of the last century. There's a statue of him in the park. His house is a nursing home now.'

'Yes, we know most of that,' said Lizzie. 'We wanted to find out about his sons really.'

'You'll have to do some searching, I'm afraid. One of you could read through the old newspapers. We've got an index that will help you find all the references to Rawlings. That might tell you something. The other one could read the census returns. They record all the people who lived here every ten years, so you can find out exactly what they were up to. After that we've got some of the family papers you might want to look through. You know, letters and diaries, that sort of thing.'

The woman burst into activity. She stood up and started rummaging through drawers for the rolls of film that recorded the census information. She shouted across the room while she was doing this. 'All right, Mr Harris, you'll have to get off that machine now. These children need it for their school project.'

Mr Harris was apparently the trembly old man in the corner, wearing a woolly overcoat and fingerless gloves. 'But I've only been here ten minutes,' he whined.

'Don't be selfish, Mr Harris. You know very well you come here every day and you're too blind to read anything anyway.' Still grumbling, Mr Harris began shuffling his papers together.

'We don't want to be any trouble,' said Jed quickly. 'We can come back later.'

'Nonsense. No trouble at all,' said the woman, showing Jed how to read an old census form.

As soon as Jed was engrossed in his task, the woman moved an old ledger away from the sleeping Mr Jenkins who had begun to dribble and showed Lizzie where to find the old newspaper volumes and the drawer of index cards. Soon she too was looking eagerly through old copies of *The Milford Weekly Intelligencer* for any information she could find on the Rawlings family. She was sitting next to the old woman who was muttering to herself but she smelt funny so Lizzie moved up the table.

After about three-quarters of an hour Lizzie was growing restless. She went over to see how Jed was progressing. Jed looked up as she approached. 'Any luck?' he asked.

'Not much,' replied Lizzie. 'I found loads of stuff about him being mayor and giving some land to build a library on but nothing to help us. Now my eyes are going funny. How about you?'

'Pretty good,' said Jed. He showed his sister what he had found. 'Look, here's Josiah Rawlings in 1851. He was 30 then and not married. Here he is again in 1861. By then he's got a wife, Sophia, and they've got a son called Edward aged five. In 1871 Edward is fifteen and William's been born. He's four.'

'That picture in the book must have been taken a couple years before then,' observed Lizzie.

'Yeah,' agreed Jed. 'I'm just looking at 1881 now.'

Jed wound the reel round until he came to the entry for Rawlings House. They both read through it. 'That's weird,' said Lizzie. 'He's on his own apart from servants. There's no sign of the rest of the family. Something must have happened to them.'

'He's got a W next to his name,' said Jed. 'That might mean widow. Sophia must have died.'

'Widower,' Lizzie corrected her brother. 'Women are widows, men are widowers.'

'Whatever.' Jed could not be bothered about grammatical errors while he was ghost hunting. 'Edward would have been twenty-something by then so he might have left home.'

'Yeah,' Lizzie agreed, 'but that still leaves William who would be fourteen. He should be there.' They were puzzling over this when Lizzie noticed something else. 'Oh look. One of the servants is called John Stokes,' she said, pointing. 'I wonder if he's our great-great-granddad.'

'Don't let that woman hear you say that,' warned Jed. 'She doesn't seem to like family history. I think most of these old people here are finding out about their ancestors, so you can understand why she gets fed up with it. Look out, she's coming over.'

A rustle of tweed and a smell of menthol announced her arrival. She had brought the box of family documents for them to look at. Before long, the two were hard at work again, searching through old papers for any clue. After about five minutes Lizzie gave up. 'This is no good,' she complained, 'I can't read the handwriting.'

'It is pretty hard,' agreed Jed. 'I can just about decipher it.'

'Well, you're used to bad handwriting.'

Jed ignored the insult and passed his sister a small red book. 'Here, try this. I think it's some sort of diary but there's some drawings in it as well. I'll carry on with these letters.' They worked on for another twenty minutes before Jed looked up again. 'I think Josiah and Edward must have argued about something. There's a very angry letter here from Josiah blaming Edward for something, and there's a very short and unfriendly note from Edward asking for his luggage to be sent on. The address says Durban. I think that's in Africa somewhere, so perhaps he moved away and that's why he's not in the census after 1871. What've you found?'

'This is pretty good,' said Lizzie. 'It's got Edward Rawlings written inside the cover and a date, 1879. There's all sorts in it. The first half is mostly pictures. Drawings of plants and machinery and stuff. Then there's some notes I can't read and some maths equations. I think he must have been a scientist or something. At the back there's a sort of diary and it's written neater so I can make most of it out. Don't know what most of it means though.' The two looked through the entries together. The dates were written in the margin and the entries varied in length from a couple of words to a few lines. 'What does this mean?' asked Lizzie. '"Apparent success. Cannot be sure but definite field weakening and visual disturbance."'

'Dunno,' said Jed, 'sounds scientific though. What about

this one? They get weirder. "Successful rabbit transport." I reckon he must have been a mad scientist. That would explain why he's not there in 1881. He could have been in a mental home.'

'Look,' cried Lizzie, excitedly pointing at the entry for June 11th. '"Have told Will all."'

'Well?' asked Jed, not sharing his sister's excitement.

'Don't you see. Will is short for William. His brother William must have been still alive and well in 1879. He'd have been about twelve by then.' They read some more. Jed pointed out an entry further on.

'"July 2nd. Will gone. Do not know what to tell Father. July 3rd. Cannot recover Will but dog returned. Hodges knows and is threatening to tell Father. Father certain to be furious when he finds out."'

'This sounds bad,' said Lizzie. 'What do you reckon he did to Will?'

'No idea. Do you think he killed him by accident?'

'Could have.' Neither said it, but both thought it. A boy killed when he was twelve fitted their ghost theory very well. Lizzie broke that train of thought when she made another discovery. 'Hey, look. There's our name again. "July 4th. Disaster. Father increasingly suspicious. Machine broken. Stokes child. Father must not find out."'

'What was he up to? It sounds like he's done something to another kid as well. Funny that our name should be there though. I wonder if there are lots of people called Stokes.'

There were no more diary entries on that page, but what was written next left them in no doubt that Edward Rawlings was certainly mad. '"*Nota Bene*. The moon of the Emperor Julius meets the merry god of agriculture on two crosses and two straights."' Jed read the entry, completely baffled by it. 'The man was a complete nutcase. "At a solitary hour, meet in Minerva's lair. There the passage can occur." What is he talking about?'

'I dunno.' Lizzie was as confused as Jed. 'I wouldn't want to meet him, though. He must have been off his trolley.' She shivered at the thought of young Will having a dangerous lunatic as a brother.

They turned the page to read on but the page was blank. Jed flicked forward, but the last third of the book was completely empty. 'That's it,' he said. 'Weird. Wonder why he stopped writing.'

'Probably because he was arrested or locked up in a padded cell,' said Lizzie wryly.

Jed laughed. There did not seem much more they could do. When the nursing home help came to wheel Mr Jenkins away, they decided they might as well go home too. They tried to thank the woman at the desk for her help but she was too busy. There was a man waiting for attention who was wearing a brown overcoat and holding what looked like a Personal Digital Assistant or palm-top computer. He seemed absorbed by what was displayed on the screen but he watched the children out of the corner of his eye. The assistant, meanwhile, was talking to another man who was much younger. He had a pleasantly tanned face and his hair was dark and curly. He was quizzing the woman about his ancestors while she frowned at him in disapproval. His accent was strange to Jed. It wasn't quite like Australian. It might be South African.

Josiah Rawlings sat frowning at the desk in his library. He had dated his letter June 11th, 1879, but he was distracted and had written nothing for the past five minutes. Everything about the room suggested that the occupier was a successful man. The walls were lined with oak panelling except where heavy, leather-bound volumes were mounted on shelves. The floor was covered in a rich, thick carpet and in the corner stood a marble statue of the Roman goddess, Minerva. The goddess of wisdom – she was a worthy patroness of any library.

Josiah was certainly a man who had little left in life to aim for. He was one of the richest men in the county. He was well respected and had twice been made mayor of Milford. His wife had been beautiful and charming, the daughter of an earl. His son had graduated from Oxford with a first class degree. His frown deepened at the thought of his son. Apart from the loss of his dear wife, the conduct of his elder son was causing him more grief than anything else. He leaned over to a cord that hung from the ceiling behind his desk and gave it a tug. Minutes later a servant arrived.

'You rang, sir?'

'Yes, Stokes. Send Mr Edward to see me, would you?'

'Very good, sir.'

Josiah busied himself with his letter until his son arrived. He did not look up until it was finished and signed, even though Edward had entered the room and stood waiting. 'You wanted to see me, Father,' the young man muttered, when finally he had his father's attention. In many ways the two men who faced each other across the desk were similar. Both had thick, curly hair, although Josiah's was grey now. Both had a slightly hooked nose and a determined look in their eyes. But where Josiah looked the image of respectability in his morning coat and gold watch, Edward had his shirt sleeves rolled up, his hair was uncombed and there was a smudge of oil on his face. It was this that Josiah commented on first.

'Yes, I wanted to see you, but not looking like a coal miner. There's dirt all over your face.'

Edward scowled but took out a handkerchief and rubbed his face. 'Is that all you wanted to say or was there a good reason for dragging me up here?' he asked sullenly.

'That's enough of your impertinence, young man! You're living under my roof and eating my food so you'll have the courtesy to do as I say.' Josiah glared at his son.

Edward glared back but eventually controlled his temper and gave a grudging reply, 'Yes, Father. I'm sorry.'

Josiah continued, 'As it happens, I did have good reason for calling you up here. I want to know if you have considered my proposition.'

Edward groaned. 'Again, Father? You must know my feelings on this. We've discussed it before and I thought I made my opinion plain last time we spoke.'

'Yes, you made your opinion plain, but you could give me no sensible reason for it. Now tell me, have you reconsidered?'

Edward summoned as much patience as he could and told his father again. 'I'm sorry, Father. I know it disappoints you but I don't wish to direct the mill when you're gone and I see no reason for me to learn the business now.'

'Then what do you intend to do?' Josiah retorted angrily. 'What have you done with yourself this last year since coming down from university, eh? Tell me what use you've been?' Edward did not get a chance to tell his father before he continued. 'I'll tell you what you've done. You've fiddled about in that laboratory of yours looking through microscopes and taking pictures and making machines that don't appear to do anything useful.'

Edward's temper could be as quick as his father's. 'If by "useful" you mean will they make you richer by weaving cloth quicker then I admit they're no use at all.' Here he leaned over the desk until father and son were almost nose to nose. 'But there's more to life than cotton and shuttles and twills and whatever else they do up at that hell hole you call the mill.' The two glowered at each other until Josiah sat back in his chair.

'I thought Oxford would make a useful man of you. I clearly thought wrong.'

'You also thought a son at Oxford would do your reputation no harm.'

Josiah leapt to his feet and took his son by the shirt. His voice was low and menacing as he spoke. 'Are you accusing me of being a proud man? Why, if you are, you're not too old for me to take a stick to you, you ungrateful boy. Don't tell me I sent you to Oxford for my sake. You know very well you wanted to go.'

Edward held his father's gaze for a moment, then looked away. When he spoke again his voice was calm. 'Yes, I asked to go,' he admitted. 'And I loved every moment of it. And I don't mean to appear ungrateful to you or the mill for giving me an education. It's just that there's so much in the world that is more exciting than weaving cotton. I'm sorry, Father.'

Josiah sighed. The Rawlings were quick to anger but quick to cool again and they seldom held grudges with each other for long. He had to admit that Edward was a lot like himself. That is probably why they argued so often. He could remember similar confrontations with his own father and knew that as a young man nothing would persuade him to change his mind either. He tried a different approach.

'Come here, son,' he said and led Edward over to the wall where a series of family portraits hung in big gold frames. There was Josiah in pride of place with his mayor's robes and chain on. There was Sophia, his late wife looking pretty and delicate in the blue ball gown he had ordered her from Paris. Her fair hair fell in ringlets around her neck and she was wearing the silver locket that had been her mother's. Both father and son lingered sadly over her painting. Even after five years they still felt her absence deeply.

Then they came to portraits of people Edward did not recognize. 'Know who that is?' asked Josiah pointing to a full-length figure pictured with an old-fashioned rifle and hunting dog. Edward could see the family likeness but shook his head. 'That's my grandfather. He was called Josiah too. You won't remember him of course. He built the first Rawlings mill back in 1793. It was a small affair then. His father had only been a weaver, but the son became a mill owner.' They moved on to another portrait. This one was dressed in a stiff white collar and tall black hat. 'What about him? You may remember him.'

'Grandfather?' guessed Edward.

'That's right. Another Josiah. He took over the mill when his father died. He did so well that within ten years he had moved to a new site and built a bigger mill. The one we have today. Your grandfather also had this house built. I remember it as a boy. It took two and a half years to finish. The stone came by barge all the way from Wales. This used to be his study.' They moved back to the portrait of the current Josiah. 'And here am I. I took over the mill when your grandfather died, as you know. I've invested in new machinery and expanded the premises. I had to borrow heavily but it's all been paid back. Rawlings Mill is now the largest employer in Milford and I am the first Rawlings to become mayor and you are the first Rawlings to go to university.'

Edward could see where the speech was heading and tried to divert his father. 'Why aren't I called Josiah, Father?'

'What? Oh, that was your mother's doing. I wanted Josiah of course, but she couldn't stand the name. She wanted Edward after her father. I let her have her way in the end. Kept her happy, and the old boy.' Edward warmed to his father when he heard this. However much he denied it Josiah was clearly a proud man and proud of his family. He must have loved his wife very much to have abandoned that particular family tradition. 'The point I am making,' said Josiah, not to be diverted for long, 'is this. For three generations Rawlings Mill has been handed down from father to son, and each generation has made it bigger and better than the last. Now tell me who is going to run the mill when I am gone?'

'Will,' suggested Edward. 'He loves the place.'

Josiah sighed again and after a pause he reluctantly accepted defeat. 'Yes, perhaps William might. Although I think he would rather operate a barge or some other nonsense. I had to speak to him only yesterday about spending all his time with mill workers and servants. Absolutely filthy he was. He'd been on a barge all morning.'

Edward quickly made his way back to his laboratory after his father had dismissed him. The air had been cleared for the time being, but Edward did not suppose he had heard the last of Josiah's views on his son's responsibilities. One thing Josiah had said was certainly true. Edward did spend most of his time 'fiddling about' in his laboratory. He had been in the middle of something exciting when Stokes had called him and he was keen to get back. The experiment with the rabbit had been successful a few days before and he was in a position to try again today.

His laboratory was not in the main house but in a remote part of the grounds. It was not much more than a wooden hut, built on a stone slab floor. He had had it built so far from the house to avoid being interrupted too often. As soon as he arrived he began taking readings from gauges and dials on a metal box that was resting on his bench. With each reading he would make small adjustments of the levers on a much larger box that was on the floor. He had not done more than five minutes' work when he heard the door swing open. He groaned, but the frown left his forehead as he turned to see who was there.

'Hello, Will,' he smiled.

Although he was eleven years older, Edward and his brother had become good friends. He and Will were quite different in looks and temperament. Will was more delicate-looking, like his mother, with straight fair hair. He did not have his father's quick temper as his brother did. It was hard not to like Will.

'What did Father want with you?' he asked.

'Is nothing a secret?' laughed Edward. 'How did you know I had been summoned?'

'Stokes told me.'

'Did he? Don't let Father know you've been mixing with the servants again. You know he doesn't like it. If you must know, Father wanted me to give up my life's ambition to become the greatest scientist the age has known and become a cotton mill owner. I declined the proposition, again. I said you'd do it instead.'

If Will was interested in becoming a rich industrialist, he showed no sign of it. He was already busy, studying the interesting things Edward had in his laboratory. He liked the stuffed animals in their glass cases best and he spent some minutes looking at them with their fur and claws and beady glass eyes. The largest case contained a magnificent eagle with its wings fully extended. It had been arranged in the act of swooping on to a kill. The poor little weasel was already struggling in its talons. Will noticed that there were titles written on little plaques mounted on the glass.

'*Aquila*,' he said slowly, struggling with the unusual word. 'What does that mean?'

'Come now, Will,' his brother answered. 'Surely you know that. What have you been learning in your Latin classes all year?'

'Oh, it's Latin, is it? I'm not much good at that.' His face was downcast for a moment but then it brightened again and a wild glint appeared in his eye. 'But I do like the stories about Roman armies and gladiators.' Glancing down he saw some metal rods that Edward had been using to construct his machinery. Seizing a longish one, he challenged his brother. 'I'm Julius Caesar and you're a barbarian so arm yourself quickly.'

Edward grinned and looked at Will's makeshift sword. 'That's a bit long for a Roman sword, isn't it? They used short stabbing swords, about this length.' He selected a much shorter rod and brandished it in front of his brother.

Will compared the two rods. 'Very well,' he said. 'I'll be the barbarian and you can be Caesar with his silly little sword.' With that Will charged at his brother who quickly parried the blow. Metal clanged against metal as they fought back and forwards around the laboratory, and sparks occasionally flew as their swords clashed. The room rang with shouts of laughter as they swung wildly at each other and there were some very near misses, particularly next to the glass cabinets. It was only when Will had his brother trapped in a corner that Edward finally called a halt.

'I surrender,' he cried, his face red and his breath short. 'The might of Rome has fallen to the barbarian horde.'

'I'm not a horde,' Will protested. 'You can't have a horde of one.'

'Whatever you say,' said Edward, bending over and resting his hands on his knees as he slowly recovered.

'So what does *aquila* mean?' Will persisted.

'Eagle.'

'Oh. I could have guessed that. Why not write it in English so everyone can understand it?'

'Scientists always label species in Latin. It's so that whatever language they normally speak, they will know they are talking about the same thing.' He stood up and wiped the sweat off his brow. 'Anyway, Will, much as I enjoyed that little battle, I'd like to get back to work on my latest invention if I may.' He gave a little flourish of his hand to indicate what he meant.

The big machine that Edward had been working on was intriguing. It was made out of a large polished wooden case held together with brass rivets. There was a series of dials and levers across one side of it. The other side was connected by cables to some sort of metal drum. On top of the machine were coils of copper wire and sockets for more cables.

'What does it do?' Will asked, as he studied the strange dials.

'Well, it doesn't weave cotton,' said Edward, laughing, 'much to Father's disgust.'

Will sensed that Edward was hiding something from him. 'Come on. Tell me what it does.'

Edward stopped laughing and considered. 'I could tell you, but you may not believe me.'

'I would.'

Edward made a decision. 'I might tell you, then, but let me show you something else first.' He went over to a desk in the corner and picked up a wooden box which he brought back to Will. 'Here,' he said, 'look at these.'

Will rummaged through the box. 'Why, they're photographs,' he said. Here's a view of the house and here's one of me. I remember you taking these last summer.'

'That's right,' said Edward. 'Now look at the others. I took them not long after I photographed you.'

'These aren't very good,' Will said critically as he examined them. 'This one's all foggy and this one is odd. It seems to have more than one picture on top of each other. They're all like that.'

'Yes,' agreed Edward, 'and now look at this last one.' He took a photograph out of an envelope and handed it to Will, looking slightly tense. Will took it, puzzled by his brother's behaviour. He was about to reject it as just another strange print when he realized what he was holding. It was another confused image with a view of the house overlaid by other things. Most of it he could not make out, but the bottom right hand corner was a little clearer than the rest. There was quite obviously a woman standing near the west wing of the house. Will's hands trembled and he spoke quietly.

'It's a picture of Mother.'

'Yes,' said Edward.

'But you said you took all these pictures last summer.'

'That's right. I did.'

Will looked up at his brother wide-eyed. 'But Mother's been dead for five years.'

When they had finished at the records office, Jed and Lizzie returned home on the bus. It was an uneventful journey until they got to the nursing home, which was one stop before theirs. There was some hold-up at the front as the driver argued with an old man about the fare. The sound of the driver's angry voice drifted up the bus.

'No! You've come too far. You can't get off until you pay the rest.'

'What's that?' came the old man's voice.

The argument continued but Jed and Lizzie were not listening. The delay had given them a chance to look more closely at the home through the bus window. They had passed it hundreds of times on their way to school but had never paid much attention to it. It was certainly a huge house for just one family. Josiah Rawlings must have been a very wealthy man. There was a short drive up to the main entrance which was impressive. Marble steps led up to double wooden doors flanked by two pillars. Stone lions sat at the foot of each pillar. The two wings of the building stretched off into the distance and rose three storeys high. Only the chair lift on the steps and the sign above the door that said 'Rawlings House Nursing Home' showed that this was no longer the private home of a successful businessman.

'Wow! He must have been rich,' said Jed.

'Yeah,' agreed Lizzie, her eyes scanning the vast number of windows. 'I wonder which was poor Will's room.'

'You needn't call him "poor Will". We don't know his brother killed him.'

'Well, something strange happened to him. What has this bus stopped for?' Brother and sister peered down the aisle to see what was happening. The driver and old man were still arguing.

'I know you only paid 87p yesterday,' the driver was saying loudly, 'but that was yesterday. See that notice? That's been there for six weeks that has. You can't tell me you didn't know that the fares was going up.'

'I can't see,' wheezed the old man. 'It's me eyes. They don't see too good.'

The driver was not sympathetic. 'That's not my problem. My problem is you owe me 9p.'

'But I ain't got 9p.'

'That's the old man from the records office, isn't it?' said Lizzie.

Jed looked. 'Yeah, it's Mr Harris who had to get off the machine so we could have a go. Shall we help him?'

Jed and Lizzie made their way down to the front of the bus. 'Why can't you let Mr Harris off the bus?' asked Lizzie.

The driver gave her an irritated look. 'Because he owes me 9p.'

'But he hasn't got 9p,' reasoned Jed. 'Go on, let him off.'

'No. He tries this every time the fares go up. 87p only got him as far as the hospital. He's come two stops too far.'

'Well, how about this,' offered Lizzie. 'He's come two stops too far, and we've both got one more stop to go. Mr Harris can have our stops and we'll all get off now.'

The driver pursed his lips. You were not strictly allowed to give half your journey to someone else, but he couldn't see Mr Harris handing over the 9p any time soon and he wanted to get on with the journey. Then Mr Harris started to have a coughing fit. That settled it. He did not want a heart attack or worse on his hands. He waved them all off. 'All right, get off then, but remember it's 96p tomorrow.' The bus roared off and Mr Harris peered at the two children through thick glasses.

'Here, ain't you the two kids from the records office?'

'Yeah,' said Jed, 'we're sorry that woman pushed you off the machine this morning. We didn't ask her to.'

Mr Harris turned and started his walk to the front door. 'That's all right. She's right. I am too blind to read anything.'

'Shall we see you to the front door?' asked Lizzie who was keen to get a closer look at the house.

'Thank you, miss. That'd be kind.'

The three walked up the drive, the gravel crunching beneath their feet. Mr Harris walked very slowly so they had a good chance to look around. There were statues and disused fountains in the gardens and an old summer house covered in ivy.

'Imagine living here,' said Jed.

'I do live here,' puffed Mr Harris.

'No, I meant imagine living here as the only family. Being rich and having all those servants and stuff.'

'Oh, you mean like old Rawlings who used to own the place.'

'That's right,' said Lizzie excitedly. 'Did you know him?'

'No. I might be old but I ain't that old. My old dad did though. He used to be a gardener here, and Granddad did too.' They had reached the front door by now. Mr Harris put his hand in his pocket and pulled out a pound coin. 'Here, have this for your trouble.'

'What?' said Jed in disbelief. 'You said you didn't have 9p for the bus driver.'

'Weren't going to give no ruddy bus driver 9p,' said Mr Harris obstinately, and he shuffled inside.

It was Dad who provided them with the next lead the following Tuesday. Mum was working a late shift at the children's hospital where she was a nurse and so Dad had cooked tea. The three of them were eating their shepherd's pie when Dad started his moan about work again.

'You'll never guess what I am this week. Rob Stokes, Psychic Sleuth, investigator of the bizarre, the unexplained and the downright stupid.' His two children looked at each other. Their Dad was weird.

'Now I remember why I never bring friends home,' said Lizzie.

'Yeah. What are you talking about, Dad?' asked Jed.

'You remember last week. The phantom woman in white haunting the common? According to the residents of Milford she is not the only restless soul to haunt this troubled town.'

'Do you mean people have seen other ghosts?'

'You name it, they've seen it. As well as the woman in white, we have the black hound, the phantom monk and, you won't believe this one, the disappearing bunny rabbit. I've got to do a follow-up story for next week's edition so I have to interview some of these cranks.'

Jed and Lizzie were curious to know if anyone else had seen their ghost but did not want to ask their father outright about him.

'Who are you going to see, Dad?' asked Jed.

'Well, the only story that seems to have any credibility is one about a boy.' Lizzie and Jed exchanged excited glances. 'Two or three people claim to have seen him and their stories seem to agree. They say a boy of about twelve in Victorian clothing appears briefly and then off he goes again, into the shades or wherever.' Jed was frantically trying to remember when Victorian times were and what sort of clothes they wore. He hazarded a guess.

'Victorian? Was that 1800 and something?'

'1837 to 1901,' Dad said irritably. 'I thought you'd been studying Victorians this term.'

Jed shrugged. 'Yeah, well, I can't be expected to remember everything.'

Dad shook his head sadly. 'If I had the money, Jed, you would go to a good school. What was I talking about?'

'About a ghost boy.'

'Oh yes. One old man says he's even got a picture he took of the phantom child, so I'm going to interview him tomorrow.'

Lizzie's heart was pounding but she tried not to sound too interested. 'Will you get a copy of his photo?'

'I'll certainly try. That all depends on whether the old man will let me. He sounded like an awkward customer. He's called Harris. He lives in the nursing home on the corner.'

Jed and Lizzie could barely contain their excitement but they had to wait until after tea before they could talk about it. They were both in Jed's room. Lizzie was sprawled on the bed, but Jed stood looking out of the window, which he often did now.

'Well, things are fitting together a bit now,' said Lizzie. '1879 is Victorian so if Will Rawlings is the boy we've seen, he'll be wearing Victorian clothing.'

'Yeah and if Dad can get hold of a picture from old Mr Harris then we'll be able to tell if we've been seeing the same boy. I hope Dad doesn't upset him. It's obvious that Dad doesn't believe any of this and if he starts joking then Mr Harris will get all grumpy like he did with the bus driver.'

'Perhaps we could ask Mr Harris,' suggested Lizzie. 'He likes us.' Jed did not answer. He was peering intently out of the window. 'What's up? Is he there again?' Lizzie quickly joined Jed at the window.

'No. I thought for a second he was. Made me jump. But there's a man down there acting a bit funny.'

The man below was certainly behaving strangely. He was a young man with dark, curly hair and he kept looking at a small piece of paper in his hands. He would look up and move a bit and then study his paper again. Finally he came to stand almost exactly where the ghost boy had stood and he looked up again. This time he stared up into the window and looked Jed straight in the eye. They held each other's gaze for perhaps ten seconds. The man was visibly shocked at the sight of Jed. Then he blinked and seemed to pull himself together. He glanced down at his paper again and walked off.

'What was he up to?' asked Jed. 'Have you seen him before?'

'I think I have, but I can't remember when.'

Neither could Jed, but he was sure he had seen the man somewhere before as well.

Will Rawlings' hands trembled as he looked down at his mother's image. He felt a mixture of emotions – grief, as always, fear and confusion. He tried to speak normally but could not disguise the tremor in his voice. 'What is it? A ghost?'

Edward could see his brother was upset. 'No, Will. I don't believe in ghosts, though I admit I had my doubts when I first saw the picture. No, there's another reason why Mother's in that picture and it's almost as hard to believe.'

'Tell me then.'

'I will, but first another surprise. I hope you can cope with another. Here, you can help me.' Edward had finished making adjustments to his machine and now he and Will moved the box and drum outside. Edward went back into his laboratory and returned with an armful of wires and metal spikes. He began to arrange the equipment.

'What are all these things?'

'This is the power supply.' Edward connected two heavy cables to the large drum. 'You have to be careful. There's acid in there. I've converted the old water mill into a generator of electricity so I can charge this supply up there and bring it down here to use.' He plugged the other ends of the cables into sockets on the wooden box. 'This box contains my greatest secret. I've been working on this since last summer when I got those photographs. I'll show you what it does in a moment but first we need to set up the field boundaries.' Will watched Edward insert the metal spikes into the ground to mark out a circle about two yards across. On each spike was mounted a small wire antenna and copper coils. Each was connected to the next by a light cable and the spike nearest the box was connected to the machine itself.

'There,' said Edward when it was done. 'Now all I need is the rabbit.'

'The what?'

'A rabbit. Every magician does this trick but never like this before.'

Will noticed there were some hutches along the side of Edward's hut which contained various rabbits and guinea pigs. Edward unhooked the catch on the nearest hutch and pulled out a large white rabbit with pink eyes which he set down within the circle of spikes and wires. It seemed a fairly docile creature, but Edward placed some lettuce leaves near it to stop it wandering off.

'And now,' announced Edward, clearly enjoying the show, 'for the first time before a select audience of one, Mr Edward Rawlings will demonstrate his newly perfected trick of the disappearing rabbit.' He took a slight bow.

'I say, you're not going to hurt it or anything, are you?'

'The member of the audience need not fear. This trick has been performed on one previous occasion and the creature suffered no ill effects. Now quiet, if you please, and the show will proceed.'

Edward started making final adjustments to the machine. He muttered to himself, saying things that Will did not understand. 'Duration – one minute. Delay – about a quarter of an hour. That ought to be about right.' He finished making his settings and looked up. 'Will, would you take my watch and tell me the time?'

'It's nearly eleven o'clock.'

'Good. Now watch the rabbit.'

Edward pulled the largest lever mounted on the front of the box and an electrical hum began to sound. Blue sparks flickered gently over the copper coils. This lasted some moments until the sound had risen to a high-pitched whine. Then Edward flicked a smaller switch and immediately the area within the wire boundary shimmered slightly and the rabbit and lettuce disappeared. Will cried out in astonishment. He instinctively moved closer to get a better look but Edward called out in warning.

'No! Don't go too close. Just watch and tell me when a minute is up.' When a minute had elapsed Will told Edward, who reversed the switch and lever. The whining noise ceased, the blue sparks faded away and the rabbit reappeared, still munching lettuce and apparently unaware that anything unusual had happened to it. 'Gentleman of the audience, I thank you.' Edward took another bow and picked up the rabbit to return it to its cage.

Will clapped with delight. 'How did you do it? Where did the rabbit go?'

'The rabbit didn't go anywhere. It was there all the time.'

'No,' protested Will. 'I saw it disappear.'

'You did indeed, but it hadn't gone to a different place. It had gone to a different time. Roughly a quarter of an hour into the future, I hope, although I can't time it precisely yet.'

'What? I don't understand.'

'I'll try to explain. I've got about a quarter of an hour before the second part of the show. It is a bit complicated and some parts of it I don't fully understand myself.' Edward lowered himself on to the grass next to his brother.

'Will, do you know how a photograph is taken?'

'Yes. You have a camera which is a kind of box thing with a glass hole in the front. You take the cover off the glass, leave it for a while and cover it up again. That sort of makes the picture, doesn't it?'

'That's how you work the camera. Do you know how the picture is captured?'

'No.'

'It has to do with light. We see things because our eyes are sensitive to light. You have to imagine light as tiny particles or waves. No one is sure what it is really. These particles travel from the things we are looking at, into our eyes and that is how the picture gets into our heads. A camera works just like an eye. Light travels through the hole at the front and on to a glass plate at the back. This plate is coated with a chemical called silver bromide, which reacts to the light and records the picture. Are you following so far?'

Will nodded. 'I think so, but I don't quite see where the rabbit fits in.'

'The rabbit comes later. Now last year I was taking a lot of photographs as you remember. I was experimenting, trying to make the chemical react to light quicker so that taking pictures wouldn't take so long. I mixed up a new batch and took those photographs that I showed you earlier. When I developed them I was surprised like you to see the pictures. I thought I must have made a mistake and taken more than one picture on the same glass. That's called a double exposure. But when I developed the picture of Mother I realized that couldn't be the explanation because I only bought the camera after Mother died. I had no idea what had happened until I realized that I was taking one picture of the same place but from many different times.'

Will was confused. 'I don't understand.'

'Let's take that photograph with Mother in it, for example.' Edward scrambled up and went to fetch it. 'There. You can see most of the picture comes from the present. It's just the house. But then there's Mother. That part of the picture must come from five years ago or more. And that. Can you tell what that is?'

'A sheep?'

'Yes. Now there haven't been sheep here since before the house was built, fifty years ago. And do you see that?'

Will frowned as he struggled to make out the half-obscured shape. 'It looks like an old woman in a chair with wheels.'

'That's what I think. I think she might come from the future because her chair looks like nothing I've ever seen before.'

Will frowned as he struggled with the idea of lots of things from different times being in the photograph at the same time. 'Unless they're all ghosts,' he suggested.

'Call them ghosts if you like but there's nothing supernatural about it. I found out what was happening. The new chemical I used on the glass plates was not only reacting to light particles, but to a different kind of particle as well. These new particles seem to behave like light. They not only move in the ordinary three dimensions of space, but through time as well. If you know how to detect them, these particles will let you see the past and the future.'

'And what about the rabbit?'

'How you go on about the rabbit. I had a lot more to dis-cover before I could start doing rabbit tricks. Having found the time particles I had to devise a way of filtering them so I could isolate the image from one particular time. I didn't want to be seeing things all on top of each other like in the photographs. Those wires do that.' Edward pointed to the two antennae mounted on top of the machine. 'They act as a receiver. After that, I found that applying electrical power through those copper coils intensified the image to the point where not only a picture of something appeared, but the thing itself would be brought here from another time. I call it temporal shift.'

Will frowned. 'What do you want to call it that for?'

'Because it means "moving time".'

'Does it?'

'Yes. You know, temporal comes from the Latin word *tem-pus* meaning time.'

Will sighed. 'More Latin.'

'Well,' said Edward, standing up. 'That's what the machine does. It separates a small area of land and moves it forwards or backwards in time. Isn't it beautiful?' He laid an affection-ate hand on the polished wood and buffed up the copper coil with his shirt cuff.

'So when you turned it on everything inside the wires moved forward in time by a quarter of an hour and we couldn't see the rabbit anymore.'

'That's right.'

'What were we seeing then? When the rabbit was gone.'

'Good question, Will. I don't know. We were probably seeing the same piece of land, but which time it came from I haven't been able to work out yet. Now then, what time does my watch say?'

'Just about quarter past eleven.'

'Then watch the same place very carefully and we should be able to see the rabbit appear again.'

Sure enough within a few minutes the air shimmered, a faint crackling sound could be heard and the placid white rabbit came into view again, still munching its lettuce. Will looked at it and then across to the row of hutches. There was the rabbit sitting in its cage and there was the same rabbit sitting on the lawn, the first traveller through time. A minute later there was another ripple and the rabbit on the lawn was gone.

Jed and Lizzie were keen to quiz their dad the following evening about his interview with Mr Harris but they did not want to make him suspicious by sounding too interested. Dad was likely to be quite sarcastic if he thought they actually believed in ghosts. They were at the dinner table when Jed casually asked the question.

'Did you discover any ghosts today, Dad?'

Dad groaned. 'I thought I'd met some nutters before, but they were only amateurs compared to today's bunch. I just hope we never have a UFO sighting. I think that would finish me off.'

'What about the old man?' asked Lizzie.

'What old man?'

'There was an old man called Hopkins or something, wasn't there?' Lizzie didn't want to let on that she knew him. 'He said he had a photo of a ghost.'

'Oh, you mean Harris. He was the worst of the lot. He was so blind I doubt he could see an elephant, let alone a ghost.' Jed and Lizzie's hearts sank. He had obviously upset

Mr Harris somehow. Dad was still talking. 'Fantastic place that nursing home. I mean it smells of wee now, but it must have been incredible when it was a private house. You should see the staircase in the main hall.'

'Did he have a photo of the ghost?'

'He had a whole box full of photos and letters and newspaper cuttings. There was a picture of him in his uniform during the war. Another of him holding a ferret. He used to be a gamekeeper apparently. Then there were some older pictures of his dad who was a gardener. After about twenty minutes of reminiscences and coughing he finally got out the ghost picture.'

'What was in it?' asked Jed, sounding more excited than he meant to.

'It was just a very old photograph of a Victorian family. The Rawlings. They used to own the big house. There was a grumpy looking old bloke and two boys.'

'Where was the ghost then?'

'There wasn't one. He kept pointing to the younger boy and insisting he was the ghost. And then he started rambling on about a rabbit he'd seen in the war. Quite mad I tell you. I don't know how I'm going to make a story out of all this.'

Jed and Lizzie would have liked to know more but Mum dished up the bolognese and the conversation turned to other things.

'I wish Dad had taken Mr Harris a bit more seriously,' complained Lizzie. They were discussing their plans in Jed's room. As usual, Jed was standing at the window.

'Well, I can understand why he didn't. You've got to admit it wasn't a very convincing ghost story.'

'But he must know something about what happened to Will. Otherwise why would he be saying he was a ghost?'

'Yeah,' agreed Jed. 'I think we need to speak to him.'

'Do you think he'll talk to us after what Dad's done?'

'I don't see why not. He doesn't know he's our dad. He just thinks we're the nice kids who helped him on the bus.'

'Yeah, you're right.'

'How are we going to get to see him then? I don't fancy just walking up to the nursing home and asking him outright.'

'Me neither.' They thought for a few moments then Lizzie continued. 'I know. He goes to the records office every day. We could go back there and try to talk to him.'

'Good idea. We'll have to wait till Saturday then. Hey, Lizzie!'

'What?'

'You remember that strange man we saw out the window?'

'Yeah. Is he back?' She stood up quickly.

'No, but I've just remembered where I've seen him before. Talking about the records office reminded me.'

'Yes,' cried Lizzie. 'He was there, wasn't he? He was the younger man who came in at the end and had a foreign accent.'

'That's right. Wonder what he's up to.'

On Saturday they could not go straight into town as they had the previous weekend. Mum insisted they take Arthur for his walk before they did anything else.

'Make sure he has a good long run,' she said. 'He's missing his old haunts and if you come back in ten minutes I'll only send you out again.'

'It's Mum who's missing the old place, not Arthur,' said Jed, when they were out of earshot.

'I know,' Lizzie agreed. 'I miss Little Moor too, but Mum's

got loads of memories. She had her box of photos out yesterday and I think she'd been crying.'

They soon arrived at the wasteland behind their house. They had already been to investigate the site and not found anything, but another look wouldn't hurt. The boy might appear again. Jed and Lizzie weren't quite sure whether they wanted him to or not. They let Arthur off his lead and he tore off into the woods immediately. He would come as soon as he was called so they let him wander while they hung around. Jed sat down on an old tyre and Lizzie continued to kick around through the weeds and long grass. 'I think there must have been a building here once,' she said after a while.

'Why's that?'

'Well, there're some slabs of stone here like a floor.'

Jed got up to have a look. 'Oh yeah. We ought to tell Dad. He was talking about building a patio. He could use these.' Just then Arthur came bounding back and started dancing around them excitedly. He had something small in his mouth.

'Hey Arthur. Here boy. What have you got there?' Lizzie tried to catch the lively dog. Arthur thought it was a great game and when they eventually got hold of him he wanted a tug of war. 'Let go, you stupid dog. You're going to hurt yourself and you're making me all spitty. There, got it.'

'What is it?' asked Jed.

'Don't know yet.' She rubbed off some of the dirt that was caked all over it. 'It's an old cigarette lighter. It's not rusty. It's made of brass.' She rubbed it some more. 'It's got some initials on it. It says *T. H.* We could clean it up and give it to Dad. It might still work.'

'Dad doesn't smoke,' Jed pointed out.

'Well, he could use it to light the fire then.'

'We don't have a fireplace anymore.'

'In which case he could use it to set fire to awkward boys who keep on making stupid objections to good ideas.'

'Yes, he could,' conceded Jed. 'Shame we don't know any of those.'

It was half-past ten before they eventually got to the records office. A similar selection of old people were reading, muttering to themselves or snoring. Mr Harris was there wearing a raincoat. He was sitting at the desk this time with an old book. The woman behind the desk recognized the children and greeted them so loudly she nearly woke Mr Jenkins.

'Back again for more punishment, eh? What would you like to do today?'

'We'd like another look at the Rawlings family papers please,' said Lizzie.

'Right you are then.' Within minutes she was back with the box of documents. Jed and Lizzie thanked her and went to sit next to Mr Harris.

'You here again?' asked the old man as they sat down. 'Want a humbug?'

Jed pointed to the sign that said 'No Eating' but Mr Harris was not impressed. 'Get on. I been coming here for years and I always sucks a sweetie.' The children accepted the sweets. They were in a plastic bag and had all stuck together in one lump.

'What you two doing?' Mr Harris asked when they had finally extracted a sweet each.

'We're investigating the Rawlings family.'

'What you want to do that for?' Mr Harris was suspicious.

'It's a school project,' said Lizzie, trying her lie again.

'Get on. You want to know about the ghost. I heard you talking last week.'

'Is there a ghost?' asked Jed innocently.

'Have you seen a ghost, Mr Harris?' asked Lizzie.

'Might have. Can you read?' The children nodded. 'I can't,' he grumbled. 'It's me eyes. Have a look in this book. You can read something for me.'

'What is it?' asked Jed, taking the old book bound in creamy-coloured leather. The words 'Burials 1854–1889' were embossed on the front in gold lettering.

'It's a burial register. It tells you all the people that has been buried up in the churchyard. Look up February 1874.' Jed turned the old pages. 'Now read the names till you find Rawlings.'

Jed read through the entries. 'I've found it. February 19th. Sophia Rawlings. Aged 45. Consumption.'

'That's Josiah's wife,' said Lizzie excitedly. 'She died in 1874. That's why we couldn't find her in 1881.'

'What's consumption?' asked Jed.

'TB. You know, too-ber-kee-low-sis. Makes you cough.' As if to demonstrate, Mr Harris had a little coughing fit himself. His face was red and his eyes were streaming by the time he had recovered. His voice was croaky when he spoke again. 'Now turn to July 1879.'

Jed did as he was told. His hands trembled as he guessed what he was about to find. Sure enough there was the entry for July 7th. William Rawlings. Aged 12. Consumption.

'He died as well. Of the same thing his mother died of.'

'Did he?' asked Mr Harris.

'That's what it says.'

The old man grunted.

'Well, why would it say it if it wasn't true?' Lizzie wanted to know.

'My granddad was gardener up at the house when young Will was buried. He says Will was right as rain just a week or

48

so before he were buried. Funny time to catch TB too, in the middle of summer.'

'How did he die then?'

'Dunno. Perhaps he didn't die. My granddad says he saw Master Will long after he was buried. After Josiah was buried for that matter.'

'What? Was Will a man by then?'

'Nope. He were still a boy exactly like the day he died.'

'A ghost then?' breathed Lizzie excitedly. 'Have you ever seen Will's ghost, Mr Harris?'

'I seen something but I ain't saying what it were.'

Mr Harris would not say anything more after that. He went back to peering blindly at the pages of the register and occasionally turning them with his trembly fingers. Jed and Lizzie decided they might as well go home. They returned the box of documents to the desk and the woman asked them how they had got on.

'Really good today,' said Jed. 'We found out loads.'

'Good. Good,' boomed the woman. 'Soon have your project done, eh? Funny that you should have been looking at the Rawlings papers. Last week I hadn't even put them away when a feller from South Africa came in wanting to find out about the Rawlings too. He wanted to know your names when he found out you'd been looking at them. Didn't tell him of course.'

'Was that the young man you were talking to when we left?'

'Yes. Silly chap was doing his family history. Had come all that way just to find out about his ancestors. More money than sense if you ask me.'

Jed and Lizzie were both intrigued. 'Then was his name Rawlings too?'

'Yes, that's right,' said the woman. 'Edward Rawlings.'

Will Rawlings pulled hard on the oars as his brother lay back lazily in the boat, his hand trailing idly through the water. Both brothers had removed their jackets and collars and rolled their sleeves up. It was Sunday so Edward was not working in his laboratory. Josiah and his two sons had walked up the hill to church that morning and had sat in the big family pew at the front. After lunch Will and Edward had decided to take a row on the lake. Edward was not much inclined to work today even if his father would have permitted it.

'The trouble is, Will,' he said, 'we seem to have reached a dead end with this line of research. I mean there is only so much you can learn from a rabbit.' It was nearly a week now since Edward had shared his secret with his younger brother and each day Will had joined him at his laboratory for more time-travelling experiments. They could not do much each day because the power supply drained quickly and it then had to be carefully wheeled up to the water mill and left overnight to recharge. Edward had two electrical drums, but even so they did not manage to transport the rabbit more than four or five times each day. One thing they had learned was that the further into the future a rabbit was sent, the quicker the power drained. The furthest they had managed so far was about a century into the future and Edward could maintain that for about four minutes.

'All we can definitely say is that we can transport things through time and bring them back without harming them. What do we do next? The rabbit can't tell us anything. What do you think would happen if someone was to step over the boundary of the time-field while the machine was on? For a moment half of them would be in one time and the other half in another time. Would they survive that?'

Will did not know so he asked a question that had suddenly occurred to him. 'Can you send things backwards as well as forwards?'

'I haven't yet, but there's no reason why I shouldn't be able to.'

'Why don't you then?'

Edward considered his answer. 'To begin with I tried sending the rabbit forwards in time so I could have the satisfaction of seeing it appear half an hour later or whenever. That helped me calibrate the machine as well so I could measure exactly how far in time the rabbit had moved. We've got it pretty accurate over short time spans now. There's no way of knowing how good it is over years of course.'

'Why don't you try backwards then?'

'I could,' conceded Edward, 'but we would have to be much more careful.'

Will stopped rowing and let the boat drift. They were in the middle of the lake and the house could be seen on the rise of the slope, framed by the trees that grew on either bank of the lake. 'Why careful?' he asked.

'I don't mind tinkering with the future because it hasn't happened yet, but if something happened in the past that shouldn't, then that might change things now.'

Will was puzzled. 'What do you mean?'

'Imagine this, Will. Let's say we send a rabbit back fifteen years in time and it appears right next to Father who is out for a shoot in these woods.' He waved a hand to indicate the direction of his laboratory. 'The sight of a rabbit appearing out of thin air makes Father leap with fright. The loaded gun goes off in his hands and Father is unfortunately killed. How would that be?'

'That would be tragic of course.'

'Yes, tragic, but think some more. What would happen to Father now?'

Will struggled with this new idea for a moment. 'I don't know. He'd disappear I suppose because he'd have been dead for fifteen years.'

'Yes and who else would disappear?'

'I don't know.'

'Think, Will, think.'

Will hazarded a wild guess. 'The rabbit?'

Edward laughed. 'No, not the rabbit. You, Will. If Father had died fifteen years ago you would never have been born.'

This was too much for Will. 'No, that can't be right. I mean I exist, don't I? I wouldn't just not exist. How could that happen? You'd remember me and that would mean I must exist.'

'I don't know, Will. You might or you might not. You can see why I'd be reluctant to send things backwards though, can't you? The risk is too great.'

They drifted some more, reflecting on this new line of thought. Will played with the oar gently in the water and watched the fish come up to nibble at the oar before diving back below. Edward was first to speak. He was still lying back in the boat with his eyes shut and his head resting on his hands.

'Of course we could go back and do some good. Just think if I went back a hundred years and invested a hundred pounds in the bank at six and a half per cent interest per annum and then came back to the present. The money would be waiting for us.' He did a quick sum in his head. 'There'd be nearly sixty thousand pounds by then. We'd be rich.'

'We already are rich,' observed Will.

'Yes, that's true, but you get the idea.'

There was silence again until Will plucked up the courage to ask what he had been thinking. 'Edward?'

'Yes?' Edward's response was sleepy.

'Could we go back and save Mother?' Edward sat up sharply making the boat rock. The two brothers stared at each other, Will's lip trembling slightly. Both their minds were racing but eventually Edward shook his head. He leaned forward and laid his hand on Will's shoulder before speaking.

'Will, we can't. Don't even think about it.'

'But why not? You said yourself we could go back and do some good and I can't think of anything better than saving Mother.'

'Oh, Will, there are lots of reasons why we can't. For one thing Mother died of a disease. Wilkes is the best doctor moncy can buy and he couldn't save her, so how could we even if we did go back?'

'We could try and find out when she caught it and stop her. I don't know. We could try.' Will's voice was pleading.

'But Will, have you thought about it? What would Mother do if we turned up looking five years older? We'd frighten her to death before she even got ill. And what if we met ourselves? Or what if Father should find us?'

'We'd have to explain what we were doing. He'd want to save Mother too.'

'But even if he believed us, that wouldn't be fair on him. What if we couldn't save her? Can you imagine being told that Mother was going to die before it happened? There would be no hope at all. It would be terrible. No, Will, don't think about trying. It would never work and you're only tormenting yourself. We have to let her go.'

53

There were tears stinging Will's eyes but he had to admit Edward was right. It was stupid dragging up all those feelings again. He would never stop missing Mother – none of them would – but she was gone and that was the end of it.

'You're right, Edward. I'm sorry. I just thought . . .' He could not finish his sentence, but Edward understood.

Will picked up the oars again and started pulling for the bank. 'What shall we do next?'

'I don't know. There are lots of things I'd like to find out but they all seem to require a person to make a trip, which is risky because we don't know if it's safe for humans.'

'It doesn't hurt the rabbits.'

'No, but rabbits' brains are much less complex than ours. They're dull-witted when they go and they're dull-witted when they come back. I don't know what would happen to a rational being like you or me. The change might send us mad.'

'You could send me on a short journey and we could find out.'

Edward looked tempted but he would not do it. The boat had reached the jetty and Edward leaped ashore to tie it to the mooring post. The two brothers walked back up to the house in the late afternoon sun. 'Will, after losing Mother and never being really close to Father, to lose you would be too much. Much as I'd like to have the opportunity to see the future I think we're going to have to confine our experiments to rabbits for the time being.'

Tom Harris was walking back to his gamekeeper's hut in the dark. It was nearly a full moon which was good because usually the blackout made walking home from The George difficult, particularly if you had drunk four pints of beer. In his moleskin trousers and knee-length coat, Tom looked like a gamekeeper, but he would not for much longer. Next week he would be dressed in a khaki uniform and it would not be a shotgun he would be carrying but a rifle. Then it would be ten weeks' basic training and he would be off to teach Adolf Hitler a lesson. The newspaper tucked into his deep coat pocket was dated May 11th 1940. There was a picture of the new prime minister, Mr Winston Churchill, on the front page, looking stern and resolute. 'I have nothing to offer but blood, toil, tears and sweat,' he had said in his first speech. Well, Tom Harris knew all about that sort of thing. He'd show them what a fine soldier he could be. He'd make John Sullivan shut his ugly face too.

Tom scowled as he remembered the countless times John Sullivan had put him down. Only that evening he had laughed and sneered in the pub when Tom had told them he had signed up to be a soldier. 'What, are they that desperate? They'll take mental cases now, will they?' Tom clenched his fists and his face flushed with anger as he remembered the taunts and how everyone had laughed – even Sally. Tom hated the way John showed off in front of Sally. Most had slapped him on the back and told him not to listen to John and said he was a good man for going, but Tom knew that nobody believed his stories. So what if they didn't believe him? Tom knew there was something strange going on.

It was his grandfather George who had first told him that something peculiar had happened near his hut. He had been a gardener back when all the land belonged to old Rawlings. His hut had been Mr Edward's then and nobody knew what he got up to with his machines and experiments. Then young Will had died and Mr Edward had gone off to Africa. Gone off in disgrace some said. George hadn't been a superstitious man but he had told Tom that strange things seemed to happen near the hut after that. He even said he'd seen Master Will standing outside the hut years after old Josiah had died and the house sold.

The moon passed behind a cloud, making the night dark. Tom pulled out his brass cigarette lighter. Blackout precautions did not allow torches even if you could get the batteries. His hut was not far ahead now, but it was rough ground so he would have to go carefully not to trip. He peered into the distance. There seemed to be a patch of light by his hut. He thought for a moment his hut was on fire and he quickened his pace, but then he realized the light was not on his hut but near it. What was that light? It was too bright for moonlight. As he neared his hut the sight became stranger still. It was ordinary daylight. A small patch of daylight in the middle of the night. And in the centre of the patch of light there sat a white rabbit eating lettuce.

Tom rubbed his eyes. He had only drunk four pints. He looked again but the daylight and the rabbit were still there. Well, Tom thought, a white rabbit was a white rabbit. His niece had been nagging for a rabbit for months. This one would do just nicely for her birthday. He cautiously stepped forwards, not wanting to frighten the rabbit off, but also feeling wary. He could hear a faint crackling noise and his fingers tingled slightly as he stretched them out into the strange patch of light. He stepped slowly forward and the tingling passed over his whole body but nothing else happened to him. He stood for a moment, surprised to feel the warmth of the sun on his face in the middle of the night. Then he bent down and picked up the rabbit. He was just congratulating himself when his stomach lurched horribly. Everything around him wobbled and he found himself standing face to face with a boy in broad daylight.

Tom Harris cried out startled and so did the boy. Tom's eyes darted wildly around him for a few seconds. Things were familiar yet strange. His hut was there but it looked different, much newer for one thing. The woods were further away and the road was not there at all. He looked at the boy again, his mind racing and panic rising in him. He'd seen that boy before, but only in an old photograph, and here he was in the flesh. It was too much. He let the rabbit drop from his fingers as he fell faint to the ground.

Jed, Lizzie and Arthur walked up the hill to St Thomas's church. They had not been there before but it was easy to find because the spire was the tallest building around. The gate creaked on its hinges and once inside they looked around at the hundreds of gravestones, not knowing where to start. There were a few other people in the graveyard, talking in low voices and placing flowers in vases. They looked at the graves near where they were standing but most of them seemed to be new. Lizzie suggested they try further up the hill where everything looked older and more overgrown.

'I don't know what else we're going to find out even if we can find a grave,' said Lizzie. Arthur was tugging at the lead but she did not like to let him run loose in a churchyard.

'No, me neither,' agreed Jed. 'But we might as well try. There doesn't seem to be much else we can do.'

There were hundreds of graves so they each took a row and started walking up and down looking at the dates. When they found a row that were mostly dated in the 1870s, they stopped and began reading the headstones more carefully to find the names of the people. This was difficult on some of them where the stone was worn or covered with moss and brambles. After about twenty minutes of searching Lizzie called out in a low voice. 'I think I've found it.' Jed quickly came to see. 'We should have guessed really,' she said, as he joined her. 'It's the biggest grave here.' The grave was certainly impressive – a big slab of blackish stone and a statue of an angel – but it was poorly kept. They had to pull the brambles away, which was not easy, then scrape off the moss which got under their fingernails.

'It's sad, isn't it, when you've got no one to remember you and keep your grave nice,' said Jed as they worked.

Lizzie was more practical. 'I don't suppose they mind now.'

When the grave had been cleared, Jed read out the inscription. '"Sophia Rawlings taken from us February 18th 1874. Also her son William Rawlings July 7th 1879. Also Josiah Rawlings husband of Sophia and father of William March 7th 1903." Then there's a verse from the Bible. There's no mention of Edward Rawlings. Do you think he died in Africa and was buried there?'

'I don't know. But I bet Mr Harris does. We should have asked him.'

They were interrupted by an agitated voice calling them. 'I say, you two children. What are you doing?' Jed and Lizzie looked up guiltily, wondering if they had done anything wrong. A man dressed in a black cassock and a white collar was walking up the path. His wispy white hair was fluttering in the breeze.

Jed spoke as he approached. 'We're only looking. We're not doing any harm.'

The vicar was clearly suspicious. 'A man has just told me that he saw you doing something to the graves.'

'We pulled the brambles and moss off this one to read the inscription,' Lizzie said. The old man looked down at the Rawlings grave.

'Well, yes, it seems much neater,' he conceded. 'I'm sorry if I sounded angry. Cleaning graves isn't what I usually find young people doing. Defacing them is more common. Can I ask why you are interested in the inscriptions?'

'Only in this one. We have been trying to find out about this family,' Lizzie said. The old man looked quizzical. 'For a school project,' she added.

The two children and their dog walked back down the slope with the vicar. He was telling them in his reedy voice about the font in the church which had been paid for by Josiah Rawlings. His voice faded into the distance and when they were gone a middle-aged man stepped out from behind a large tomb and walked up the hill to look at the Rawlings grave. He took his computer from his brown over-coat pocket and held it up to the grave. It must have been one of the latest models with image capture because, at the touch of a button, a digital picture of the grave appeared on the screen. He saved the image and closed the case. The children had found out far more than he'd expected them too. It was about time he paid them a visit.

Will stared in disbelief at the strange man lying at his feet. Edward left the controls of his machine and rushed over to stand next to his brother. 'Will, we've brought a man back from the future. Look, it's amazing. That man's older than me and he hasn't even been born yet.' Edward seemed very excited and worried at the same time.

'What's he doing here?'

'He must have walked into the time-field to pick up the rabbit and was still there when we switched the machine off.'

'Is he all right? Have we killed him?'

Edward bent to look at the body of Tom Harris. 'He's unconscious but he seems healthy. I can't tell if his mind's all right until he wakes up.' Edward sniffed. 'He smells of alcohol so it may be some time before he does wake up.'

'But what are we going to do with him? We can't just go taking people from the future. They'll miss him. And what will he do here? Father's sure to find out. I don't think he'd like what we're doing here.'

'Father won't find out. We'll have to send him back.'

'How?'

Edward's mind was racing. 'We'll leave the settings exactly as they are. We'll lie him inside the time-field and switch the machine on again.'

'Is there enough power in the drum?'

'No. Quick, Will, we need to change the drum.' Edward rushed into his hut to fetch the spare drum while Will pulled out the cables. Five minutes later they were ready to work the machine. The man still lay unconscious on the grass. Will had been thinking.

'This isn't going to work.'

'Why not?'

'He's asleep. If we switch the machine on and leave it for a few minutes, then he might still be asleep when we switch the power off again. He'll come straight back to us. And we'll have used all the power in both drums and we won't be able to try again till tomorrow. Who knows what will have happened by then?' Will was beginning to panic a bit.

Edward paced up and down as he thought. 'I think there

are two things we can do,' he said at last. 'We can wait until he wakes up, explain everything and tell him he needs to step over the boundary into his own time when we've switched the machine on.'

'He might not like that. He might be really angry or get frightened and run off.'

'That leaves the other option. One of us needs to go forward in time with him while he's asleep, drag him outside the boundary, then step back inside and wait for the machine to be switched off.' Edward's eyes were shining. 'Will, I'm going to travel through time.'

'But you don't know if it's safe.'

'I'll have to risk it.'

'Why don't I go?'

'You're not strong enough to move him.' Will bent down and tugged at Tom Harris's coat lapels.

'You're right,' he said after straining for a while. 'But I can't work the machine either.'

'Yes, you can. You've seen me do it. You need to pull this lever and watch this gauge until the needle reaches the red bit. That means the machine is ready. Then you simply flick this switch and I'll be sixty years away. Give me two minutes. That should be plenty of time to get him clear and get back inside the time-field. Then pull the switch and lever back.' Will looked worried but a moan from the unconscious man spurred them into action. 'Quick, Will, we need to hurry.'

Edward stepped inside the wires and made sure none of Tom Harris was lying outside. Will pulled the lever and the electrical whine began and the blue sparks flickered over the copper coils. When the needle showed ready, he flicked the switch. Edward and Tom Harris faded away. Will spent a very anxious two minutes looking at Edward's watch, then he turned the machine off. The air rippled, the noise stopped and Edward reappeared alone.

He was reading a newspaper.

'This is amazing,' said Edward later. They had decided to go boating again because the middle of the lake was one place they could talk in private. Will rowed as Edward read the paper he had stolen from Tom Harris. 'There's apparently some war going on against Germany in 1940.'

'That can't be right. We like the Germans. Queen Victoria married one.'

'Her Majesty has died by 1940. There'll be a King George on the throne by then. Will, this really is extraordinary. Look at this picture. I think it's some sort of vehicle that powers itself around the streets. I wonder how it runs? There's no funnel on it. And look at this. That's a machine that flies. Not a balloon but a heavy metal machine with wings like a bird. Apparently the two sides are using them to drop explosives on each other's cities.' Edward flicked through some more pages, his eyes darting from one marvel to the next. 'I wonder what radio is. And what is cinema? And vacuum cleaning? What do they want vacuums for and why would anyone want to clean them? Will, the future is amazing. I must go there again.'

'I don't want to get explosives dropped on me.'

'Well no, nor do I. I think we better avoid 1940 anyway. We don't want to chance meeting that man again. He seems to be living in my hut in 1940.'

'What did it look like?'

'It was hard to tell. It was dark. I could make out some new buildings over there and the woods had grown a bit. Apart from that it all seemed the same.'

'And you're sure you feel all right?'

'Absolutely fine. I felt a bit sick when it all happened but that passed straight away. Then I dragged the man out. It feels a bit strange as you leave the time-field but it didn't seem to do me any harm.' Edward closed the paper and folded it up. 'Let's go and get those drums recharged and tomorrow we can start travelling through time.'

Lizzie was busy at the kitchen table cleaning dirt from the old cigarette lighter when the doorbell rang. Mum was preparing vegetables and Dad was washing up so Jed answered the door. On the doorstep stood a man with close-cropped grey hair, wearing a brown overcoat.

'Jed Stokes?' he asked.

'Yes,' Jed admitted.

The man took out some ID which he showed to Jed. 'Inspector Morgan, U Division. Are your parents in?' He spoke in short, clipped sentences.

Jed immediately felt uneasy. 'Yes, they're both in the kitchen. Is everything all right?'

'That remains to be seen,' the inspector said. 'Can I see your parents please?'

Jed took the inspector through to the kitchen. They all looked up, surprised to see the stranger. Dad immediately dried his hands. 'Hello,' he said. 'Can I help?'

'Possibly. My name is Inspector Morgan.' He held out his hand for Dad to shake but with the palm facing downwards. Dad frowned slightly in confusion but took the inspector's hand and shook it awkwardly. He studied the ID briefly as it was given to him.

'Is anything wrong, Inspector?'

'Not wrong, but I would like to ask Jed and Lizzie a few questions.'

The children jumped at the sound of their names. Mum looked anxiously from their faces to the inspector. 'What is it?' she asked. 'Are they in any trouble?'

'Not trouble as such. I'm sure they're going to co-operate and everything will be fine. Now then, Jed.' The inspector turned to the boy with what he intended to be a disarming smile. Jed instinctively drew back from the almost hungry expression on his face. 'I'm sure you'll agree with me that strange things have been happening.' The forced cheerfulness suggested Inspector Morgan was not used to dealing with children. Jed did not know how to answer him. Strange things had been happening of course, but this policeman could not possibly be investigating a ghost.

'I . . . I don't know,' he stammered at last.

'Don't worry, son. I know you're reluctant to talk about it.' He gave an unnatural laugh. 'Worried I'll think you're mad?' He moved nearer to Jed. 'You can tell me. I'll believe you.'

Jed glanced at Lizzie who shook her head quickly. 'I don't understand,' he said.

Inspector Morgan had not missed the little shake of Lizzie's head. The unnatural cheerfulness slipped and his voice was darker, almost sinister when he next spoke. 'I think you do understand, both of you.'

'Well I don't,' said Dad. He was never patient at the best of times and Inspector Morgan was beginning to irritate him. 'Are you going to explain yourself, Inspector, or just make cryptic comments all afternoon?'

The policeman scowled at Dad. 'I will explain and then perhaps Jed and Lizzie can add anything they know.' Morgan pulled out one of the kitchen chairs and took a seat which nobody had offered him. 'I work for U Division. You will not have heard of us or know what we do. We are an intelligence branch. U is for unexplained. We investigate some of the more unusual things that happen, particularly if we think they are a threat to national security.

'Something very strange happened here over a century ago. All this land where your house is now built used to belong to a family called Rawlings.' Dad turned his head slightly, a thoughtful look in his eyes. He remembered hearing about the family in his interview with Mr Harris. Inspector Morgan continued. 'One member of the family, Edward Rawlings, created a machine of such potential that even our scientists today would like to know how he did it.'

'What machine? What did it do?'

'Ah! that would be telling.' Morgan tapped the side of his nose with his forefinger and nodded knowingly. 'Something went wrong in 1879. Edward's younger brother William disappeared or was killed and Edward left the country in disgrace. He went into business abroad and seems to have abandoned his experiments after that. It is not known what happened to the machine but we assume the father destroyed it. Since then, this site has been the occasional centre of some very unusual activity, which seems to have been increasing in the last few weeks. I believe there may be a way to learn something about the machine and I would like Jed and Lizzie's full co-operation in achieving that.' He smiled again, trying to regain some of his earlier friendly manner, but Dad was having none of it. He was really losing patience now.

'Inspector Morgan, I don't know what you think my children can do to help you with a crime that happened 120 years ago.'

'Did I say a crime had been committed? I don't think I

65

said that, Mr Stokes. I think Jed and Lizzie can help us with this *mystery* because they are witnesses to it.'

'Are you mad? You said it happened in 1879.'

Mum laid a hand on Dad's arm. 'Quiet, dear. He is a policeman.'

'Thank you, Mrs Stokes. Now then, Jed and Lizzie. What can you tell me?' The two looked blank. They really did not want to tell this policeman anything. If Dad knew they were hunting ghosts they would never hear the last of it. 'All right, then,' he said more menacingly, 'perhaps your parents would like to learn about *your* unusual behaviour in the last week. Your trips to the library and the records office, for example. Reading through old documents is a new hobby of yours perhaps. Or why you spent this afternoon clearing up grave-stones. That is a little unusual for teenagers, isn't it? The vicar seemed to think so, didn't he? And what about your inter-view with old Tom Harris?'

'Is Tom his first name?' Lizzie asked, before she could help herself. Jed gave her a scowl and Inspector Morgan looked smug.

'Yes, I know all about Tom Harris.' He got no further as Dad interrupted.

'What? Do you two know what this man is talking about?' The two children looked down at the table and remained stubbornly silent.

'Your father asked you a question,' said Inspector Morgan, but this was a mistake. Dad did not like him and he turned on him.

'Thank you, Inspector. I'll ask you not to interfere when I'm talking to my children.'

'I am a policeman, Mr Stokes, and this is an issue of national importance.'

'Well, I assume you have a warrant of some sort. We've

humoured you so far in your bizarre questioning, but as far as I can see the only accusations you can bring is that my children have been going to the library and performing works of public service in the local cemetery. Now I'll admit that is unusual but it hardly warrants arrest. If you have nothing further to say I'll ask you to leave my house and go and investigate some real criminals.' Dad was standing looking determined and Mum looked worried. Inspector Morgan stood up.

'As you wish, Mr Stokes,' he said stiffly. 'I have just one request for Jed and Lizzie before I go. Do not tell anyone else about what you have seen, and if you see anything else unusual at all, call me at once.' He left a card on the table. 'Call at any time, day or night.'

Dad showed him to the front door and then came back into the kitchen. 'I think you two have some explaining to do,' he said.

Edward Rawlings was sitting on the grass next to his machine. The sky was a rich blue and the late afternoon sun beat down without a cloud in sight. But Edward was looking at a small patch of intense rain that was falling just a couple of yards away. Puddles were forming in the area inside the time-field and raindrops were hitting the ground hard and splashing up again. Whenever a raindrop or splash passed through the boundary it sparkled and glistened as it disappeared, turning the whole time-field into a spectacular fountain of light. Edward's watch and chain were lying on the grass next to him. He glanced at it occasionally until it showed that Will had been gone for five minutes. Time to bring him back. He stood up and reversed the switch and lever on the machine. Immediately the rainfall shimmered and vanished, leaving Will standing in its place. Will looked slightly disorientated as he always did after a time trip.

'How was 1910, Will?'

Will's eyes gradually focused. 'A lot like now actually.'

'Was it raining?'

'No. Why?'

'The area inside the time-field was full of rain while you were gone. I had this theory that the two times simply change places when we operate the machine. You know, this piece of land goes forward to 1910 and at the same time the same piece of land from 1910 comes back here. But if you say it isn't raining in 1910, then I can't have been seeing 1910 while you were gone.' Will was finding that conversations often became complicated when they discussed time transfers. He shook his head now as he grappled with this idea, but it was no good.

'I don't know what you're talking about,' he said.

'Never mind, Will. Tell me what you saw. Did you learn anything about the future?'

'It really hasn't changed. I saw someone though.'

Edward was excited. 'Really? Who?'

'George Harris, the gardener. He looked much older. His hair was all white but I could tell it was him. He's still wearing the same cap. He came out of the woods over there with a gun over his shoulder and he had two dead pheasants in his hand. He jumped when he saw me.'

'I'll bet he did. Did you speak to him?'

'No. He looked terrified but he started to walk towards me. Then the time was up and I came back here before he got near enough.'

Edward thought about the implications of meeting people

68

from the future. 'It might be good to meet someone. We could ask them some questions. We're not learning anything at the moment. I'd love to have some more newspapers from the future.'

Will disagreed. 'I don't want to meet anyone I know. George looked really frightened. Like he'd seen a ghost.'

'That's true. We don't want to disturb people.'

'I don't want to find out what's going to happen to me either. It might not be nice and I'd rather not know.'

Edward sat back down on the grass. He idly tugged at a few tufts of grass while he thought about this. Suddenly he seemed to make a decision. 'Let's go much further forward in time. We'll both be dead by 1970 even if you live to be a hundred. Let's go as far forward as we can. I think we can manage trips of about three minutes if we go forward 120 years.' His face brightened as an idea occurred to him. 'No. Let's make it 121 years. That will take us to the year 2000. A new millennium!'

Their planning was interrupted when Will noticed a familiar figure approaching. Josiah Rawlings had appeared around the corner of the trees and was walking across the grass towards Edward's hut. 'Look out, it's Father,' he warned his brother.

Edward leapt up quickly. 'What does he want?' He sounded exasperated. 'He never comes down here. He just sends Stokes to fetch me. Quick, Will, help me get the machine away. I don't want him asking questions. If he knew what I was doing he'd send me away to sea or something. He hates anything he doesn't understand.'

Will bundled up the cables and metal spikes while Edward wheeled the machine into his hut. By the time Josiah arrived only the large power drum remained on the grass outside.

'Hello, Edward. Ah! There you are, William. I've been looking for you. You've been spending a lot of your time over here this last week or so, haven't you?' He clearly did not like the idea of Will passing his time at Edward's laboratory. Perhaps he thought he might be influenced by Edward's feelings about cotton mills. 'What have you both been up to? What was that equipment I saw you putting away?'

'I've been showing Will what electricity can do,' said Edward quickly. This was true, if not completely honest.

'I see.' Josiah sounded deeply suspicious. 'And what can it do? What's that metal drum doing there?'

'This is a supply of electricity. I can't show you now because it's drained but when it's charged up I can make motors run and glass bulbs glow brighter than any gas light. It's marvellous, Father. I've converted the old water mill to generate electricity, you know. You really ought to allow me to wire up the house, then we could have lighting for free.'

'We have gas lighting, Edward. That's good enough for me.' His words sounded final and Edward's face fell.

'Yes, Father.' His eyes were fixed firmly on the floor so Josiah could not see the hurt look in them.

'Good. But now I have a little surprise for William.' The old man turned to his younger son, smiling. 'There's something for you up at the house that might tempt you away from here for a while.'

Will looked up, intrigued. 'What is it, Father?'

'Why don't you run along and see. It's leaning on the door to the kitchen at the moment. Edward and I will follow at a more leisurely pace.' Will set off immediately.

Edward was uneasy, thinking that Josiah would start discussing his future role at the cotton mill again. But as they walked up to the house together, Josiah seemed more ready to talk about Will than Edward.

'I don't think it's entirely healthy for Will to spend all his time in your laboratory, Edward.'

'We do most of the experiments outside, Father. He's getting plenty of fresh air.'

'Even so. I'd rather he spent some of his time in more usual boyish pursuits.'

'Like mixing with barge men and mill girls?'

Josiah frowned. 'You know what I mean, Edward. Boys of William's age should be swimming and walking and playing with the dogs. That sort of thing. I'd like you to encourage him in that if you would.'

Edward sighed. He was very reluctant to let Will go because he needed him for the time transfer experiments. 'I did promise to teach him photography this summer. Would that be appropriate?'

His father brightened. 'Yes. I think he'd enjoy that. Perhaps he would like to photograph me when he is proficient in the art.'

Josiah cleared his throat and looked slightly bothered about what he had to say next. Edward sensed his discomfort and they walked on looking resolutely straight ahead. 'Edward, since your mother died I have only had you boys as company.' Edward said nothing. 'Now I may not seem like an affectionate man, and I know you and I have had our disagreements, but I do care for you both very much and in every decision I make, I have both of your best interests at heart.'

Edward was not used to such plain emotion from his father and did not know what to say. An uncomfortable, 'Yes, Father,' was all he could manage.

'I am not going to forbid you from teaching William certain scientific experiments but I want you to know this. I do not entirely trust science. I believe you may be meddling with things that God never intended men to know.' Here he turned to face Edward. He gripped him hard by the elbow and looked him fiercely in the eye. 'That boy means the world to me and if ever you let him come to any harm, then I will never forgive you.' The sudden intensity of Josiah's words took Edward by surprise and he thought guiltily about all the risks Will had already been exposed to. He was about to reassure his father that Will would not come to any injury when they were interrupted. Excited cries of delight were coming from the direction of the house.

'Thank you, Father. It's magnificent.' Will's shouts could be heard long before he came into view. When he did appear, it was at high speed as he careered wildly around the corner on his new bicycle. The front wheel was much larger than the rear wheel and Will was perched high on the saddle with his legs racing around recklessly.

Josiah and Edward leapt out of the way in alarm as the machine narrowly missed them. They spun around to follow the course of Will's first voyage. 'I say, William. Slow down,' Josiah shouted. 'You must learn to control the machine before you go so fast.' But it was too late. Will was riding far too fast as he came to a corner. Unable to slow up, he left the path and the bicycle bounced over the rough ground with Will shouting wildly – half from fear and half from delight.

'Slow down, Will! Apply the brake,' Edward shouted through cupped hands. But Will gathered more speed as the slope got steeper and he disappeared from view around the corner of the woods.

Josiah Rawlings clutched at Edward's elbow again, this time in apprehension. 'I do hope he hasn't forgotten about the lake,' he said. A moment later the sounds of a loud crunch followed by a louder splash announced that William had indeed forgotten about the lake. The two hurried to see if Will was all right and they found him up to his waist in the muddy water. His eyes were shining and his spirits were not dampened, even if the rest of him was soaking.

'That was amazing,' he managed to say between big gulps of air.

Edward turned to his father, laughing. 'Is that your idea of a safe boyish activity?'

Josiah had the grace to look embarrassed. 'Yes. Quite,' he said, before he too burst out laughing.

The three Rawlings made their way back up to the house together, Will's excited voice carrying over the grounds as he described his first bicycle ride. Josiah laid a hand on Will's shoulder, being careful not to get his own jacket wet, as Edward pushed the bicycle. It was one of those moments, all too rare since Mother had died, when they felt like a family.

Tom Harris woke with a groan. He felt terrible. His head ached, his joints were sore and he was so cold. He blinked in the early morning light and tried to remember what had happened to him. He did not normally wake up soaked in dew and staring up at the trees. As memories of the night came back to him, a horrible sight appeared in front of his eyes. John Sullivan was leering down at him with that infuriating grin of his. His face was so close that Tom could see the hairs that grew out of his nostrils and feel his hot breath on his face. 'Just when I thought things were bad,' groaned Tom. His voice was croaky because his throat felt all dry.

'Morning, Tom,' sneered John. 'Had a rough night, did you?'

'None o' your business what I do,' growled Tom, struggling to sit up. There was no way that Tom was going to tell

73

John what he had seen last night. He would never hear the end of it. 'What are you doing here anyway?'

'Just passing.'

Tom was suddenly suspicious and he quickly felt his pockets. This was difficult because his coat was soaking wet and his fingers were cold and fumbling. His wallet was still there. His newspaper was gone. That was no real loss, but his lighter was gone as well. He rechecked his pockets. 'Where's my lighter?' he demanded.

'What lighter? What are you asking me about your lighter for?' John seemed genuinely puzzled but then he grinned again as he realized what must have happened. 'You don't mean to say you've lost the lighter that Sal gave you? The brass one with your initials on?'

'Don't talk about my Sally like that, you toe-rag. Now stop messing and give me my lighter back.' Tom was still sitting on the wet grass but he made a grab at John who jumped back laughing.

'Steady now. Don't want to hurt yourself fighting an Englishman. Save that for the Germans. I ain't got your lighter and I don't think Sal is going to be too happy when I tell her you lost it.'

Tom was in a real rage by now. 'You ain't going to see my Sally. You stay away from her.'

'Oh, but I am going to see her. Got a package for the big house.' John waved a brown paper parcel in front of Tom's face. It was addressed to Rawlings House where Sally worked as a maid. 'In about ten minutes' time I'll probably be sat nice and snug in the kitchen having a cup of coffee with her. She'll be upset of course when I tell her how careless you are with her presents, but no matter. She can cry on my shoulder.'

Tom staggered to his feet as quickly as he could but John

was long gone and all he could do was shout after him. He dragged himself into his hut rubbing some feeling back into his numb body. A hot cup of coffee was just what he needed. He put the kettle on and started to get out of his wet clothes. He carefully went through all his pockets again and then began to look around for his lighter. He had to find it. Sally was paying far too much attention to John Sullivan as it was. If he were to leave next week after arguing with her then who knows how long it would be before Sally left him for John. Tom searched in vain for his lighter because although it was just outside his hut it was lying there over sixty years ago.

Jed and Lizzie kept their heads down as they sat at the kitchen table. Their dad was standing over them and they didn't want to look him in the eye.

'Well?' said Dad. 'I'm still waiting for an explanation. Do either of you know what that idiot was talking about?'

'Rob!' Mum interrupted Dad indignantly. 'You're talking about a policeman.'

'He may be a policeman,' Dad defended himself, 'but he was still a complete plank.'

'Rob, that is enough!'

'Oh, all right.' Dad dismissed the issue with a wave of his hand. 'I'm sorry. Do either of you know what that policeman was talking about?'

There was an awkward silence for a few moments before Lizzie answered. 'Not really.'

'What do you mean "not really"? What was all that about you studying old documents and gravestones?'

'Er, yeah. That was sort of right.' Jed blushed.

'Sort of?'

Jed sighed. 'He's right. We have been studying old documents and graveyards and we've been talking to old Mr Harris.'

'Right. Well there's nothing illegal about that. I would like to know why though.'

Dad waited expectantly until Jed, having been nudged by Lizzie, reluctantly answered. 'We wanted to find out about a boy called Will Rawlings.'

'Yes?' Dad clearly expected more.

Jed, now red to the ears, spoke in a low mumble. 'We thought he might be a ghost.'

Dad made an impatient noise in his throat and shook his head in disbelief. 'A ghost. I would have thought there were better ways to spend your spare time.' The children said nothing. 'And what about that machine he was talking about?'

Both children looked up at their dad. They had nothing to hide here so Lizzie shook her head as she answered. 'No idea what he was talking about.'

Dad gave them a penetrating stare for a moment and the children held his gaze. 'OK. I believe you.' He sat down looking thoughtful and for almost a minute nobody said anything. Mum eventually broke the silence.

'What did he want then?'

'I don't know,' said Dad slowly. 'He can't have been looking for a ghost, but it must be something important. There's more to this than meets the eye. What is Morgan trying to hide? Why wouldn't he tell us what that mysterious machine did?' Dad pondered for a few moments and then seemed to make a decision. He turned to his children. 'Jed, Lizzie, there are no such things as ghosts. I don't know what Morgan wanted but I mean to find out if I can.' Dad sensed a possible story here. 'If you see Morgan again, you are to let me know what he wants. Is that understood?'

'Yes, Dad,' the children answered sullenly.

'Good. Then we'll say no more about ghosts.'

Jed now had a grumble to make to Lizzie. 'Why did you have to let on that we knew Mr Harris?'

'Sorry. I didn't mean to. It's just he took me by surprise when he told us Mr Harris is called Tom. I was cleaning this lighter, see, and it's got the initials *T.H.* on it.'

Dad took a look at the lighter. 'This is nice,' he said, as he turned it over in his hands. 'My dad used to have one a bit like it. It must be fifty years old or more. Where did you get it?'

'Arthur dug it up in the woods at the back.'

Dad gave it a shake and flicked the mechanism. It gave a satisfying click but no flame emerged. 'You've done a really nice job of cleaning it up. It needs some fluid and a new flint but it should work fine then. If you like I'll get you some on Monday. I can pop out at lunch-time.'

'Thanks, Dad.' The tense atmosphere was beginning to fade. 'I was going to give it to you, but now I know that the initials are the same as Mr Harris's I thought I'd give it to him. Do you mind?'

'No. I don't need it. Give it to the old boy. He might like it.' He turned back to the sink to carry on washing the dishes. 'He may not be able to see it but he might like it.'

On Tuesday afternoon Mr Harris was sitting next to his window at the nursing home. There was a cup of tea on the table but it was going to go cold as Mr Harris rummaged through a wooden box balanced on his knees. His shaky hands picked up photographs and news cuttings as he went over in his

77

mind some of the events of his life. At eighty-seven he had much more to look back on than to look forward to. He picked up a small jewellery box and had another look at the ring he had never had the chance to give to Sally. Then he came to the bundle of letters at the bottom of the box. He slipped them out of the old knotted string that held them together and turned them over one by one until he came to her letter. He held it close to his face as if to read it again. His weak eyes could hardly make the writing out but he knew it by heart anyway. It was short and not unkind, but even after sixty years his eyes were damp as he reread the letter from Sally telling him that she was going to marry John Sullivan.

'Visitor for you, Mr Harris.' A woman with curly hair and a pale green uniform came into the room followed by a slightly shy-looking Lizzie. 'Oh Mr Harris, you've let your tea go cold. I'll get you another one. Would you like a drink, dear?' This question was to Lizzie.

'No, thank you. I don't need anything.'

'Right, I'll leave you two together then.' She left carrying the cold cup of tea.

Mr Harris peered short-sightedly at Lizzie when she was gone. 'Oh, it's you.'

'Yes.' Lizzie felt awkward and did not know what to say.

'Your brother about?'

'No.' Lizzie saw the pile of papers and photographs on the table and she remembered that Mr Harris had a picture of Will taken when he was older than in the picture they had seen in the book. 'Oh,' she said excitedly, 'can I see your picture of Will Rawlings?'

'How d'you know I got a picture of Will?' Lizzie had forgotten that Mr Harris did not know that she was the daughter of the journalist who had been to see him. She would have to tell him now.

'My dad told me. He came to see you from the newspaper.'

'Oh him. I showed him the picture. He didn't believe me.'

'I believe you,' said Lizzie. 'And Jed does. Dad still doesn't though. We had a policeman come to question us but Dad wouldn't listen to him.'

'Police come to see me too, in 1940. Didn't tell 'em much.'

Lizzie smiled at the obstinate old man. 'No, neither did we.'

Mr Harris shuffled through the collection of old photos and handed her the one that he selected. 'That's him. The youngest one. You seen him?'

Lizzie looked at the family photograph. There was Will in his jacket and Eton collar and knee-length trousers. 'Yes,' she whispered. 'That's him.'

'I seen him too.'

The moment was broken by the uniformed lady returning with a fresh cup of tea. She handed it to Mr Harris who wobbled most of it into the saucer as he held it. 'What you come for?' he asked, when the woman had gone again. Lizzie smiled as she remembered.

'I've got a present for you, Mr Harris.' She pulled the old lighter out of her pocket and handed it to him. Dad had managed to get it working and now when you struck the flint, a fierce flame burst out of the top. Mr Harris took it and held it up close to his glasses. His voice was strange as he asked, 'Where'd you get this from?'

'Our dog found it in the woods behind our house. I cleaned it up and I saw the initials on it and when I found out you were called Tom I thought I'd give it to you.' Mr Harris's shoulders had begun shaking slightly as Lizzie spoke and there were tears in his eyes.

'Oh, Sally,' he said after a while. 'I looked for it. I really did. I didn't mean to lose it. I'm sorry, Sally.'

Lizzie was alarmed. She never knew what to do when grown-ups cried. She realized that Mr Harris did not know what her name was so she reached over and placed her hand on Mr Harris's arm. 'I'm not called Sally, Mr Harris. My name's Lizzie.'

Mr Harris pulled out a handkerchief and wiped his eyes and blew his nose. 'Sorry, miss. Didn't mean to cry, but you took me by surprise.'

'I'm sorry I upset you, Mr Harris. I thought you might like the lighter.'

'I do miss. I like it very much. I been looking for it for sixty years.' He ran his fingers gently over the shiny brass before putting it in his box with his other precious things. 'This lighter lost me a wife.'

Edward and Will were almost completely in the dark. Edward had put thick black coverings over both the windows in his laboratory and blocked off the light that came in around the door frame. The only light came from a dull bulb on the corner of the workbench that had a red glass cover over it. The red light shining upwards on their faces gave the brothers eerie-looking expressions – a bit like pantomime devils. Edward was teaching Will how to develop the photographs he had taken that morning.

'What are we fumbling about in the dark for?' Will asked, as he bumped into a cupboard and sent a pile of cans flying to the floor.

'I would have thought that was obvious, Will. What did I tell you made a photograph appear on a glass plate?'

'Light shining on it.'

'That's right, which means we have to keep them in the dark until the image is fixed. Otherwise all our pictures will be wiped off by the extra light shining on them.'

Edward showed Will the lengthy process of turning an image recorded on the glass into a printed version on paper. This involved lots of soaking in chemicals, careful timing and rinsing in water. The smell of chemicals was strong and overpowering. If Josiah had thought photography was a healthy activity for boys, he might have changed his mind if he could have smelt this part of the process. At last they were nearly completed.

'This is the most exciting part of making a photograph, Will. Even if you've done it a thousand times, the part where you first see your picture appearing is always fun.' Edward picked up the sheet of photographic paper with a pair of wooden tongs and carefully lowered it into a metal tray of strong-smelling liquid. 'The image is already on the paper but it won't appear until we soak it in the developing fluid. Watch, Will, this is like magic.' Edward and Will both leaned over the tray and watched as the image, at first faint and ghostly, appeared on the paper. It was a picture of Will proudly holding his bicycle on the drive outside the house. Will was delighted.

'It's wonderful. Can I hold it?'

'No, not yet. First I have to fix it and then rinse it and then leave it to dry. You'll be able to hold it by this afternoon.' Edward transferred the picture to another tray of chemical fluid, then to a tray of water. Finally he clipped the finished photograph to a piece of string that was strung across the room to let it dry.

'There now, let's do the next one.' The second picture was rather special because it was a trick photograph. Edward had set the camera up on the edge of the woods and started to take the picture, but he had only kept the shutter at the front of the camera open for half the time needed. Then he had shut the camera up and got Will to stand among the trees and opened the shutter again to take the other half of the picture. The result of all this was that the trees looked real and solid, but Will looked faint and transparent. The trees could be seen showing through him. 'There,' said Edward, as he lifted the finished picture. 'The Ghost of Will Rawlings.' Will looked at his own ghostly image, his eyes full of wonder.

There were five photographs altogether. One of Edward smoking his pipe. One of Josiah as he had suggested, and finally one of all three Rawlings together. They had to make two prints of the last image because they had promised one to George Harris whom they had got to work the camera while the three of them posed for the picture. Soon all of the photographs were strung like washing on a line and Edward said it was safe to let the light in again.

'There, that should keep Father happy,' said Edward as he lifted down the blackout material.

Will stood looking at the photographs with his hands behind his back. They looked even better in the daylight. An idea occurred to him. 'Would it be safe to take the camera when we travel in time?'

Edward turned to face Will, looking thrilled.

'Yes! That is a brilliant idea. We could take some photographs of the future.' He continued folding the blackout material while he made his plans. 'We could start this afternoon. You ought to go and ride your bike around for a while now. Make sure Father sees you having fun. I've got some entries to make in my journal and then after lunch I think Father is going to meet a man from the railways to talk about cheaper transport. While he's gone we'll send you to the year 2000 like we decided yesterday.' Will agreed and moments later he was wobbling away on his bicycle back up to the house. Edward took out his small red book and began making some notes in it.

Dad was peering carefully out of the living room window. He made sure he stayed behind the net curtains because he did not want to be seen. It was very early on Sunday morning and Jed was rubbing his eyes sleepily when he wandered into the room a moment later. 'What's up, Dad? It's still night.' He came to the window and was about to pull the curtain back to look too when his dad caught his arm.

'Shh,' he hissed. 'I heard a noise so I came down to see what it was. That lunatic policeman's over there.'

'Who? Inspector Morgan?'

'Yes. Not so loud,' Dad whispered.

'These windows are double glazed, Dad. He can't hear us. What's he doing?'

'I don't know. He's fiddling about with that rubbish skip. Hang on a minute, he's going. Jed, go over and see what he's done, will you?'

'I'm in my pyjamas.' Jed was indignant.

'Oh, all right. I'll go.'

'You're in your pyjamas.'

'I'll put my dressing gown on then,' said Dad, sounding exasperated at Jed's lack of initiative.

Dad was really quite embarrassing sometimes. Jed watched him incredulously as he ambled casually across the road in his tartan dressing gown and slippers, and then leant on the rubbish skip trying to look inconspicuous. Luckily it was not yet five o'clock and only a ginger tom-cat was there to stare at him. A minute later Dad was back in the living room, outraged.

'There's a camera fixed to the skip. He's spying on us. It's incredible. The camera is tiny. You'd never see it unless you were looking for it.' Dad had seen a lot of cameras in his newspaper work but never anything like this. 'It must be cutting-edge technology and they complain about being under-funded.' Dad was not going to tolerate being placed under police observation. 'Jed, when you're dressed I want you to go and pull faces at the camera. I'll show them you can't . . .' He tailed off and his expression changed as he became more thoughtful. 'No, let's leave it there. Let's pretend we haven't noticed it.'

'Why, Dad?'

'He's up to something, isn't he? It must be really important. This could be a big story.' Dad looked more excited as he spoke. 'I could get myself a job in a national newspaper if I can pull this off. We'll leave the camera there and pretend to co-operate with his investigations. That way we won't raise his suspicions.'

'You don't think that the sight of you walking around the street in your pyjamas and dressing gown will raise his suspicions then?'

Dad waved this objection aside. 'He's only just left. He can't be monitoring us yet.' Dad left the room to make an early morning cup of tea, leaving Jed thinking. A job on a national newspaper would mean more money, but they would have to move to London, wouldn't they? Jed did not want to move again and he was sure Mum and Lizzie wouldn't either.

Edward fidgeted with impatience as the machine hummed and sparked. He could not look at his watch as Will had taken that with him to measure the photograph exposure. Instead he had brought out an old carriage clock which was now balanced on top of the machine with its brass ball mechanism spinning, first one way, then the other. It did not have a second hand so timing the trip was going to be less precise this time. He made a note in his red book to remind himself to include an accurate clock if ever he built another machine.

It had been over a week since Will had had the idea to take the camera, but this was the first time they had managed to do it. With Josiah keeping a closer eye on Will's activities, they had found less opportunity to use the machine. On the few occasions they had had the chance, they had used their trips to find a time when something was happening that was worth photographing. Most trips had taken them to times that looked disappointingly like 1879. Finally, however, they had come across a moment in the year 2000 when some new buildings were going up close by.

The minute hand on the clock seemed to have moved on about three minutes. That should be plenty of time for Will to have taken the photograph. Edward switched the machine off. As the hum died, Will reappeared with the camera.

'Well?' asked Edward eagerly. 'How did it go?'

Will was readjusting to his surroundings. Before he had the chance to answer, the brothers were interrupted by a quiet cough attracting their attention. Edward immediately spun around to see who the visitor was and found himself facing a youngish man in a policeman's uniform. His hard hat came down low over his brow and his dark blue jacket had rows of bright brass buttons. 'Good afternoon, sir, Master Will,' he said, nodding a slight bow with his head.

Edward was shaking. They had never been interrupted while using the machine before. He managed to compose himself and speak to the officer.

'Good afternoon, constable,' he said. He looked at the man more closely. 'Hodges, isn't it?'

The policeman was pleased at being recognized. 'That's right, sir.'

'You're here to see your sister, I suppose.' Sarah Hodges worked in the kitchen up at the house.

'Not today, sir. I hope you will excuse me for interrupting you like this. I have occasion to visit your father in his capacity as Justice of the Peace. I took the liberty of walking through the woods as it is quicker.'

'Yes. That's fine,' said Edward, not really meaning it. Hodges had very nearly witnessed the machine in operation.

'That machine, sir?'

'Yes?' said Edward anxiously.

'May I ask what it does, sir?'

Edward's face reddened. He felt a drop of sweat trickle down his back. 'The machine? Yes. Certainly. It . . . it takes photographs.'

Constable Hodges smiled. 'No, sir. Not that machine. I recognize a camera. We use them in the force sometimes. I meant the other machine.' He looked intently at Edward, who found it hard to hold his gaze.

'Oh, that machine.' He laughed nervously. 'That machine's a bit of a secret at the moment, Hodges. I haven't patented it yet, you see.'

'I do see, sir,' said Hodges, significantly. 'Right then. I won't disturb you any longer. I'll be on my way up to the house. Good afternoon, sir, Master Will.' Constable Hodges nodded again and left them. The two brothers watched him until he was out of sight and then let out a deep sigh of relief.

'Do you think he saw us?' Will asked.

'I don't know,' said Edward. 'He sounded suspicious, but then policemen usually do. That's part of their job. I think we had better get the machine away in case he says something to Father. We'll put it in the corner and cover it with a cloth. Did you take the photograph?'

'Yes. It was early afternoon and the light was still good.'

'Excellent. Let's get it developed then.'

An hour later Edward and Will stood in the laboratory looking at the still-glistening photograph hanging from the string. There were five houses in the picture. 'Amazing,' said Edward. 'Houses from the twenty-first century. What can you see different about them?'

Will looked closely. 'Not much really. Only small things. I've never seen roof tiles like that before.'

'What about the chimneys?'

Will looked. 'There aren't any. How do they keep warm?'

'Electricity of course. I tell you, Will, everyone will have electricity in the future.'

The two brothers continued to study the picture and then Edward pointed to an upstairs window in the middle house. Will followed his finger and gasped. There was a boy looking intently back at the camera. Even at that distance the look of fascinated fear was clear.

'It looks like you were seen, Will,' said Edward.

On Sunday morning the whole family decided to take Arthur for his walk. They usually did when Mum was not working. Walks on Sunday morning had been a big part of life at Little Moor. The roast dinner would be left cooking in the range and they would spend an hour or two walking through the woods and down country lanes. Arthur would race on ahead excitedly and lag behind when he found an interesting smell. Walks were best on frosty winter mornings with the grass crunching underfoot and the countryside glistening as the sun slowly melted the ice. They would arrive back feeling cold and hungry to be greeted by the smell of roast chicken and the warmth of the kitchen. Nothing could compete with that in their new house, and by trying to continue the tradition they probably missed their old home more.

They found themselves walking to the wasteland behind the house again. There weren't many other places to walk and Dad wanted to have a look at the slabs of stone the children had mentioned. Lizzie had told the family about Mr Harris's reaction to the lighter and it was this that Dad was talking about now.

'If old Tom Harris is right about his lighter, then he must have lived around the back of our house sixty years ago.'

'What do you mean "if" he's right. He'd recognize his own lighter if it was a gift from his girlfriend, wouldn't he?' Lizzie was defensive about Mr Harris. She was quite fond of him now, particularly since she had heard the sad story of how he lost his sweetheart after they argued over the loss of the present. She did not like the way Dad ridiculed him.

'I mean the old man's half blind and I'm not completely convinced he'd recognize a double-decker bus let alone a little cigarette lighter.'

Mum intervened again. 'Rob, that's unkind. If Mr Harris says that he lost his lighter sixty years ago and it has unexpectedly turned up, I don't think you should make fun of him.'

Dad backed down. 'Right. Sorry. I am too cynical. It comes from being a journalist.'

They had reached the spot where Will appeared and Dad had a good look at the stone slabs while Arthur raced off into the woods again. 'I may have been wrong about Mr Harris,' Dad said after a while. 'He showed me a picture of himself back in the 1930s and he was standing outside his hut clutching some ghastly ferret. There were trees in the background. Now there was definitely a building here of some sort. There's slabs for a floor and concrete footings where a wooden frame might have gone. If I stand just about here ...' Dad walked about seven or eight metres away from the site of the old hut towards their house. The others joined him.' ... and imagine a hut just there, then it looks pretty much like that old photo did. Perhaps he did lose his lighter in these woods after all.'

The four of them stood still, thinking about Mr Harris before Dad stirred. 'Right, shall we go on?'

The children were reluctant. 'There's not much elsewhere to go,' said Jed.

'What about the woods?'

Their looks betrayed their lack of interest and Dad lost his patience. 'Well, we can't go home yet. I for one am going for a walk in these delightful woods.' He waved a hand in the direction of the trees. Just visible in a clearing were the remains of some rusted-out cars and a discarded washing machine. 'Would you care to join me, ma'am.' He gave a half bow and held out a hand to Mum, who giggled girlishly.

'It would be an honour, sir.' She linked her arm with Dad's and the two set off with Arthur bounding around them. In a few moments they were out of sight.

'How embarrassing are parents?' Lizzie asked.

Jed shook his head in exasperation. 'Just be grateful that Dad isn't in his pyjamas.'

They were still in the same spot when it happened. There

was a faint crackling noise, the air rippled slightly and all of a sudden Will Rawlings was standing in front of them. They both gasped and Will's jaw dropped in surprise. Jed and Lizzie were standing face to face with the boy from the past. For about thirty seconds no one did anything. The Stokes were trembling with fear. They had seen Will before but never this close. Besides, seeing Victorian children materializing out of thin air is something you never really get used to. Will was less frightened than the Stokes but he had no idea what to say. He just stood there open mouthed.

It was Arthur who eventually broke the lull in activity. Never one for keeping pace with the people he was walking with, he had come loping back to investigate where the children had got to. He was dragging a huge stick for a game of fetch. He dropped his stick as soon as he saw Will and stood there, his ears pricked up and his tail wagging relentlessly. Here was somebody new to play with. He bounded forward barking excitedly and Will spun around as he heard the noise. Will was well used to dogs and he should have seen that Arthur's tail was wagging and he only wanted to play. But he was already unnerved by the shock of appearing right in front of people from the future and now the sight of a large, strange dog racing towards him and barking was just too much. He cried out in alarm and backed away. He caught his foot on an old brick and fell over backwards, completely outside the time-field. Arthur bounded towards Will and took a giant leap to land next to him. He never arrived. He was still in mid leap when the air shimmered and the dog vanished just as Will had done before. Everyone stared in amazement. One moment Arthur had been there, the next he was gone. His barks had stopped abruptly, as if someone had switched them off.

There were perhaps five seconds of shocked silence until

Will scrambled up and ran back to where he had been standing. 'No!' he cried. He sounded desperate. 'No! I've only been here about a minute. Turn the machine on again. Edward, please. I'm still here. Please. Oh, it's no good. He can't hear me.' Will broke off, looking utterly lost and alone.

'He's not behaving much like a ghost, is he?' Lizzie was recovering from her shock now. She stepped forward and plucked up the courage to speak. 'Er . . . Hello. Are . . . are you the ghost of William Rawlings?'

Will turned and looked sadly at them. 'No. I am Will Rawlings. Can you tell me what year it is?'

Josiah strode purposefully down towards Edward's laboratory. Will was wasting his time with his brother again. He had seen him from the library window a quarter of an hour before, riding down there on his bicycle, and he had not returned yet. He neared the corner of the woods, where the path turned and brought the laboratory into sight but even before he could see the building he started calling. 'William. William, do you hear me?'

Edward jumped with fright at the sound of his father's voice. Will was time-travelling and Father must not find out what was happening. He quickly reversed the switch and lever to bring Will back before his father rounded the corner. Edward was seething with frustration. He had built his laboratory for privacy but he was constantly being interrupted. Really, it was becoming like Piccadilly Circus. The air rippled as the blue sparks faded away but Will did not reappear. Instead a large red setter dog flew through the air barking wildly and skidded to a halt nearly bowling Edward over. The dog looked around disorientated and confused. It turned sharply to look behind itself and ran a few paces backwards sniffing the ground and clearly looking for something. It whimpered a little from fright and having snuffled around the ground for a while longer, it sat back on its haunches and began to howl.

Edward was as confused as the dog. Where was Will, for goodness' sake? What was this dog doing here? What was he going to tell his father? He tried to pacify the strange dog, but did not have long before Josiah was with him. 'Edward,' the older man thundered, 'what the devil is going on? What is that dog behaving like that for? Can't you make it quiet?'

'I'm trying, Father. Here boy. Be quiet.' He patted and fussed the dog but it was no good. Arthur's howls continued and in the end Edward dragged him by his collar to the laboratory and shut him in. He continued to whine and scratch the door with his paw while Edward turned to face his father.

'What in heaven's name are you doing, Edward? Why was that dog howling like that? What have you done to it?' He eyed the machinery suspiciously.

Edward was in a state of shock bordering on panic. His brother Will was trapped somewhere in the future and he had to act quickly to get him back. He did not want to spend time dealing with an angry, suspicious father. 'I didn't do anything to it. He just took fright at a noise.'

'I don't recognize the dog. He's not one of ours, is he?'

'Yes, he's mine. I got him a few days ago. George Harris knew someone who wanted to get rid of him.'

'Wouldn't have thought you had time for a dog with all your experimenting.' Josiah looked around sharply. 'Where's William?'

Edward tried to sound relaxed but his voice was strained and it betrayed him. 'Will? I don't know. He's not here.'

Josiah frowned. 'His bicycle is,' he said meaningfully. Father and son both looked towards the laboratory where the bicycle was leaning against the wall.

'Yes. His bicycle is.' Edward repeated the words vaguely. It felt as if he was not really there. As if he was witnessing the whole terrible scene from somewhere else. His own voice sounded distant and he felt a heaviness coming over him. He swayed slightly but pulled himself together. He must not give Father any more reason to grow suspicious. 'Yes,' he said more purposefully, 'he was here a while ago, but he didn't stay long.' Edward tried to think of a lie that would make Josiah happy. 'He said he didn't want to bother with me today. He said he was going to explore in the woods.'

Josiah relaxed a little. 'Did he? Good.' He was not completely convinced and he had not missed Edward's strangeness, but he let his suspicions drop for now. 'Are you all right? You look like you've seen a ghost.'

'Yes. I'm fine. I did feel a little strange then. I was up late last night.'

'If you ask me, these experiments of yours aren't healthy. Are you sure that electricity contrivance is safe?' He looked again at the machine. Hodges had said something about a machine, hadn't he?

'Yes. Quite safe, Father.'

'If you say so.' Josiah turned to go and Edward stood still, trying to appear unruffled while his father walked away.

As soon as he was around the corner and out of sight, however, Edward leaped into action. He rushed to the machine, pulled the big lever and waited for the electrical humming noise and blue sparks to begin. Nothing happened. He frantically pulled the lever back and forward again and again and tapped furiously on the gauge. The needle refused to move. Edward felt faint. He slid down to the

93

grass and sat propped against the wooden side of the machine his mind reeling, his body feeling sick. Will was somewhere in the future and the power supply was completely drained.

It took a while for the implications of Will's words to sink in. How could this be Will Rawlings? He was born in the 1800s. He'd be dead by now. Lizzie moved closer to Will and peered intently at him. No, she couldn't see through him, however hard she tried. She tentatively reached out to touch him. Will drew back a little, uncertain of Lizzie's intentions, but then stopped as he realized what she was doing. She touched him slowly on the shoulder, ready at any moment to pull her hand back if by some horrible chance it should pass through him. But no, the boy was flesh and blood. She could feel him trembling and noticed his face was very pale.

'You're not a ghost,' she said.

'I know,' said Will.

'But what are you doing here then?'

'It's complicated.'

'I'll bet it is.'

Jed stepped forward to join his sister and Will looked at him. His eyes narrowed in concentration.

'I've seen you before,' said Will. Jed was confused for a moment but then his face cleared.

'You've taken my photograph.'

Will looked from Jed's face away to the row of houses. He smiled.

'Is that your house?' he asked, pointing.

'That's right,' said Jed.

Will held out his hand to Jed. 'I'm Will Rawlings.'

Jed took his hand. 'Pleased to meet you, Will. I'm Jed Stokes and this is my sister Lizzie.'

They were interrupted by the sound of Mum and Dad returning from their walk in the woods. Jed tensed. What would Dad say if he saw Will? He turned to Lizzie with a questioning look on his face. She shrugged. They were getting closer. They could clearly hear Dad grumbling about Arthur. Jed made a quick decision and turned back to Will.

'Will, I don't think you ought to meet my Dad just yet. Not until we've found out a bit more.' Will could hear Dad's loud complaints and looked nervous. He quickly nodded in agreement. He knew all about angry fathers. 'You could hide in the woods until they're gone.' Will turned and ran for cover, and a moment later Mum and Dad were back on the scene.

'Where has that idiot dog got to?'

'I don't know,' said Lizzie. 'He did come back for a while but he seems to have disappeared again.' Little did Dad know how accurate Lizzie's words were. He made impatient noises and started calling out for the dog again. Jed and Lizzie joined in, knowing they would never find him this way, but wanting to stop Dad from becoming suspicious. Dad soon lost his patience.

'Oh, well. He'll turn up. Let's go in.'

'We'll stay out a bit longer,' said Jed. Dad seemed surprised.

'I thought you were bored of this walk.'

'Well, yeah,' Jed said tentatively, while he racked his brains for an excuse to stay out. 'We'll wait for Arthur to come back.'

'OK,' agreed Dad. 'See you later.' He turned and walked home with Mum.

When they were safely gone, Jed and Lizzie turned back

to Will who was anxiously peering out from behind a tree. 'OK Will,' said Jed. 'Tell us everything.'

Twenty minutes later Will had finished his tale. The three children had sat down on whatever they could find – Lizzie and Will on a dumped fridge lying on its side and Jed on an old car seat he had dragged out of some tall grass. Jed thought he had found the best seat until he realized that the foam upholstery was full of dirty water which had been seeping into his trousers the whole time Will was speaking. He jumped up quickly, grumbling. Will's mind was wandering to his surroundings now he had finished his story. He got up and pulled at a piece of twisted metal and looked at it curiously.

'Is this a bicycle?'

Jed managed to drag his attention away from his wet bottom. 'Yeah. It's broke now. That's why someone's dumped it here.'

Will looked at the tangled chain and gears and punctured tyres. 'I've got a bicycle, but it's nothing like this.'

Lizzie was sitting deep in thought as she considered everything Will had told them. 'Let's get this straight,' she said at last. 'You're here because your brother sent you forward in time from 1879?'

Will dropped the bike and turned back to Lizzie. 'Yes.'

'Where's our dog then?'

'He was inside the time-field so he'll have gone back to 1879 instead of me. Don't worry about him,' Will added, when he saw Lizzie's look of concern. 'Edward will look after him and send him back as soon as he can.'

Lizzie shook her head. 'I'm not worried about Arthur. I'm worried about you.'

Will suddenly looked more serious. 'Why?'

'You need to get back to your own time.'

'Yes, I do. I'll have to get into the time-field next time it appears.'

Lizzie looked doubtful. 'But you say your brother can only switch it on for three minutes each day.'

'Twice a day,' Will corrected her. 'We've got two power drums.'

'Well, that's still not very long each day, if you don't know when it's going to happen. You can't just sit here all day waiting.'

No,' agreed Jed. 'Particularly with Inspector Morgan hanging about watching everything we do.'

'Who?'

Jed explained about Inspector Morgan.

'Do you think we should tell him about Will?' Lizzie asked.

Jed looked uncertain. 'I don't know. I mean I know he's a policeman and everything but I don't trust him. I think he wants the machine for himself. I don't know if he'd want to help Will get home. Anyway Dad told us not to talk to him.'

'Shall we tell Dad then?'

'Do you want to tell him we've found our ghost?'

'But that's just it,' Lizzie persisted. 'Will's not a ghost. Dad would have to believe us if he met Will.'

Jed considered this for a moment. 'I'm not sure about Dad either,' he said at last.

'What?' Lizzie sounded shocked. 'He'd want to help Will. You know he would.'

'Yeah, he would, but . . .'

'But what?'

'It's just that Dad thinks there's a really big news story behind all this and if he knew about that time-machine he'd want to find out all about it and then he'd sell the story and

Will might get forgotten in all the fuss.' Lizzie was thought-ful. 'And,' Jed added, 'if Dad got that story then he'd get a job with a big newspaper and we'd all have to move to London.'

That settled it in Lizzie's mind. 'Right,' she decided, 'we'll just have to find a way of looking after Will until we can get him back home without Inspector Morgan finding out he's here and without Mum and Dad knowing who he is.'

'Easy then,' said Jed bitterly.

Will looked from Jed to Lizzie as they spoke, his appre-hension growing as he listened to them discussing his fate. The seriousness of the situation was only just dawning on him.

Ten minutes later Jed was at his front door. He let himself in to be greeted by the smell of roast dinner. He wandered into the kitchen nervously. Dad looked up from his newspaper.

'Hello, Jed. Any sign of Arthur?' Jed shook his head. Dad made more impatient noises and went back to reading.

'Where's Lizzie?' Mum asked.

'Er . . . she's still out there looking for Arthur. I've only come in to change my wet trousers.'

Dad smirked. 'Jed! I'm surprised at you. A boy of your age ought to have his bodily functions well under control by now. What happened? Did you see your ghost again?'

Jed tensed but managed to answer naturally. 'Ha ha! Very funny. If you must know I sat on a wet car seat.' He changed the subject quickly. 'Mum, I've met a friend. Can he come to lunch?'

'Yes, of course. Who is it? Daniel?'

'No. He's called Will. I don't think you know him.'

'Will who?'

'Will R . . .' Jed just managed to stop himself saying Will's real name. 'Roberts,' he finished.

'Will R . . . Roberts?' Dad looked at Jed strangely. 'You're stuttering now. Get a grip, son.'

Jed was exasperated. 'Hiccups,' he said and he hiccupped again loudly to prove it.

In another ten minutes he was back with Lizzie and Will in dry trousers and carrying a spare set of clothes. 'It's OK,' he said. 'Mum says it's all right for Will to come to lunch. I've said his name is Will Roberts because Dad knows the name Rawlings. Dad's seen your picture as well,' he said to Will, 'but if you change into these clothes he probably won't recognize you.' He handed the boy a pair of his jeans and a T-shirt. Will examined them dubiously before going behind a tree to change.

'Is this going to work?' asked Lizzie in a low voice so Will wouldn't hear.

'I don't know,' Jed answered. 'What else can we do?'

'What *are* we going to do?'

Jed shrugged. 'Spend the afternoon looking out of my window until we see the time-field appear and then make a run for it I suppose.' Lizzie seemed unsure but this wasn't the end of their problems. 'Oh no!' Jed said.

'What?' his sister asked anxiously.

'Morgan's got a hidden camera pointing at our front door. How are we going to get Will in without him finding out?'

Lizzie put her hand to her forehead in despair. 'We're going to have to climb over the back fence.'

'What and trample through the flower beds and walk mud into the kitchen? Mum's going to love that.'

'Any better ideas?'

Jed had none. Will emerged from behind the tree carrying his own clothes and wearing Jed's. Will was two years younger than Jed and about a head shorter. The T-shirt Jed had given him nearly reached his knees and the jeans had had to be rolled up. With the old-fashioned lace-up boots and Will's long flowing hair, the overall effect was strange to say the least.

'This is never going to work,' said Jed despondently.

Five minutes later the three children trooped into the kitchen through the back door. Dad looked up sharply.

'What are you up to? How did you get round to the back garden?'

'We, er . . . climbed over the fence.'

'What?' Dad was incredulous. 'What did you do that for?'

'It was quicker,' Jed defended himself.

'What about the flower beds?'

'Um . . .' Jed shuffled his feet trying to hide his muddy shoes. 'Dad, Mum,' he said quickly to change the subject, 'this is my friend Will.' Jed and Lizzie moved aside to reveal Will in his ill-fitting clothes, his mouth open as he stared in wonder at the electric spotlights in the ceiling.

Dad and Mum were slightly taken aback at Will's appearance and for once Dad was momentarily silenced. Mum recovered first.

'Pleased to meet you, Will.' Will did not respond. The bright lights seemed to have mesmerized him.

'Is your friend all right?' asked Dad in a low voice. 'You know.' He tapped his head to make his meaning clear.

'Course he is,' hissed Jed. 'Will,' he said more loudly and nudged his new friend. 'This is my mum and dad.

Will tore his eyes away but couldn't focus for a while. Little blobs of coloured light in the shape of light bulbs seemed to be dancing in front of his eyes. 'Pleased to meet you, Mr and Mrs Stokes,' he said vacantly while he blinked. Mum was impressed.

'What a polite young man,' she said approvingly. She looked at Will more closely. 'Jed, isn't that your T-shirt?'

Jed started guiltily. Then he looked at Will and groaned inwardly. He had given Will the bright orange T-shirt they had bought on holiday last year. Why hadn't he picked out a less memorable one? 'Er . . . yeah it is. I . . . I lent him some clothes because he got wet as well.'

'I see. Shall I have Will's clothes then? I can get them clean and dry before he goes home.'

A hunted look entered Jed's eyes. 'No!' He thrust the bundle of Victorian clothing behind his back. They were a dead giveaway. Mum was taken aback by the ferocity of Jed's reply. 'I mean no thanks,' Jed said more calmly. 'They're all right really. I'll just put them on my radiator.'

'OK,' Mum replied. 'You're just in time all of you. Lunch is in ten minutes. You'll need to take those muddy shoes off and wash your hands and Will, do you want to phone your family to tell them where you are?'

A look of panic passed over Will's face. 'I don't know,' he said. Lizzie came to his rescue.

'There's no need for that. They won't mind.'

'Lizzie!' Mum frowned. 'What am I always telling you about letting me know where you are? Of course Will must phone home.' She picked up the mobile handset. 'What's your number, Will?'

'My number of what?' he asked, his eyes darting around the kitchen like a frightened rabbit's. Dad's look grew more and more quizzical and even Mum was a little taken aback. Jed intervened again.

'I know it,' he said quickly. He grabbed the handset and dialled the speaking clock. 'Here,' he said, handing it to Will. 'Speak to your Dad and tell him you're staying here for lunch.'

Will looked doubtfully at the handset and then back at Jed, who nodded encouragingly. Will tentatively took it and after more desperate looks from Jed began to speak. 'Hello, Father,' he said at the top of his voice holding the telephone in front of his face. Jed cringed and grabbed Will's hand to move the phone into the right position.

'Talk normally,' he whispered. Nothing happened. Will was now holding his head on one side as he listened transfixed to the man telling him that on the third stroke it would be twelve fifty-three precisely. 'Talk,' pleaded Jed. Will started into action.

'Hello, Father,' he said, 'I am at my friend Jed's for luncheon.' He handed the phone back to Jed, who desperately tried to put things right. 'Hello, Mr Roberts,' he said. He paused for a moment as if someone was answering him. 'Yes, that's right. Will's staying for lunch. He'll probably stay here all afternoon.' Another pause. 'No it's no problem. Right. Bye then.' He hung up and ushered Will to the door. 'We'll wash our hands upstairs,' he said.

'Not until you've removed your shoes,' said Mum. The three children hastily kicked their muddy shoes off by the back door and escaped upstairs.

'That kid is odd,' said Dad when they had gone. Mum couldn't help but agree. Dad pondered a bit. 'His face seems familiar,' he said. 'Jed hasn't brought him home before, has he?'

'No,' said Mum. 'I think I would remember him.'

Dad nodded in agreement.

Lunch was excruciating for the Stokes children. They were constantly on edge as they worried that Will might give himself away. Fortunately Will was quiet most of the time because at home he was not allowed to speak at the meal table unless an adult spoke to him first. Unfortunately Mum and Dad would keep asking him questions. He always answered politely, but it usually took a while to get his attention. His gaze would be firmly fixed on the gravy jug slowly rotating inside the micro-wave or on the electric mixer Mum was using to make the custard. By the end of the meal Mum still thought Will was a sweet, polite child if a little strange and Dad was convinced he was a half-wit. They had learned a bit about his background and although none of it gave him away, the children were relieved when the meal was over and they could disappear to Jed's room.

'I'm glad that's over,' said Lizzie.

'Yeah,' agreed Jed. 'They suspect something's up though. Let's hope we can get Will back before anyone finds out.'

'What do we do now then?' asked Will.

'We're going to have to take it in turns to look out of the window and hope we see the time-thingy appear.'

'Very good,' said Will. 'Where is it?'

'You can see it if you look,' said Jed, crossing to the window. 'It's near that fridge you were sitting on.'

'What's a fridge?' asked Will as he joined Jed. But he didn't get an answer. Instead the older boy pushed him firmly away.

'What?' cried Will in surprise.

'Sorry, Will,' said Jed, taking a step backwards himself. 'Morgan's down there.'

'What?' Now it was Lizzie's turn to cry out. 'Where?'

'Almost exactly where Will appeared.'

'Oh no!' Lizzie crossed to the window to look, but Jed held her back.

'You don't want to be seen,' he said.

Very carefully the three of them crouched down at the window sill and carefully peered over the top to see what the inspector was doing. He was poking about in the grass with a stick and occasionally picking something up, examining it and throwing it back down. The children watched anxiously. What if the time-field appeared now with Morgan there? Not only would he learn the secret of it, but they would not be able to rush down there and send Will back home. Gradually the tension lessened as the policeman worked further and further away from the site.

They were still kneeling together when Dad came into the room. They looked around guiltily as the door opened. Dad rolled his eyes to the ceiling in disbelief. The madness seemed to be spreading.

'Very devout,' he said. 'I mean I know it's Sunday but it's still sweet to see you saying your prayers.'

'We weren't praying,' said Lizzie defensively. The three of them scrambled quickly to their feet.

'No?' said Dad.

'No, we were . . .' Lizzie struggled for a plausible reason to be kneeling at the window. 'We were looking for Arthur.'

'Ah,' said Dad. 'Now that's what I came to see you about. Mum's going out to look for him again. Do you want to go with her?' The children thought about Inspector Morgan sneaking around in the undergrowth and quickly shook their heads. Dad shrugged. 'Oh well,' he said. 'It's up to Mum then. I'm going to watch *Star Trek*.'

Half an hour later Lizzie was growing restless. They were still peering through the window and nothing had happened. Inspector Morgan hadn't returned, but neither had the time-field.

'I'm going to watch telly with Dad,' she declared.

Jed grunted in response. His eyes were fixed on the scene outside. Will was lying on Jed's bed so that he could not be seen from the window. He had one of Jed's magazines and was looking at pictures of boys on BMX bikes. His mouth was open in amazement at the tricks they could perform.

'Can you really do all this on a bicycle?'

'What?' said Jed, turning briefly away from the window. 'Oh yeah. Hops, jumps, wheelies – all that sort of stuff.'

'Amazing,' said Will, as he went back to turning the pages. 'I like your mother,' he said some moments later.

Jed turned his head, a bit puzzled. That was an odd thing to say. He had had loads of friends around to his house but none of them ever commented on his parents. He wouldn't either if he were at a friend's house. Then he remembered Will didn't have a mum. He immediately felt a bit awkward. He wanted to be sympathetic but didn't know what to say. 'Yeah. I like her too,' he managed at last. 'And Dad's all right really, when you're used to him.'

Will nodded. 'Like my father. He seems fierce but he's really kind as well.'

Jed turned back to the window. He hadn't thought about his parents like that before.

Downstairs the closing credits of *Star Trek* were rolling while the theme music played. Lizzie had only seen the last quarter of an hour and hadn't really grasped what was going on.

'I don't get it,' she said.

'Don't get what?' asked Dad, as he flicked the telly off with the remote control.

'What was happening. Why was Dr Spock behaving like that? I thought he was supposed to be all cool and unemotional, but he was shouting and fighting and stuff.'

'That's *Mr* Spock if you don't mind. Dr Spock is someone else entirely.'

'Yeah, whatever you say. I still don't get it.'

'Well,' Dad explained. 'It was all to do with time travel.' Lizzie sat up sharply causing Dad to give her another strange look. 'What *is* going on today?' he asked. 'What are you twitching for?'

'Nothing,' said Lizzie, forcing herself to relax. 'You were saying?'

'Yes,' said Dad. '*Mr* Spock had been thrown back in time by some sort of anomaly in the gravitational field of the planet and so he reverted to the savage behaviour of his primitive ancestors.'

'Really?'

Dad ignored her sarcasm. 'Really,' he said. 'It wouldn't happen like that of course. I mean, Mr Spock would stay part of his own space-time continuum, wouldn't he?'

'Oh, absolutely,' agreed Lizzie.

'People wouldn't change just because they had gone back in time or forward in time for that matter. I mean, let's say people develop the ability to read minds in the twenty-fifth century. If I went forward to that time I wouldn't immediately be able to read minds, would I? I'd still be me.'

Lizzie looked thoughtful. She'd never admit it out loud but her Dad was sort of making sense.

'What could you do with a time-machine then?' she ventured.

Dad was really warming to his theme now. His eyes gleamed with excitement. 'If you had a time-machine, you'd be the most powerful person in the world.'

'How come?' Lizzie was puzzled. 'It's not like a bomb or anything.'

Dad tutted in exasperation. 'Power isn't only to do with force. It's more subtle than that. If you got hold of a time-machine you could do anything. You could go back in time and kill Hitler when he was only a baby, for example. That way you'd be able to prevent World War Two without any-one ever having any idea that it might have happened.' Lizzie's eyes were now opened wide. There was more to her Dad than she had thought. 'You could really do some dam-age as well. I remember reading a story once about a man who went back in time and accidentally killed a dog. That dog, if it had lived, was going to wake its household that night and save them all from a fire. The dog couldn't bark its warning because it was dead so the whole house full of people died.' Dad's voice lowered as the tension in the story built. Lizzie leaned forward as she was gripped by what her dad was saying. 'The man's own great-grandfather was in that house so he died as well and throughout history all his descendants disappeared, including the man himself.' Lizzie sat there stunned for a moment and then with a little cry she ran from the room. Dad was left looking at her empty chair in bewilderment. There was definitely something up with the children today. End-of-term feelings perhaps.

Lizzie burst into Jed's bedroom. 'Will! We have to get you home,' she cried.

Jed turned to his sister in exasperation. 'Which is exactly what we're trying to do while you lounge around watching telly.'

'No, it's more important than that. Will might cause an anomaly in the space-time continuum.'

Will and Jed gave Lizzie a look somewhere between baf-flement and concern. 'I don't think you ought to watch any more *Star Trek*,' Jed said carefully. 'It seems to affect you.'

Lizzie clutched her head in exasperation. 'No, you don't understand. If you go back in time, you can change the past and that will change history. Dad was telling me a story about a man who killed his own great-grandfather.'

'Well, that's a nice way to spend your afternoon. What happened to the man? I hope he went to prison.'

'Of course he didn't go to prison. He disappeared because he didn't have an ancestor anymore.'

'Edward thought of that,' said Will. 'That's why we only went forward in time.'

'But it works both ways,' said Lizzie, almost crying in desperation to make herself understood. 'Good grief, Will, you could be our great-granddad.'

This was too much for Jed. 'Don't be stupid, Lizzie. Our great-granddad is called Percy Stokes. We see him at Christmas and he always calls me John.'

'You're not even trying to understand,' said Lizzie, really crying now. 'What I mean is, what is going to happen to all of Will's descendants if he can't go back to 1879 and grow up and get married and have kids and do all the stuff he's supposed to do?' With that she turned and stalked out of the room, slamming the door after her.

Jed turned back to the window thinking deeply. He hoped he hadn't missed the time-field during that conversation. Lizzie had a good point but there was a nagging doubt in his mind that something was not quite right about what she said.

By teatime the time-field had still not reappeared and the children were forced to go downstairs to eat. It was dreadfully frustrating to think that they might miss their only chance to send Will home. If it didn't come soon, they would have to try and persuade Mum to let Will stay the night.

Their meal was interrupted by the doorbell. Will looked around trying to place the source of the noise while Jed got up to answer it. The patterned glass of the front door made everything wobbly but there was no mistaking the short grey hair and brown overcoat. Inspector Morgan. Jed hung back, reluctant to open the door in case the policeman should try to force his way in and find Will in the kitchen. He tentatively put the security chain on and peered through the crack in the door.

'Hello, Inspector.'

The policeman seemed surprised to see Jed. 'What are you doing here?'

'I live here.'

'I know but . . .' The inspector tailed off confused.

Jed looked at the policeman equally baffled until he realized what the trouble was. Morgan had their house under surveillance and hadn't seen him return from the morning walk because he had climbed the fence. Well, Jed knew that Morgan was spying on them, but he wasn't going to let the inspector know that. He watched him steadily as the unfortunate man opened and shut his mouth like a suffocating goldfish a few times.

'Did you want something, Inspector?'

The inspector pulled himself together. 'Yes. Is your father in?'

'I'll just run and find him for you.'

Inspector Morgan had had his face pressed close to the door throughout this conversation and now Jed slammed the door while he left to get Dad. He did not want the nosy policeman to have any chance of hearing Will while he opened the kitchen door. Inspector Morgan jumped back quickly to prevent his face being hit by the door, but not quickly enough to prevent his tie getting trapped. A moment later when Dad arrived he found the unhappy inspector pressed right up against the door, caught there by his tie. His face looked grotesque squashed against the glass.

Dad was delighted. He enjoyed the scene for a moment before approaching the door.

'Yes, Inspector?' shouted Dad through the door. 'Can I help you?'

'I wonder if you would open this door,' came the muffled reply.

'I'm sorry, Inspector. You'll have to speak more clearly than that.'

'Open this door!' The inspector shouted.

'Why certainly.' Dad released the unfortunate inspector. 'Now what can I do for you?'

Inspector Morgan was rubbing feeling back into his nose. 'Can I come in, Mr Stokes?'

'No, I don't think that's necessary. What did you want?'

'I was wondering if you or your children had observed anything further since my last visit.'

'What sort of thing?'

The inspector seemed reluctant to say. 'Er . . . you remember our conversation?'

'I remember a lot of strange hints about machines and boys disappearing, but really, officer, if you could be more specific?' The thought of that big story was still in Dad's mind. 'What did it do, Inspector? That machine?'

'I can't say.' His voice was sullen.

'Then neither I or my children have anything to report,' said Dad obstinately. 'Good day, Inspector.' Dad began to shut the door.

'No!'

Morgan shouted and threw his weight against the door as if desperate to prevent it shutting. Dad stepped back, shocked. Immediately the policeman realized he had gone too far. He stood up straight again and looked ashamed. 'I mean, please, if you have any information concerning a machine or a boy – he might appear lost or confused – you should tell me.'

Dad looked at the man curiously. 'Yes, Inspector I should,' he said enigmatically. He shut the door. 'But I probably won't.'

Dad was thinking deeply as he returned to the kitchen. The inspector seemed desperate – far more involved than he should be in an ordinary case. Clearly this wasn't an ordinary case. What did that machine do? And all these hints about a boy from the 1870s. Dad's mind flitted to Will who was at this moment sitting at the kitchen table, but he shook the thought from his mind before it could settle there. Don't be stupid, he told himself. You're getting as bad as the kids.

After tea it was suggested that Will should go home.

'Where do you live, Will?' asked Dad reaching for his car keys. 'I'll run you home if you like.'

Will looked confused. Why would Mr Stokes want to run home with him? His own father never ran anywhere. It was too undignified. He was about to answer when Jed butted in.

'Can he stay the night? Please?'

Dad looked to Mum who always made these sort of decisions. Mum shook her head.

'No, I'm sorry, Jed. It's school tomorrow and Will will need to go home for his books and uniform and things.'

'My school has finished for the summer already,' Will volunteered.

'Really? I thought you went to Jed and Lizzie's school.'

'I go to Randall's,' said Will, before stopping to wonder if his school was still there after 121 years. Fortunately it was.

'Randall's eh?' Dad was impressed. 'Good school. Well, darling, what do you think?'

Mum shook her head again and was about to speak when

Jed caught her eye. 'What?' she said. Jed beckoned her into the hall. 'What is it?' she asked again when they were alone.

'Please let him stay.' He sounded desperate.

'Jed, what's all this about? Why do you want him to stay so badly? It's not as if you can spend any time with him. You still have to go to school.'

'I know, it's just that . . . he can't go home.'

'Can't?' Mum looked inquisitively at her son. 'Why ever not?'

Jed looked at his feet. He was going to have to lie. 'He's not very happy at home.'

Mum's face was instantly filled with compassion. 'Oh, the poor dear. What's wrong?'

'I dunno,' said Jed, his eyes still down. 'I don't think he gets on with his Dad.'

'Oh, Jed, that's a real shame but we won't solve his problems by taking him away from home.'

'I know, but he'd really like to stay for a while. He needs to think and stuff.'

'A while?' Mum looked surprised. 'How long were you thinking?'

Jed looked up at his mum. 'A day or two?'

Mum returned her son's pleading gaze for a moment and then relented. 'All right. He can stay – just for a day or two.'

'Thanks, Mum.' Jed gave his mum a quick hug.

'We'll need to phone and tell his parents though,' said Mum reaching for the phone. Jed grabbed it quickly before she could.

'I'll do it,' he said.

Edward strained as he pulled the two power drums on their trolley along the track to the old water mill. Sweat dripped off his forehead and his feet slipped on the gravel. He would normally only take one drum at a time, but today he was desperate. He had just lost his brother in the future and he needed to get his power supply working again. He was being foolish really because he could only charge one at a time, so there was no particular advantage in dragging them both over there at once. The hard work helped though. It gave him a sense of purpose when there was nothing else he could do. Being forced to wait was unbearably frustrating.

Edward's slow progress could be seen quite easily from the kitchen window where Constable Hodges was having a cup of tea with his sister. 'What's Mr Edward up to? Why doesn't he get a servant to help him do that?'

Sarah Hodges crossed the room to join her brother at the window. 'Oh, it's nothing,' she answered when she had seen him. 'He always takes those drums up to the mill in the evening and then he brings them back in the morning. Something to do with his experiments. He doesn't like anyone to help with his experiments except Master Will.'

'But it's not evening. It's not even lunch-time.'

'That's true. Perhaps he's finished early today.'

'Perhaps.' Hodges tugged absently at his moustache for a moment. Something strange seemed to be going on down at Mr Edward's laboratory. That machine of his did something peculiar. He had not seen clearly, but Master William had been flickering somehow as he had rounded the corner of the hut. He had blinked and assumed his eyes were deceiving him, but Mr Edward's manner had been very strange afterwards. 'Sarah do you know what Mr Edward does down in his laboratory?'

'Oh Lor! No. I wouldn't understand even if he told me. He's terribly clever is Mr Edward. He's been to university.'

'I don't trust him, Sarah.'

'What? Not trust Mr Edward? Why ever not? He's a proper gentleman.'

'A gentleman he may be, but he's got a strange machine which looks dangerous.'

'Get on with you. You're too suspicious, Frank Hodges. That comes from being a policeman.'

'Maybe I am suspicious,' he admitted, 'but I'd like you to keep an eye on him and tell me if anything at all unusual happens.' Hodges drained his tea and got up to go. Sarah passed him his helmet and jacket and offered to walk with him as far as the gate.

Edward connected the two heavy cables to the first of the power drums and pulled the lever that would start the generator. There was a crunch as the cogs engaged and then the constant rumble of machinery as the drive shaft started turning. Edward sat down exhausted on the bare wooden floor and leaned against the wall. The feel of the cold stone pressed against his back was a welcome relief and he took out his handkerchief to wipe his face. Now there was nothing he could do but wait – wait and plan.

There were two things he needed to decide. One was how was he going to explain to Father where Will was. The other was how was he going to get Will back. The first should be straightforward enough. He could tell Father that Will was staying with friends for a day or two. That often happened and fortunately Will had mentioned the idea at breakfast the day before. The second was going to be much more difficult. As far as he could see there were three possible ways of rescuing Will, but none of them seemed very good.

The first possibility was that he could go forward in time and try to find Will. That was pointless of course because there would be no way of getting back and then they would both be trapped there. The second was more promising but he rejected that too. This idea was to go back in time to that morning and warn himself that Father was going to interrupt them. This seemed a good idea until Edward began to think about the implications of changing the past again. If he were to tell himself what was going to happen then of course they would not send Will on the time trip today. But then the disaster would not have happened for him to know that Father was going to interrupt them, so then he would not be able to go back and warn himself. If he did not go back and warn himself . . .

Edward tied his mind in knots grappling with this one and in the end he did not have the courage to do it. He imagined himself trapped forever in an everlasting loop of telling himself and then not telling himself. No, the only option seemed to be the third choice which was to switch the machine on as often as possible and hope that Will was nearby and could see the time-field. This seemed a slim hope but his only one. He stood up and prepared himself to go and meet his father.

Sarah Hodges half ran back up the drive to the house. She should not really have walked with Frank to the gate; lunch had to be served soon and they would be missing her in the kitchen. She could save a bit of time if she used the front door rather than going all the way round to the kitchen entrance. She glanced left, climbed the steps and quietly edged through the door. She closed it softly behind her and turned to find herself standing face to face with Josiah Rawlings.

'G'morning, sir.' She did a slight curtsey and stared at the floor, her face reddening.

'Good morning, Sarah. The kitchen entrance is your usual way into the house, I believe.'

'Yes, sir. Sorry, sir.'

'Very good then.' He made to pass her and leave through the front door but turned to speak to her again. 'Oh, Sarah. You can inform cook that Master William will not be with us for a day or so.'

'Yes sir.'

'I've just heard from Mr Edward that he's staying with the Bradshaw boy for a few days. Apparently Mr Edward met one of the Bradshaw servants with a message at the gate ten minutes ago.'

'Very good, sir.' Josiah left and Sarah breathed out in relief. That would teach her to try and sneak through the front door.

Frank might be right about something strange going on Sarah thought to herself as she made her way to the kitchen. How could Mr Edward have met the servant at the gate ten minutes ago? She had been walking up to the gates and back all that time and had not seen him. And how could Mr Edward have got from the old mill up to the gates so quickly? Something was wrong but she did not have time to think about that now. Lunch needed preparing.

The next morning, immediately after breakfast, Edward pulled the first fully charged power drum back down to his laboratory. He had hardly slept the night before and had woken from his fitful sleep at five o'clock. It was already light and he had wanted to try to get Will back right then. He persuaded himself to be patient, however; he did not want to make Father any more suspicious than he already was by unusual behaviour. As the trolley came to rest outside his laboratory, he pulled the key out from his pocket and slid it into the lock. The sound of the unlocking door attracted the strange dog's attention and it was there to greet Edward as the door opened. Its tail wagged frantically as Edward bent to pat it on the head. The dog had calmed down considerably since yesterday. Edward had fed and watered it and taken it for a walk in the afternoon, and now it bounced around excitedly, expecting more treats. Edward had been glad of something to do through the long afternoon of the previous day.

He had decided to send the dog back to the future during the first attempt to recover Will. Yesterday he had sent a boy forward and got a dog back, today he hoped to send a dog forward and get a boy back. Sending the dog back, though, was not going to be straightforward because, although it seemed intelligent enough as dogs go, it could not understand complex instructions. You cannot tell a dog to stand here until you switch the machine on and when you are back in your own time, walk out of the time-field. Edward toyed with the idea of turning the machine on and throwing a stick for the dog through the time-field. The dog would chase the stick into the time-field and Edward could quickly switch the machine off. He realized soon enough, however, that this plan would not work. If the machine was already switched on, the dog would not be walking into its own time but some unknown time. Edward still did not know what time appeared to replace the current time when the machine sent the time-field forward.

In the end Edward decided he would just have to settle the dog inside the boundary, turn the machine on and hope that the dog would walk out of the time-field when it saw that it was back home. Settling the dog was difficult enough, but

Edward eventually managed it and his fingers were on the lever to activate the machine when he suddenly had an idea. The dog must have had something to do with Will leaving the time-field. Maybe the dog had frightened Will. This well-groomed, healthy dog was certainly not a stray and if dogs have owners, they are usually nearby. Did the dog's owners see Will's arrival? Perhaps Will was with them now. Edward broke into a clammy sweat as he thought again about Will trapped in the future, possibly with someone hostile and dangerous. He forced himself to calm down. Panicking was not going to help Will at all. He had to hope that Will was with someone good.

If Will was staying with the dog's owners, hopefully the dog would wander home, and if he attached a note to the dog's collar then he could communicate with Will, telling him when he would switch the machine on. Edward became excited about this possibility and took out his red notebook to write the letter. He chewed his pencil stub for a moment as he considered what to say. He had to tell Will enough, but he did not want to put in so much detail that he would give away his activities to anyone if Will was not with the dog's owners. In the end he wrote the following: 'Will, Father interrupted experiment and so trip finished early. Could not reactivate transport as power was drained. Be at the usual place at four o'clock this afternoon. Edward.' That should do it. His fingers trembled as he tore the page from the note-book. He folded it into a long strip and wrapped it around the dog's collar. This got the dog all excited once more, and so it was some minutes before Edward was ready to activate the machine again.

'Goodbye, dog,' he said when everything was finally ready. 'Take my message to Will.' With that he pulled the lever, watched the needle rise as the humming noise increased and then he flicked the switch. With a ripple of air, the dog was gone. Edward gave the dog the full three minutes to move. Also, the longer he kept the machine on the more chance Will had of seeing it. When the time was up he reversed the switch and lever and the time-field returned to normal. The dog was gone but Will had not returned. Edward's heart sank a little but he had not really hoped to be successful first time. He would just have to hope that the message got to Will in time.

He picked up the handle of the empty trolley and began to pull it away to fetch the second drum. As soon as he was out of sight, the blue-uniformed figure of Constable Hodges stepped out of the trees and walked over to the deserted machine. The policeman spent some minutes looking at the box with its copper coils and strange levers and dials. He knelt down on the grass to examine the little spikes that marked the boundary of the time-field. He took off his helmet and scratched his head. If he had not seen it with his own eyes he would never have believed it. This machine had made that dog disappear. He had not been mistaken – something very strange indeed was definitely going on down at Mr Edward's laboratory.

Jed and Lizzie returned home from school together the day after Will had arrived. It was hard to concentrate on school work with all that had been happening racing through their minds. Luckily it was near the end of term and very little work was being done anyway. Tomorrow would be the last day and then it was summer holidays from Wednesday onwards. They stopped suddenly as they turned into their street. Inspector Morgan was walking towards them. After a moment's hesitation, Lizzie set off again followed by Jed. They had nothing to hide. They were allowed to walk home from school, weren't they?

'Hello, Inspector,' they greeted him cheerfully as they passed. The policeman grunted a reply. He didn't seem too happy, which must be a good sign. He can't have found out about Will yet.

As they opened the front door a blur of rusty-red fur and flailing legs bombarded them. 'Arthur!' they both cried out with surprise and spent a happy few minutes petting him. He rolled over on his back with his gangly legs sticking up in the air and the children tickled his tummy as the dog wriggled with pleasure.

In the kitchen Mum and Will were sitting at the table. Mum was drinking a mug of tea while Will was twiddling with the knobs on the radio. He held his ear close to the speaker and grinned with delight as voices and music phased in and out of the fizz and crackle between stations.

'Hello, Mum. Hi, Will,' the children greeted them.

'Will,' said Jed a little urgently, 'what are you doing?' Will looked up guiltily.

'It's all right, Jed,' said Mum, 'I've offered to tune it in for him, but he seems to want to play with it.'

'Shouldn't you be upstairs, Will?' Jed persisted.

'Oh, don't you start,' complained Mum. 'He was up there all morning and it was all I could do to drag him down here for lunch. Then he wanted to dart straight back upstairs as soon as he'd eaten a sandwich.'

Arthur had followed the children into the kitchen and while Jed was talking Lizzie continued to stroke his head. As her hand brushed his collar she felt the bit of twisted paper and looked down in surprise. She carefully slipped it out, making sure her mother wasn't watching, her hands trembling a little as she realized what it might be. Turning her back on the others she uncurled the note and read it, her heart beating quickly. Four o'clock! She looked at her watch. There were only ten minutes to go.

'I think we all need to go upstairs right now,' she said wildly. They all stared at her in surprise and seconds later Jed and Will were scrambling after her, leaving a bewildered Mum alone.

'What's up with you?' Jed demanded, as soon as they were safely in his bedroom.

'There's a note here. It was attached to Arthur's collar.'

Will snatched at it. 'This is from my brother,' he cried excitedly. 'It's his writing.'

'Yes,' said Lizzie, 'and it says that the machine is going to be switched on at four. That's ten minutes' time.'

'What are we waiting for?' Jed exclaimed. 'We've got to get Will there now.' He was halfway to the door before Lizzie could answer.

'But what about Inspector Morgan?' Jed stopped in his tracks.

'What?' asked Will.

'We saw the inspector outside just before we came in. If we go out now we're likely to bump into him.'

'We'll have to go out the back door then and over the fence,' Jed suggested.

'Mum's in the kitchen. She'll see everything from the window. She's sure to stop us if she sees us trampling on the flowers again.'

Jed looked at his watch. 'We've got five minutes at the most to make a plan. Think, everybody.'

Everybody did think. There was about a minute's silence as the three of them racked their brains for a solution. Jed crossed to his window and surveyed the scene below, hoping it would provide some inspiration. His eyes scanned the garden and then the wasteland behind. His heart jolted as his gaze became fixed on a now familiar scene. The time-field was already there. He made a sort of strangled noise in his throat and Lizzie and Will immediately joined him at the window.

'That's not fair,' cried Lizzie in outrage. 'It's early. Can't your brother time it right?' she demanded. Will simply looked pale and frightened and didn't answer.

'It's no good grumbling. We're just going to have to run for it,' said Jed. 'Ignore Mum and go.' Just then the doorbell rang and a look of hope appeared in Jed's eyes. 'The door! Mum will answer the door,' he cried. 'You two can run through the kitchen and get over the back fence while she's in the hall.' He ran to the bedroom door, pulled it open and stood to one side. 'Be quick. I'll stay here and keep an eye on everything. I can warn you if anyone comes.' He looked expectantly at the others. 'Well, go on then. Run!'

Lizzie and Will ran.

Mum was rummaging through the freezer wondering what they might have for tea when the doorbell rang. Sighing, she pushed the frozen peas back into the drawer and shut the freezer door. In the hallway she recognized the figure behind the frosted glass door even before she opened it.

'Hello, Inspector,' she said, a little nervously. Inspector Morgan was pleased to see Mum answer the door. He had the idea that she might be more co-operative than her children or husband had been.

'Ah, Mrs Stokes,' he began smarmily. Then he stopped. He had briefly seen the shapes of two children flit past from the foot of the stairs across the hall and into the kitchen. He stared in puzzlement. They had been very quick but he could swear that the boy with Lizzie was not her brother. 'Mrs Stokes,' he said feverishly. 'Two children just ran across your hallway.'

Mum turned and looked but the hall was now empty again. She turned back to the policeman. 'That's quite possible,' said Mum puzzled. 'I have two children and they're acting very strangely.'

'But one of them wasn't yours.'

'Oh, that would be Jed's friend, Will, then.'

Inspector Morgan looked at her intently for a second while the implications of what she'd said sunk in. Then without a word he turned and ran back down the garden path and up the road. Mum stared after him. What was getting into everybody today?

From his bedroom Jed could see everything clearly. It was a matter of seconds before Will and Lizzie burst out of the back door and into the garden. Moments later Lizzie had cupped her hands to give Will a leg up over the fence and it was only then that Jed realized that he had not had time to say goodbye. He pushed the window open.

'Goodbye, Will,' he called. Will turned as he was poised at the top of the fence. He smiled up at Jed and waved and then, jumping down, he set off at a run for the still visible time-field.

Jed watched as the twelve-year-old Victorian boy dashed away. He felt a pang of sadness as he realized that he would never see Will again. If everything worked out right, in a few minutes that young boy would suddenly become an old man who had been dead in his grave for years. But no! Wait a minute! That wasn't right, was it? The word 'grave' had triggered a memory in Jed's mind. He had known there was something wrong with Lizzie's reasoning when she had started talking about Will's descendants. Will never had any children. He never even grew up. He died when he was only twelve. They were not sending Will back to grow old. They were sending him back to his death.

Jed felt the shock of this realization like a physical blow. Feeling dizzy, he leaned on his desk for support but he couldn't waste time. He had to stop Will right now.

'Will!' he cried. His throat was suddenly dry and his voice no more than a strangled whisper. 'Will!' he shouted more strongly. 'Come back. Please.' Will did not respond. He was either already out of earshot or too intent on reaching the time-field to pay attention to anything else.

'Jed! What are you doing?' Lizzie looked up at her brother in disbelief. 'Are you mad? This is his best chance of getting back. What do you want to stop him for?'

'He dies of tuberculosis when he's twelve,' said Jed in despair. 'We're sending him back to die.'

Lizzie looked stunned for a moment, her eyes glazed and her jaw dropped. Then suddenly the truth seemed to register and she leaped into action. She quickly turned and, hanging on to the top of the fence, she pulled herself up to look over. Will was already halfway to the time-field. The fence wobbled as she swung herself over the top and on to the ground on the other side. She staggered a little and set off after Will as fast as she could. Will was a good fifty metres away from her and it was probably that far again to the time-field. She began gaining on him with her longer stride, but there was no way she was going to catch him. Her only hope was that the time-field would disappear before Will could get there. She wondered how long there was left. It couldn't be more than thirty seconds at the very most. It was going to be close whatever happened. Lizzie was beginning to despair. The thought of Will dying so young was too horrible to face. She forced the thought from her mind and put on an extra spurt of speed. But just then a strange voice called out.

'Will Rawlings!'

The voice was that of a young man with a foreign accent. The sound of his own name from a unknown voice caused Will to stop in astonishment. Who would recognize him here? All thoughts of reaching the time-field were momentarily banished from his mind. He turned to see where the strange voice had come from and started with surprise. The young man was still a long way off, but from this distance he looked a bit like his brother. The man started to hurry towards Will who suddenly remembered the urgency of reaching the time-field before it disappeared. He turned and set off running again. Fifty metres to go. Forty. The field was still there. Thirty metres. Twenty. The slight shimmering in the air could be clearly seen at this distance. Just ten metres to go. He was sure to make it now.

'No!'

Will could not help crying out in despair. With just five metres to go the air rippled and the time-field disappeared. He almost threw himself the remaining distance, but the short neat grass had vanished and he staggered and fell into the usual weeds and rubbish. He hung his head for a moment or two, taking great lungfuls of air as he recovered. Then he lifted his head, a look of anguished bewilderment on his face. He had been so close. The stranger was still running towards him and so was Lizzie. He dragged himself to his feet and waited dejectedly until they arrived.

A thousand thoughts were buzzing around in Lizzie's

head as she covered the remaining few metres between herself and Will. She was finding it hard to keep up with the pace at which their problems seemed to shift course. First there had been the desperation to get Will to the time-field in time. No sooner had they succeeded in that, then the new problem became stopping him from reaching the time-field. Now that that had been achieved, yet another danger presented itself. In her desperate flight she realized that the man she'd seen talking to Mum was Inspector Morgan. Who very likely saw Will. Even now he could be on his way, and here was Will in the open.

Lizzie skidded to a halt and after catching her breath she looked up at the man standing next to Will. She gasped in astonishment.

'It's you.'

The young man grinned down at her. 'It's me,' he agreed. Will was looking at the man curiously.

'You're Edward Rawlings,' Lizzie said. 'We saw you at the records office and you were looking at our house the other day.' The man nodded. 'How do you know about Will?'

'I know lots of things,' the man began, but Lizzie suddenly interrupted him.

'No! There isn't time to talk now,' she said urgently. 'We've got to hide. There's a policeman coming who must not know anything about Will. Try and get rid of him, please.'

The man looked troubled. 'Okay, but I just shouted out his name. I don't know how I'm supposed to deny all knowledge of him now.'

Lizzie grabbed Will's arm and hurried him towards the trees. 'You'll think of something,' she said. Seconds later they were crouching out of sight behind the rusted-out hulk of a Ford Cortina, and they were not a moment too soon. They could hear Inspector Morgan calling in the distance.

'Hey! You there.'

The inspector continued to call out as he approached. Edward Rawlings was there waiting to meet him, a forced smile on his face, but his mind racing.

'Good day to you,' he said when Inspector Morgan finally arrived. 'Can I help you?'

'Yes, you can. Why did you just shout out "Will Rawlings"?'

'I didn't.' Flat contradiction seemed a good start, thought Edward.

'Yes, you did. I heard you.'

'I'm sorry, but I didn't. Why are you interested, anyway?' Divert him now. Another good way of winning time.

Inspector Morgan was becoming impatient. He took out his ID to show the man. 'I am a police officer investigating a case concerning a William Rawlings. I need you to tell me what you know about him.'

'I don't know anything.' Edward Rawlings looked puzzled and then he let a look of understanding pass across his face. 'I see what must have happened,' he said. 'I didn't say "Will Rawlings", but I did say "good morning" to someone who was passing. You must have misheard me.'

The officer looked distinctly suspicious. 'Good morning?' Edward nodded. 'It's four o'clock in the afternoon,' the inspector said.

'Is it really?' Edward looked surprised. 'I've only just had my breakfast. You'll have to excuse me, officer. I only arrived from South Africa yesterday. My body clock isn't running on British time yet.'

Inspector Morgan's eyes narrowed. 'South Africa, you say?'

'That's right. Just visiting. My ancestors came from around here so I'm doing some research into my family history.'

'Really? What's your name?'

'Edward Raw . . .' He broke off quickly. 'Smith,' he corrected himself.

'Edward Rawsmith?'

'No officer, just Smith.' He gave the inspector one of his open smiles. 'Can I help you with anything else?'

Inspector Morgan looked as if he might continue his questioning but then seemed to change his mind. 'No. No, thank you Mr *Rawlings*.' He looked sharply at Edward, watching for his response.

'Er . . . that's Smith, officer,' said Edward without hesitating. 'I think you must have the name Rawlings fixed in your brain.'

'Perhaps I have, Mr Smith,' said Morgan studying Edward closely. There was something familiar about this man. 'Perhaps I have.' The young South African kept his expression carefully neutral until the inspector gave in. 'Good afternoon, Mr Smith,' he said and he turned and walked away. Edward Rawlings watched him anxiously until he was out of sight and when he was gone he breathed a deep sigh of relief. He turned towards the trees.

'You can come out now.'

Lizzie and Will slowly emerged, looking around carefully to make sure Morgan was really gone. 'Good morning?' said Lizzie incredulously.

Edward was quick to defend himself. 'Well, I'd like to see you do better on the spur of the moment. Anyway he's gone, hasn't he?'

'Suppose so,' acknowledged Lizzie. She looked at the young man. 'I'm not sure who you are or what you're doing here, but you've just saved Will's life.'

'What?' Will had been standing by miserably ever since he had missed reaching the time-field, but this news shocked him out of his silence. 'What has he done? How has he saved my life?' Edward seemed keen to know too. Lizzie took Will's hand. There didn't seem to be any good news to comfort him with. It was either stay here and never see your family again or go home and die.

'Jed and I need to talk with you,' was all she could say. She turned back to Edward. 'I'm Lizzie Stokes,' she said determinedly. 'I'm grateful to you for saving Will's life and getting rid of Morgan, but I want you to know that we want what's best for Will and you'd better not interfere if you want anything different.'

Edward put up his hands in defence. 'Hey! Not so fierce. I want what's best for Will too.'

'How come?' asked Lizzie suspiciously. 'Who are you? Are you really called Rawlings? What are you doing here?' Edward smiled at the barrage of questions.

'Yes, I really am called Ed Rawlings and yes, I come from South Africa. My family used to live here until about a hundred years ago.' He turned to Will and held out a hand. 'I'd like to introduce myself, Will. You are my . . . let me get this right.' He counted the greats on his fingers. 'Great-great-great-uncle.'

Edward Rawlings' hand hovered over the lever on his machine. He hardly dared to switch the machine off in case Will did not appear. This was their best hope and if he did not arrive now Edward wondered if he ever would. It was still morning in 1879. Edward had gone to fetch the second drum and had got back to his laboratory by ten o'clock. He thought initially he would have to wait until four o'clock that afternoon before the second rescue attempt, and he had resigned himself to another tense day of waiting and worrying. Then he had clutched his hand to his forehead as he realized his own stupidity. He did not have to wait. He had a time-machine, for goodness' sake. He simply had to change the settings to four o'clock and he could work the machine immediately. This had opened up a whole new line of thought. Should he change the settings to the time just after Will had got left in the future, hoping that Will was still there? In the end he decided not. He couldn't remember the exact time Will had disappeared and he wasn't completely sure how accurate the machine was. It would be just his luck to activate the time-field just before Will got stuck in the future, not just after. No. He had sent the note so four o'clock of the following afternoon seemed the best option. A few adjustments of the dials on the machine and Edward had been ready to go. Now the three minutes were up.

He kept the machine on as long as he dared, but then with his eyes shut tight he pulled the lever and flicked the switch. The humming noise died. Edward slowly began to open an eye but in his heart he already knew the truth. If Will had been there he would have spoken by now.

Edward opened his eyes and cried out in alarm before he could stop himself. He was not looking at his brother, but at the frowning face of Constable Hodges. His moustache was trembling with emotion.

'Good heavens, constable! You gave me a fright.'

'Indeed, sir. A bit jumpy this morning, are we?' There was no warmth in the policeman's enquiry.

Edward tried to give a natural laugh but it sounded more like he was being strangled. His nerves could not take much more of this sort of stress. He just wanted to be alone and now he had to explain his actions to this policeman again. 'A little jumpy perhaps. I didn't sleep too well last night.'

'You were expecting to see something else when you opened your eyes, perhaps?'

Edward began to panic. What did he know? 'I don't know what you mean,' he said.

'Let me make myself a little clearer then, sir. Were you expecting to see a dog?'

'A dog?' Edward was confused.

'Yes, sir. The dog that disappeared earlier this morning. Maybe you were expecting it back.'

Edward's mind was in turmoil. Fear was rising in him and he was finding it difficult to think clearly. Hodges must have seen him send the dog back to the future. That was bad, but he did not appear to know about Will yet. That situation would not last long, though. He could not hide Will's disappearance forever and as soon as it became known that Will was missing, Hodges would immediately suspect his machine. Then he would inform Father or worse. No one would believe the time-travel story and they would assume that he had somehow killed his brother. He had to decide what to do. Admit nothing – that was the best plan. 'I don't know what you're talking about, Hodges,' he said defiantly.

'I think you do, sir. I witnessed it with my own eyes. There was a dog sitting there inside that ring of wire. You turned your machine on and he completely disappeared.'

'Are you saying the dog just vanished into thin air? Are you mad, constable?'

Hodges' face darkened with anger but he spoke with chilling politeness. 'With all due respect, sir, I ask you to be civil when talking to an officer of the law. I know what I saw so you need not try and deny anything.'

'I will deny it if it's not true. I don't know anything about a dog, I tell you.'

'Very good, sir. If that is the attitude you wish to take, I see no further reason to continue this conversation. However, your father might wish to hear what I have to say.'

It was no good backing down now. Edward took a gamble. 'Go ahead, Hodges. By all means go and talk to my father and tell him you've been seeing disappearing dogs. My father is not given to flights of fancy or practical jokes so I wouldn't want to be in your shoes when you tell him. But don't let me stop you. Go ahead and tell him.' Edward held out a hand in the direction of the house, inviting Constable Hodges to visit his father. He had the reckless courage of a man with nothing to lose now and held Hodges' gaze fiercely. The policeman looked undecided for a moment, but then surprisingly backed down.

'I don't think that's necessary at the moment, sir. Just as long as we both understand each other. I know what I saw. It isn't natural and it isn't right. You might be happy to conduct experiments on animals but it's my opinion that that machine is not safe. If I hear of anything else unusual happening, then I won't hesitate to go to your father. Good morning, sir.'

The policeman turned and left. As soon as he was out of sight Edward relaxed and put a hand up to massage his temples. He was getting a headache.

Jed and Lizzie pushed their way through the revolving doors of The George Hotel. They glanced nervously at the plump man in a waistcoat behind the reception desk who was looking at them a little severely through his glasses. Then a friendly greeting from a South African voice made them relax and they hurried over to where Edward was sitting. It was school-time so they didn't have long. There had been no chance to talk the day before, and there was no way that Mum and Dad were going to believe that a South African in his twenties was a friend of Jed's, so Lizzie had arranged to meet Edward at his hotel to find out what on earth was going on. This Edward Rawlings was clearly the descendant of the other Edward Rawlings – Will's brother exiled to South Africa in 1879. This had made the discussion with Will all the more painful as they had had to tell him all they had found out about his family. Not only was he now destined to stay in the future to avoid dying as a boy, but he knew as well that his only family had argued and never spoken to each other again. Will had not taken it well.

'You're Edward's grandson, aren't you?' Lizzie blurted out before they had sat down.

Edward smiled. 'Close. His great-great-grandson actually.'

'How do you know about Will? Have your family always known?'

'No,' said Edward. 'I didn't know anything at all until a month ago and even then I found it too strange to believe. That was when we got the letter from Edward.'

'What? How?' The Stokes children were incredulous.

'Deposited with the family's lawyers shortly before Edward's death, sealed with a great blob of red wax and marked, *To be delivered to the descendants of Edward Rawlings on 1st June 2000*. It had been in their vaults all that time.'

'What did it say?' asked Jed eagerly.

Edward took a large, creamy-coloured envelope out of his pocket and pulled out a sheet of folded paper, yellow with age and covered with loopy old-fashioned handwriting. The children leaned forward keenly to look. It was definitely the same handwriting as the note they had got yesterday, but it was shakier. It was the writing of an old man. It read as follows:

To my eldest living descendant in June 2000,

It is not often that one considers communicating with one's remote descendants. I shall be long dead by the time you read this, but it is of utmost importance that you understand the events of 1879, which have long shamed me and of which I have told no one. I pray that with your help I may be able to undo some of the wrong done then.

A shadow hangs over that fateful time when, because of my meddling, I lost for ever my brother Will, the person dearest to me. I do not know how science will have advanced by the year 2000, or if what is rare now might be commonplace then, but please believe me when I tell you that in 1879 I hit upon the secret of time and devised a machine that enabled a person to be projected forward in time and safely brought back. Proof of this is the enclosed photograph which, although now of great age, shows a scene from the year 2000. If the manner of the buildings is not proof enough, then a visit to Milford, England, should show that these buildings were erected in the year 2000 in the grounds of Rawlings House – if it still goes by that name.

Travelling through time was a great wonder to me when I first discovered it, but in my excitement I did not consider carefully enough the risks involved. Foolishly I allowed my brother Will to bear most of the risk, for it was he who chiefly made the trips into the future and it was he who took this photograph. He made many journeys safely to different times throughout the twentieth century but then on July 2nd 1879 we were interrupted by our father, part way through a time journey. I immediately switched the machine off, but to my horror Will did not return – he had remained in the year 2000.

Despite frequent attempts to recover my brother with the time-machine I was unsuccessful, and when my father learned of my actions he was understandably furious. He confiscated my machine and later I believe he destroyed it. I tried to persuade him that the machine was our only hope of recovering Will, but in his grief and anger he would not listen. We had already lost our dear mother five years before and now Will was lost also. My father was a man of great standing and influence and wished to avoid any scandal being attached to his name. He enlisted the help of our family doctor, Wilkes, who was willing to issue a false death certificate showing that Will had died of consumption, and on the 7th July a coffin full of builder's rubble was buried in my mother's grave. The world believed Will dead, but I knew he was alive and caught in the year 2000. My father's anger was now fully directed towards me. He bought me a passage to South Africa, gave me £100 and cut me off from my inheritance. I left England that week and never returned. My father and I did not speak again.

I have done well in South Africa, although I have never again dared to meddle with time. Already I have grand-children and am confident that some of my descendants will be alive in June 2000. I entreat you, my descendant, please travel to Milford, England, and find Will Rawlings when he arrives on July 2nd. I do not know how he would survive alone and your help seems to be my only source of hope. Please, too, give him the enclosed letter. Ask him if he remembers our conversation in the boat? I have done what I suggested and he should have no shortage of money. I would give everything to have him back, but this is all that I have the power to do.

　　Your ancestor,
　　　　Edward Rawlings

When Edward had finished reading, he folded the letter, placed it on the low table between them and sat back in his chair to survey the children and see their reaction. They were both reflecting deeply on what they had heard because there was a lot to take in. He took out a small piece of card from the envelope and placed it on the table with the letter. Jed was curious and leaned over to pick it up. It was a photograph of the back of their house. He looked closely at his bedroom window and his eyes opened wide in wonder. There he was. He was in a photograph that was over 120 years old.

'This is incredible,' he said to Edward. 'You were holding this when we saw you wandering around out the back, weren't you?'

'That's right. I must have seemed crazy to you. I was trying to find exactly where Will was standing when it was taken. I was almost convinced the whole mad story was true, but standing where the photograph was taken and seeing you looking at me exactly as you are in the picture, that finally proved it.'

Jed passed the photograph across to Lizzie so she could look at it. 'Why didn't you come and see us, once you knew it was all true?' he asked.

'I nearly did. I didn't know your name because the old woman at the records office wouldn't tell me. She couldn't really, I suppose. You can't go around giving kids' names to strange men. I knew you were researching the family though, and I suspected you knew something but I didn't want to see you until I was sure. It's a bit embarrassing asking someone if they've seen your twelve-year-old great-great-great-uncle.'

Lizzie was gazing intently at the photograph but her mind was buzzing as she tried to take in everything the letter had told her. She looked up as she realized the implication of one very important fact. 'Will never did die of TB then. That was just a story to cover up his disappearance.'

'Right again,' said Edward.

'Then there wasn't any reason to stop him returning to 1879. He could have gone back yesterday and carried on as normal.'

This profound observation absolutely stunned Jed. They had been through so much the day before: the excitement of the note from Edward, the tension of trying to get to the machine secretly, the worry of Inspector Morgan's interference, the panic as they realized Will was going back to die and then the relief at Edward Rawlings last-minute intervention to stop him. All that turmoil and emotion had been for nothing.

Jed clutched his head in despair. 'No!' he groaned. 'We were so close. Will was just five metres from the time-field and you stopped him from going back. We thought you'd saved his life but you haven't. You've just made sure he'll never get home.'

The children both looked at Edward accusingly and he stared back confused.

'Hang on a minute,' he said defensively as they glared at him. 'I don't know what you're talking about. I didn't see any time-machine. All I saw was Will Rawlings being chased across the grass by you.' He nodded at Lizzie. 'I recognized him from the family photo album and naturally called out his name. Minutes later I'm being hailed as a hero for saving his life, after fending off a mad policeman and now I'm being accused of deliberately spoiling your plans to save Will. I just don't get it.'

This did seem reasonable and despite their disappointment the children had to admit that it was not Edward's fault. 'Sorry,' said Lizzie. 'Of course you don't how the time-machine works. It's not your fault.' She explained about the time-field to Edward who listened, fascinated.

'And the crazy thing is,' Jed said when his sister had finished, 'is that your great-great-granddad was only trying to help his brother, but all he did was stop him getting back. If he hadn't written that letter, you wouldn't be here now and you wouldn't have stopped Will from reaching the time-field.'

'It's not over yet,' said Lizzie, a determined look on her face. 'The letter says he made frequent attempts to recover Will. We've only had two so far. The first yesterday morning when Arthur came back and the second in the afternoon when we nearly did it. Edward will try again. We just have to keep a really close watch on what happens at the back of our house.'

Jed seemed pessimistic. 'So it's back to hoping we happen to see the right three-minute slot at a time when Morgan isn't around trying to mess things up. Don't hold your breath anybody.'

'It's not quite as straightforward as that, I'm afraid.' Edward hesitated. He had something he had to say but he knew it was not going to be popular. 'It's like this. Although I didn't know about the time-machine, and I didn't mean to stop Will getting back to 1879, I'm very pleased I did.'

'What?' The children were outraged.

'Listen,' he quickly defended himself. 'If Will had got back home safely then I would have ceased to exist.'

There were confused expressions on their faces momentarily until Lizzie understood and groaned with horror. 'No,' she whispered. 'This is too much. What do we do now?'

Jed was impatient. 'What? Would one of you two like to

explain what you are talking about? What do you mean Ed will cease to exist? Why should he?'

'It's more of that space-time continuum stuff I was talking about,' said Lizzie sadly. 'If Will goes home then his dad won't get angry at his brother Edward. That means he won't be sent abroad. That means he won't meet his South African wife and so all his descendants in South Africa won't exist anymore.' Jed's mouth dropped open in despair. 'Now we've got to choose,' she said. 'We can let Will go home and Ed will disappear forever, or we can keep Will here and let Ed live. It doesn't seem like much of a choice to me.'

Will sat at the window of Jed's bedroom, his eyes gazing dully at the wasteland behind the house. He didn't really know why he was bothering to do it. Even if the time-field did appear again, which seemed doubtful, he couldn't try and use it to return home because then he would die. But if he didn't go home then Edward would go off to South Africa leaving his father to grow old and die alone. He had cried a lot the night before when he understood the situation. He was sleeping on the floor in Jed's room and Jed had tried to speak to him when his sobs became noticeable, but Will had simply buried his head deeper in his pillow and ignored him. The tears welled up again as he thought about the impossible situation. He brushed them away angrily but his eyes were still red when Mum came in a moment later.

'Hello, Will,' she said. 'You've been up here on your own all day again. Why don't you come downstairs?' Will mumbled a reply, trying to hide his face from Mrs Stokes, but she was not easily fooled. 'What's wrong, Will?' she said, crossing over to lay a hand on his shoulder. 'What is it?' For an answer Will's shoulders began to shake as his sobs renewed and Mum held on to him, bewildered, until his crying stopped.

'Now then, tell me the problem,' said Mum again.

'I'm worried about my family,' said Will quietly between sniffs. He didn't think he ought to tell Mrs Stokes the whole story but he wanted so much to talk to her. He hadn't had the chance to talk to his own mother since he was seven.

'Worried? What on earth for? Is there trouble at home?' Will nodded. 'What sort of trouble? Do you want to talk about it?' Will nodded again.

'My father is very angry with my brother and I think he might send him away.'

'Send him away?' Mum looked concerned. 'How can he do that?'

Will shrugged. 'Tell him to go, I suppose. He is old enough to leave,' Will explained as he saw Mum's confused expression. 'He's twenty-three.'

'Oh,' said Mum. 'Well, everyone has to leave home some-time, Will. Twenty-three is quite old to still be at home. You never know, if your brother leaves home he and your father might get on better.'

Will didn't think so but he couldn't explain that to Mrs Stokes without saying too much. Mum continued. 'What about your mum? What does she think?'

'Mother died five years ago.'

Mum's face creased into a look of pity. 'Oh, Will, I'm so sorry. That's terrible. You must have been so young. How old were you? Eight?'

'Seven,' said Will.

'That's awful. No wonder you don't want your brother and father to argue. When you lose someone or something, what you have left becomes so much more precious.'

Will nodded again. 'I know.'

Mum hesitated before asking the next question. 'What was she like? Do you mind talking about her?'

'No, I don't mind,' Will said, smiling for the first time. 'I like talking about her. She was kind and very pretty.'

Mum smiled back at Will. 'Of course she was. She was your mother. Mothers are always kind and pretty when you're seven. When you're just a bit older they become embarrassing and nag you a lot.'

Will couldn't help laughing. 'That's not true. Jed and Lizzie don't think of you like that.'

'Don't they? I don't know what they think. They certainly don't tell me.'

Will laughed again and Mum laughed with him. Then a moment later his face was serious again. 'She died of consumption.'

'Consumption?' Mum could not keep the surprise out of her voice. 'Do you mean TB?'

Will wasn't sure. 'I think so. Father always said it was consumption. Are they the same thing?'

'Yes, they are, but it's very unusual for anyone to die of it now. If you treat it early enough a simple course of antibiotics clears it up.'

'What?' Will grabbed hold of Mum's arm. 'What did you say?' There was an almost desperate look on his face which startled her.

'I said you can treat it with antibiotics.'

She looked at Will closely as he turned back to the window deep in thought. He was a strange boy. She could not agree with Rob that he was mentally unstable, but he was certainly a little odd. He didn't seem to want to talk anymore so Mum got up quietly and left. Will did not even notice her go. His mind was racing with what he had just heard. They could cure consumption now. A cure was all they needed to go back and save Mother.

★

On Wednesday morning Jed got up late and wandered downstairs in his pyjamas. It was the first day of the summer holidays and he had the incredible sense of freedom that comes from knowing you have no school for the next six weeks. Next year he would be starting his GCSEs so he was going to enjoy this break before the hard work really began. He poured himself a bowl of cereal and carried it through to the living room to see where everyone else was. Mum and Dad he knew were both at work, but Lizzie and Will ought to be about.

He found Will sitting on the floor with his nose almost touching the television screen. The volume was turned right down but he was so absorbed by a cookery programme that he did not notice Jed enter.

'Morning, Will.'

Will jumped and turned. 'Good morning, Jed. Lizzie's taken Arthur for a walk. She showed me this thing because I can't go outside.'

'It's called a television.' Jed smiled at Will's ignorance.

'It's amazing,' Will said dreamily. 'These pictures really move. That man's a magician, I think.'

Jed doubted this. 'No, Will. Magicians wear black top hats and wave magic wands. That man is a chef. You can tell by his floppy white hat and because he's cooking.'

'Yes, but you didn't see him a moment ago. He put that chicken in that oven just like your mother did on Sunday, and a moment later he pulled it out and . . .' – Will's voice lowered reverently to almost a whisper – 'it was completely cooked.'

Jed let the matter drop. 'It's better than that,' he said. 'For a start you can turn the mute button off.' Jed pressed the remote and immediately the sound of the chef's voice filled the room.

'He speaks!' There was a look of almost religious awe on Will's face.

'And you get a choice of what you look at.' Jed flicked through the channels and Will was in raptures of delight. Cartoons, foreign soap-operas, news programmes, adverts all danced before his astonished eyes.

'I won't ever need to go outside,' he said. 'The outside can come in to see me. Television is amazing. I wish Edward could see this. He'd be so excited.'

Jed smiled again at Will. 'You'd be surprised how dull television can get once you're used to it. Anyway you can't stay inside forever. If you do stay here, you'll have to go out eventually.'

Will frowned. 'I don't want to stay here, Jed, and I don't need to now.' There had been another tense conversation between the three children the previous evening. Will had been delighted at the news that his early death had only been a cover-up story, but less than happy with the idea that perhaps he should stay in the future to prevent the latest Edward Rawlings from disappearing. Will had not said much the remainder of the evening. He had spent his time reading and rereading the letters from his brother.

'I know, Will, but you might have to. We don't even know if we'll get another chance to send you back.' Jed tried to be as positive as he could about the prospect. 'If you do stay here you'll have to go to school.'

This made Will think. 'I go to Randall's. Is it still here?'

'Randall's? Yes. It's the big old building a couple of miles out of town. We used to pass it coming into town when we lived in the country.'

'It was new when I went there. Do you go to school there?'

'No way. It costs a fortune. Dad could never afford to send me there. I wouldn't want to either. They wear a weird school uniform. The Randall's boys always get laughed at when they're seen by kids from our school.'

'Really? What do they wear?'

Jed was about to describe the collars, jackets and knee-length trousers when he realized Will had been wearing exactly the same when they first met him. 'Never mind,' was all he said.

Will's attention was drawn back to the television. They had settled on watching a cartoon and he was jumping with terror and covering his eyes every time Jerry hit Tom in the face with a baseball bat.

The doorbell rang and Jed left Will to go and answer it. The broad smile and sun-tanned face of Ed Rawlings greeted him as he opened the door. 'Hello Jed. Just thought I'd come by and show Will something. Is he in?'

'You shouldn't have come,' Jed whispered urgently.

Edward's face dropped at this reception. 'What, are you still angry with me for wanting Will to stay?'

'No. It's just there's a camera pointing at our front door. Inspector Morgan's already suspicious about you and now he'll know that you know us.'

'Oh hell! I forgot about the camera. That's why Lizzie was clambering over the back fence on Monday. Should I go and climb over the fence?'

'No. It's too late now,' said Jed wearily. 'He'll have seen you. You'd better come in quickly.' Edward stepped into the hall and Jed shut the door behind him. 'Inspector Morgan is bound to be around soon. We'll just have to think up a story to keep him happy. Will's in the front room discovering TV. I don't know if he wants to see you though. He thinks you're the enemy that's trying to keep him here.'

Edward grinned ruefully. 'So nice to be popular. I'll do my best.'

'There's someone to meet you, Will.' Will jumped up as Jed entered the room with Edward. They had seen each other on Monday afternoon but had not got much further than brief introductions before Lizzie had ushered Will back over the fence. Will stood by the sofa in his outsized T-shirt and rolled-up jeans looking suspiciously at Edward.

'Good morning, Edward,' he said at length.

Edward took this as an encouragement and did his best to put Will at ease. 'I've brought you something you might be interested in seeing,' he said as he took out a large book with red leather on the spine.

'What is it?' asked Will.

'It's the family album. I've got photographs in here going back to your father's time. I'll show you Edward's family if you like.' Edward waited for Will to answer, looking hopeful. Will did not respond for a few seconds but then his curiosity got the better of him.

'Yes, please,' he said, his eyes lighting up a little with interest.

Jed sensed this was a special moment for Will and Edward and he felt like an intruder. 'You two carry on,' he said. 'I'll just go and get dressed.' He picked up his empty cereal bowl and left the two Rawlings seated together on the sofa turning the old pages of the family album. He left his bowl in the kitchen sink and made his way up the stairs to his bedroom. He had just reached the top stair when the doorbell rang. He groaned to himself. Inspector Morgan. He went back down into the hall and opened the door.

'Hello, Inspector,' he said wearily.

The policeman was looking smug. He was clearly pleased at catching Edward visiting the Stokes. 'Hello, boy. Is Mr *Smith* in please?' He placed emphasis on the word 'Smith' and then looked expectantly at Jed.

Jed was baffled. Dad was right; the inspector was mad. Who was Mr Smith? 'Er . . . I'm not sure who you mean, Inspector. My dad's called Stokes not Smith.'

'Not your dad, boy. Mr Smith – the man who called a few minutes ago.'

'Oh, you mean Ed. He's not called Smith. He's called . . .' He stopped himself just in time. The inspector raised an eyebrow quizzically. 'He's called Smith,' Jed finished lamely.

'I see,' said the inspector. 'He's not called Smith; he's called Smith. Might I see Mr Smith-not-Smith, then.'

Jed scowled at the smirking policeman. 'Well, he is a little busy now. I'll just tell him you called.'

'Busy? What's he doing?'

'Inspector, I don't know why you keep asking all these questions. If you must know he's showing his photographs to . . .' Jed broke off again, shocked at the mistake he had just been about to make. He paled slightly and Inspector Morgan quickly picked up on Jed's behaviour.

'To who exactly?' His eyes were fiercely fixed on Jed and there was menace in his voice. 'Your parents are at work. Your sister is walking your dog. So tell me, please, who is Edward Smith showing his photographs to?'

Jed tried to look confident as he held the policeman's gaze. 'To me,' he said as calmly as he could.

'To you. A stranger from South Africa is showing you his photographs.' Inspector Morgan looked sceptical.

'Well, he is. And he's not a stranger. He's an old friend of the family.' About two days old actually, he thought to himself. 'And you are interrupting us, so if you've finished I'll go back to him.' The policeman looked as if he were about to tell Jed that he had not finished but he never got the chance. Jed shut the door firmly in his face and turned to go back upstairs to dress.

★

In the living room Will was looking at a photograph of his brother, Edward, in middle age. The likeness to his father was even more noticeable now that Edward's hair was grey, and he might easily have been mistaken for Josiah had it not been for the different style of clothing. Will was fascinated by what he was seeing – his brother twenty years older. Another picture of Edward as a very old man seated with a rug over his knees and children and grandchildren around him. He reached out a hand and touched the old picture, trying to imagine Edward growing old. There were other people in the album as well and Edward was pointing them out and telling Will the names of wives and children as they turned the pages. Half an hour later they were laughing at a picture of Ed as a child with chocolate ice-cream all over his face. Finally they closed the book.

'There, Will,' said Edward. 'That's the Rawlings family from your time till now. What do you think?'

'I think they're fine. I wish Father could have met them. He must have been a very lonely man without any of us.'

Edward nodded but said nothing. After a moment he began again. 'The next thing we have to think about is what is going to happen to you now.' He looked at Will who returned his gaze before looking down at his feet.

'I don't know what's going to happen to me,' he said quietly. 'I want to go back home but I don't think anyone's going to let me.'

'Oh, Will,' said Edward shaking his head sadly. 'You know the problems with that.' Will nodded. 'Do you blame me?' Edward asked. Will hesitated and then nodded again. Edward sighed. 'I'm sorry, Will. Obviously I don't want you to go back. It's vital for me that you stay here. I can't stop you going but I really hope you don't.'

Will spoke with difficulty. 'I understand how you feel,' he said at last, 'but I hate the thought of never seeing Father and Edward again. And I hate the thought of Father growing old alone. I wish none of this had happened and I wish I was back home with Edward and Father now.'

'I know, Will.'

There was another awkward pause before Edward tried again. 'Life isn't so bad now, you know. I see you've already discovered television.' Will smiled. 'And there's all sorts of things you can do now that you couldn't have dreamed of in 1879. You'll be all right when you get used to it. I gather from the letter that Edward must have arranged some money for you?'

'I think so. I didn't really understand that part. Here, I'll show you.' He pulled out the letter that his brother had written to him. This had been sealed when it was given to Will so this was the first Ed knew of its contents. He blinked with surprise when he found the relevant part of the letter and then gave a low whistle as he read it through carefully.

'Well, Will,' I can't tell you exactly how much you have but you are a very wealthy boy indeed.'

'Am I?' Will did not sound that interested.

'Yes. Your brother must have been a very clever business-man. He's bought you shares in some companies. He must have bought them cheaply, but these are some of the most successful businesses in the world now. They must be worth hundreds of thousands of pounds. Maybe millions.'

'That's nice.'

'You'll never have to worry about working. You'll be able to do whatever you want.'

Will looked at Edward. 'You know what I want, and even millions of pounds won't get me that.'

Edward cursed himself inwardly. He kept saying the

wrong thing. 'No. That's true. I'm sorry, Will.' The two sat in silence for a moment before Edward continued.

'If you have to stay in this year, Will, where would you like to live? You're welcome to come and live with us in South Africa. It's a beautiful country and you'll be able to see all the places that Edward knew. I can take you to his grave.'

'Thank you, Ed. I'd like to visit but I think I'd rather stay here if the Stokes will have me.'

Jed came back into the room before Edward could respond. 'Are you two finished or shall I leave you a bit longer?'

'It's all right, Jed. We're finished.' Edward got up to leave. 'I'll leave the album for you to look at again, Will. I can always come back and get it later this week. Shall I climb over the fence next time I come?' This last question was to Jed.

'No. You needn't bother. Inspector Morgan knows about you visiting now and I've told him you're an old friend. He doesn't believe it, of course, but there's no point trying to hide from him.'

'Right. I'll be going then.'

Jed saw Edward out but as they opened the front door they were nearly knocked over by a frantic Arthur who was racing up the drive, yelping. He burst through the door, ran to the back of the hall and cowered there whining and trembling, his tail firmly between his legs. Edward and Jed watched him in astonishment and Will came out into the hall to see what was happening.

'What is it, boy? What's wrong?' Jed patted Arthur's head to comfort him. 'Where's Lizzie, hey?' The dog of course could not answer, but gradually it began to calm down. Jed was about to turn and look for Lizzie when the sound of running footsteps reached their ears. 'That will be her,' he thought. But it wasn't. A horribly familiar voice interrupted them.

'Hey!'

They all froze. Inspector Morgan was outside, the door was open and Will was standing in the hall.

Lizzie walked along the path with Arthur straining at the lead. He was sniffing eagerly at the ground and tugging her first this way, then that, as he detected new and interesting smells. She just let him drag her along, her mind on other things. She loved the first day of the holidays as much as Jed, but she was thinking more about their dilemma with Will and Ed than what to do in the next six weeks. There did not seem to be a solution to the problem. She liked Will a lot. He had been so excited when she'd shown him the television and she would happily have him as another brother. She was sure Mum and Dad would welcome him too if they could be persuaded to believe the truth, but there was no denying that Will wanted to go back home. Now that she had met Ed, though, she could not face the thought of him just disappearing. It made her almost sick to think of him not existing – having never existed. A person but not a person. What would he be? A memory? Perhaps not even that. Maybe he would simply disappear and they would not even remember having met him. That itself was another horrible thought. She did not like the idea of her mind changing and not being aware of it. She shook her head to clear away the conflicting thoughts. Maybe the decision would be taken out of their hands. If they could not get Will to the time-change place when the machine was switched on then Will could not go back anyway.

Almost without being aware of where she was going, Lizzie found herself standing in the wasteland that backed on to the house. She let Arthur off the lead and picked up a stick for him. Throwing it as far as she could, she watched the big puppy race off, barking excitedly, before he came running back with the stick in his mouth. Then it was a brief tug of war before throwing the stick again. They did this three or four times and in between throws Lizzie would walk on a little so that slowly she was approaching their back fence. She threw the stick again. Arthur raced off but suddenly his barks stopped with a yelp. Then he growled. Lizzie looked up quickly to see what the problem was. Arthur was crouched nervously and for a moment Lizzie could not see what was scaring him. Then she realized what it was – the time-machine was on and the stick was lying inside the time-field.

She hurried over to where Arthur was and laid a comforting hand on his neck. He obviously remembered his last experience of time-travel and was now terrified of it. Lizzie did not know what to do. The machine was on but Will was not here. It was so frustrating. Should she run and get him? She did not know how long the machine had been on. It might go off at any time. She calculated that to run and climb over the fence and hammer on the back door to get someone's attention before running back with Will would take at least two minutes, maybe more. Would the machine still be on when they got back?

'Hey!'

Lizzie spun round in alarm. That tore it. Inspector Morgan in his brown overcoat was waving in the distance and walking towards her. He would not be able to see the time-field yet, if he even knew what it looked like, but there was no way she could go and fetch Will now. But the time-machine was on and this might be the last time they saw it.

In the pressure of the moment Lizzie began to think very

clearly and all her mixed emotions left her. She became suddenly detached as if she were watching herself thinking and making decisions and acting on them. She realized that what was most important was for Will to be able to go back home to his family. He was not here so she would have to do what she could to help. Lizzie saw herself look around for means to write a message to send to Will's brother. There was an old envelope blowing around on the floor so she stooped to pick it up. Lizzie patted her pockets but found she had nothing to write with. The envelope fell from her fingers and she turned to see the policeman still heading towards her. He was close enough to see the strange look in her eye by now and he broke into a run, but to Lizzie's strange perspective he seemed to be moving in slow motion. She turned back to the time-field and now her every movement seemed as slow as if she was moving through syrup. She saw herself release her hold on Arthur's neck and slowly step forward. Part of her realized what she was doing and wanted to scream, 'No!' But she couldn't. The figure of Lizzie stepped into the time-field. The air rippled and tingled over her body as she did so. Then slowly she turned and watched the running policeman approach her. His mouth was open and he was shouting and waving but the words meant nothing to her. They sounded distorted as if played through a tape machine slowed down. Nearer and nearer he came until she could see every detail of him clearly. The last thing she noticed was that he had spilt gravy on his shirt. She stood utterly still and calm as he bore down upon her. Then suddenly he was gone.

Edward pulled wildly at the two heavy drums on their trolley. He had reached the downward slope and it was becoming easy now. They were moving so fast in fact that at the corner where Will had left the path on his first bicycle ride, the trolley wobbled and the drums leaned over dangerously. Slow down. Being drenched in strong acid would not help anyone. Edward was absolutely frantic but he forced himself to go more carefully. 'It was utterly unfair,' he complained to himself. He had thought to get at least three days' relief from the story about Will staying with the Bradshaws, but that very morning at breakfast Josiah Rawlings had announced that he needed to see Bradshaw and that he might as well take the carriage over that morning and see Will at the same time. Edward had been powerless. He could not try to persuade Josiah not to go without rousing his suspicions. His only hope was to take the drums down to the laboratory as quickly as he could and have two more attempts at recovering Will before Josiah got back demanding to know what was going on.

Edward laughed bitterly as he realized he had used the word 'hope'. He no longer felt any hope at all. He ought to forget any more attempts with the time-machine and just admit everything to his father. In one way it would be a huge relief. He felt under such pressure being the only one who knew. Still, he had dragged the drums down, he might as well have a last try before the inevitable happened.

Without even thinking he set out the wired spikes and plugged them into the machine. He connected the first drum, adjusted the dials on the machine and he was ready. He could operate the machine quickly and efficiently now but he got no pleasure from it at all. He wished wholeheartedly he had never made the discovery. He pulled the lever and watched the needle rising as the machine hummed and the blue sparks danced over the copper coils. When the machine was ready he flicked the switch and the time-field appeared.

He had three minutes to wait. He looked at his watch wearily and then looked with equal lack of interest at the time-field. His eyes narrowed. Something was lying inside it. It was only very small but there was definitely something silver glinting in the grass. He walked up to the edge of the wired boundary and peered more closely. It looked like a coin. Worried though he was, there was still a little scientific curiosity left in him. He badly wanted to see what date was on that coin. It might give him a clue as to what year appeared in the time-field when the machine was switched on. It was a risk but he decided to get the coin.

A look at his watch showed him that only one minute had passed. It would not take him more than a few seconds to retrieve the coin. Gingerly he stepped over the boundary feeling his skin prickle as he did. He felt the slight nausea of being half in one time and half in another. He bent and picked up the coin and looked at it. It was a King George II shilling dated 1756. It did not look worn so it couldn't have been in circulation for more than a year or two. Now why would the late 1750s appear when the machine was on? All this time Edward had been standing inside the active time-field. He suddenly came to his senses and realized he needed to get out to switch the machine off. He slipped the shilling into his pocket and reversed the lever and switch. What happened next drove all thoughts of the old coin from his mind for a long time.

Edward thought he had had many shocks in the past few days, but this was perhaps the worst yet. Two things happened at once. The first was that as he switched the machine off he heard his father shouting in the distance. He was obviously on his way down to see Edward and he could guess why. The second was that there was a strange girl standing inside the inactivated time-field. He had a visitor from the year 2000. Edward assumed it was a girl anyway. She certainly had a girl's face and figure but her hair was cut in a short bob and she was wearing trousers. Edward did not have time to think about fashion trends of the future. His father was probably nearing the corner of the trees even now and he must not at any cost discover this girl here. There was enough to explain as it was. He stepped out from behind the machine and approached the girl.

'Hello, miss,' he said urgently, taking her by the elbow. 'I don't know who you are or why you are here, but it really is very important that you are not seen by anyone else. Please, wait in my laboratory until my father is gone.' The girl did not respond. She seemed to be in some kind of daze. Edward pulled her towards his laboratory and sat her down in the corner on an old chair. He held her shoulders and shook her gently to get her attention. 'Please, wait here and say nothing until I get back.' The girl still seemed confused but she returned his gaze and nodded. Relieved, Edward went outside to face his father.

'Edward? What in the name of thunder is going on?' Josiah's face was twisted with fury. Even Edward could not remember seeing him so angry.

'Father?'

'Where is Will?'

Edward did his best to seem natural. 'At the Bradshaws' surely.'

Josiah struggled to master himself. He twitched slightly and leaned forward as if to make a lunge but checked himself. He spoke with difficulty. 'He is not at the Bradshaws'. He has not been at the Bradshaws'. I had it on good authority from you that William was staying with the Bradshaws so imagine my feelings this morning when I called and asked to see William, only to find him not there.'

Edward began to defend himself. 'Father, I . . .'

'Be quiet!' Josiah thundered. 'You will hear me out. I have never been so ashamed in all my life. I looked a complete fool. Not knowing where my own son is. The idea is absurd. Now tell me two things. Why did you lie to me about William's whereabouts and where is William now?' He glared at Edward who began to think of a story to explain his actions. Nothing seemed plausible. He racked his brains but found no inspiration. He simply did not have the energy. He hadn't slept for days. His nerves were stretched to breaking point. He was feeling weak and light-headed. He could not manage another lie and he felt strangely calm as he told himself he did not have to struggle any longer.

'Father. I don't know where Will is, but I am trying to get him back.'

The furrow on Josiah's brow deepened. 'What do you mean, you don't know where he is? You were the last to see him. He left his bicycle here.'

'Yes, Father, I was the last to see him. I cannot explain it but I am doing my best to get him back. Please trust me.' He returned his father's gaze but could not hold the steady, accusing glare of Josiah. He inadvertently looked away and glanced at the machine. Josiah followed his gaze and suddenly seemed to go berserk. He roared an accusation at Edward.

'It's that infernal machine, isn't it? You've done something to William with that damned machine!' Edward said nothing but his expression gave him away. All Josiah's pent-up anger suddenly erupted in a burst of violence. He spun around and looked about for a suitable weapon. Finally he saw one and he bent to pick up the stout stick that Lizzie had thrown for

Arthur. He stood up and swung the stick with all his might. Edward cowered at first, thinking his father meant to attack him. He hadn't been beaten by his father for years, but he remembered very well the ferocity of Josiah's swing. A moment later, though, he realized that he was not the object of his father's attack, and when he saw what Josiah meant to do he wished that he was. Josiah brought the stick down with a sickening crunch on his machine. Glass splintered from the gauges and the large copper coil was crushed out of shape.

'No!' Edward screamed and lunged at his father as he raised the stick for a second blow. 'No! That's our only way of recovering Will.' He leapt on to his father, gripping him round his upper body and pinning one arm to his chest. The momentum of the dive carried them both away from the machine and on to the floor. The stick hand was still free, however, and already Josiah was swinging it down hard. Edward felt the pain burn across his back as the weapon hit him. He screamed with agony but he clung on. 'No, Father! Don't! I promise you, if you break that machine you will regret it forever.' His father kicked and struggled, but Edward was younger and stronger and managed to hold the older man until he'd calmed down enough to speak.

'Unhand me. Let go, do you hear? Do you dare to assault your own father you . . . you ungodly boy. Let go of me, I tell you, or you're no son of mine.' Edward saw that the worst of the rage was over so he let go and slowly and painfully climbed to his feet. His back was in agony and his clothes were twisted and stained with grass. His face was red and he stood there gulping lungfuls of air as Josiah struggled to his feet in a similar state. He was wary of his father attacking the machine again and so he stood between him and the broken machine. He offered his father a hand to help him rise but it was coldly ignored. His father brushed his clothes down in silence before speaking. 'Is William hurt? Is he dead?'

'No, Father. I assure you . . .' His voice faltered. He realized he couldn't answer honestly. Will might be hurt. Or worse. 'He's just lost,' he finished weakly.

Josiah glared at him. He ought to report this immediately. Alert the police and organize a search. But that would expose this affair to the entire neighbourhood. He was a proud man and acutely aware of his social position. He clenched his jaw as he struggled to reach a decision.

'Very well. I want him found.'

With that, he turned and strode off back to the house. Edward watched him until he was out of sight. Then he turned with a groan to survey the damaged remains of his machine.

'Hey! Stop right there everybody.'

Inspector Morgan was walking up the drive towards the front door, his face red and glowing from running. Nobody did as he said. Will quickly stepped back into the living room out of sight, a moment before Jed moved to push him there. At the same time Edward slammed the door on the policeman blocking his view and entry. The three looked at each other in despair as the inspector began hammering on the door and shouting. What were they going to do? Inspector Morgan must have seen Will. Jed decided they would have to take action at once.

'Ed. Can Will go with you?'

The South African caught on quickly. 'Good idea! I'll take him to the hotel. Morgan doesn't know where I'm staying so we'll be safe there.'

'Can you get there without being seen?'

'Sure. Just keep Morgan occupied here for ten minutes. Ready, Will?' Will looked nervous but he nodded. 'Right, let's go then.'

The three of them went through to the kitchen and Jed unlocked the back door. 'Don't worry, Will. Everything will be fine.' Jed was trying to stay calm but he had no idea what would happen now that Inspector Morgan had definitely seen Will. There wasn't even the option of letting Will stay with them anymore. Edward and Will slipped through the back door and Jed relocked it after them. Then he went back to face the angry police inspector.

'Will you open this door?' Inspector Morgan was still pummelling on the glass as Jed turned the latch.

'Hello, Inspector.'

'What did you shut the door for? I told you to stay where you were.' His face was furious.

'Sorry, Inspector. I didn't shut the door. Edward did.'

'Who else was that with you in the hall?'

Jed played innocent. 'That was Edward Smith. You know him. He was the one who shut the door on you. I think he thought you were a salesman or a Jehovah's Witness or something.'

The inspector made an inarticulate noise of impatience. 'Not him. The boy.'

'What boy? Do you mean me?'

'No, I do not mean you. There were three of you in the hall. You, Edward *Smith*,' here the inspector made quotation marks in the air with his fingers, 'and there was a third person. It looked like a young boy.'

'A young boy? Are you sure, Inspector?'

'Yes, of course I'm sure.'

'It might have been my sister.'

At the mention of Lizzie, Inspector Morgan's attitude changed and his voice became quieter. 'It wasn't your sister. Do you know where she is?'

The sudden change of manner disarmed Jed momentarily.

'Lizzie? Er . . . yes. She's walking the dog.' Arthur chose that precise moment to come and nose around at the door. He sniffed the floor a little and wagged his tail.

'That dog, or another one?'

Jed laid a hand on Arthur's neck. 'Quiet, boy.' Jed had not had a moment to think in the last ten minutes, and he now realized that Lizzie was still missing. Arthur had returned looking terrified and Lizzie had not followed. Fear began to creep into Jed's mind. Where was she? He did not know what to say.

'Where do you think she is?' he asked finally.

'Listen, boy,' the inspector said coldly. 'You don't know where your sister is, do you? You're right. She was walking the dog. I saw her less than ten minutes ago.' Jed said nothing. What was the inspector hinting at? 'I also saw her disappear.'

Jed paled and the policeman noticed the effect of his words. Jed tried to appear calm. 'Disappeared? Too quick for you, was she?'

'No, Jed. She disappeared. One moment she was there, the next moment she wasn't. Have you ever seen something like that happen before?' Jed had of course but he said nothing. Inspector Morgan became more urgent. 'Come on. This isn't a game any more. I know none of you have been co-operating with me, but your sister is in danger now. It's time to stop hiding things and tell me all you know.'

There was a steely look in Morgan's eyes and Jed found it hard to think straight under his glare. Lizzie must have used the time-machine and now she was somewhere in the past. Why? Perhaps Inspector Morgan was right. This was no longer a game. Perhaps he should tell him everything. Maybe he could help.

'What do you think has happened to Lizzie?' Jed asked meekly.

'I think she has been caught in Edward Rawlings's time-machine and is now in the past.' Jed remained silent. This was the first time that Inspector Morgan had been open about how much he knew. 'I also know,' he continued, 'that Edward Rawlings got into considerable trouble with his father over that machine and he lost the use of it. There won't be many chances to use the machine again, if any at all.'

'A time-machine?' Jed was still unwilling to be honest with the man. The inspector scowled.

'Don't mess around, boy. We both know the truth.'

Jed paused with indecision for a moment more. 'If there is a time-machine – and I'm not saying I believe you – if there is, why should I help you?'

Inspector Morgan was becoming impatient. 'Because I'm a policeman.'

'Yes,' agreed Jed tentatively. 'But what would you do with it?'

A look of unmistakable greed flashed across Morgan's face, an almost hungry look which passed as quickly as it had appeared. 'Why I'd help you recover your sister and return Will. Then I'd hand the machine over to the proper author-ities before it does any more damage.'

Jed had not missed that look and he was not fooled. The time-machine would give enormous power to whoever controlled it and Jed did not want it falling into the hands of someone like Morgan.

'I'm sorry, Inspector,' he said, 'I don't know what you're talking about.'

A terrible fury seemed to seize the inspector. He grabbed Jed by his T-shirt and pulled him near, but he did not shout. He spoke in a low, menacing hiss. 'You stupid boy. You can't hide this forever. People notice when other people go missing, you know. Questions will be asked. You could be in big trouble.'

Jed's face filled with fear. The inspector seemed really out of control. He tugged at his shirt to try and get away but the inspector was strong. Jed leaned over and grabbed the telephone handset. He tried to punch the keys with his thumb. Morgan stretched to snatch it away from him but Jed managed to keep it just out of reach.

'What are you doing?'

'I'm phoning the police.'

Morgan immediately let go and looked anxious. 'I am the police,' he said.

'Yes and I know you're not allowed to attack me. So unless you get out of here right now, I'm going to dial 999 and get you into trouble.'

Morgan looked distinctly worried now. He backed off and held up his hands. 'All right. I'm going.' He turned and walked away and Jed shut the door. He was trembling. In a daze he walked through to the kitchen and sat down at the table, his head in his hands. Lizzie was gone. What was he going to tell his parents?

Edward looked over the machine to see how much damage had been done. It was vital that he got it working again and he did not know how much time his father was going to allow him. The glass from some of the dials lay splintered on the grass. That would not take much fixing. The huge copper coil on top of the machine was badly bent, but did not seem ruined. It might still work. That only left the inside to check. Hopefully the box would have absorbed most of the impact, but some of the internal mechanisms were very delicate and may have been broken. For that he would need a screwdriver.

He took out his handkerchief, wiped his face and loosened his collar as he walked over to his laboratory. When his eyes had adjusted to the gloom inside the building, he saw a girl fiddling with Will's bicycle. Edward groaned. He had momentarily forgotten about his visitor. 'Hello, miss,' he said wearily.

Lizzie turned at the sound of his voice. She was more her old self again and she managed to smile at him. 'Hello,' she said.

'I called you "miss". That is right, isn't it?'

Lizzie was puzzled. 'What do you mean?'

'I mean you are a girl, aren't you?' Lizzie frowned and was about to say something indignant when Edward hurriedly continued. 'No offence, I hope. You do look like a girl of course. It's just that I'm not used to girls in trousers with short hair.'

Lizzie looked down at herself. 'Yes. I suppose I am dressed a bit like a boy from your point of view, but I'm definitely a girl. I'm Lizzie Stokes.' She held out her hand.

'Pleased to meet you, Lizzie Stokes.' Edward was lying. He wished he'd never set eyes on her.

'You must be Edward,' she said as they shook hands.

'Yes. How do you know who I am?'

'Two reasons,' she said. 'One is I've seen your photograph

163

in a history book. The other is I've met Will and he's told me all about you and your time-machine.'

Edward started in surprise. 'What? You've seen Will?' he cried. 'Where is he? Is he all right?' A wave of relief passed over Edward. This was the first positive piece of news he had had in days. Now he really was pleased to see Lizzie. 'You must tell me,' he insisted.

Lizzie smiled at Edward's excitement. 'Yes, he's all right. He's staying with my family, and Jed and I are doing all we can to keep him safe and get him back. It's quite complicated though.' Lizzie explained as quickly as she could their half of the story. How they had seen Will's appearances and done some investigating to find out all they could about him. How their dog had chased Will out of the time-field. How they had attempted to get him back, but had been interrupted by Inspector Morgan. Finally she explained their predicament with Ed Rawlings.

Edward groaned as he heard the tale unfold. He wiped his hand over his face in despair as if trying to wipe away the problem, but he only succeeded in smearing the dirt from his hand through the sweat on his face.

'I had no idea what I was doing,' he said at last. 'I've done a very bad thing, haven't I? I didn't go back into the past for fear of things like this happening but I didn't even think about what I was doing to people in the future.' All the elation he had felt at news of Will's safety drained out of him and he felt as miserable as ever. He sat down heavily on the chair but immediately wished he hadn't. The pain in his back gave a sharp twinge and he clutched his hand to his side in agony. 'Ow!'

'What is it?' Lizzie was concerned.

'It's my back. My father was attacking the machine and I got a blow from the stick when I jumped in to stop him.'

Lizzie looked serious. 'I heard all the shouting. Is the machine all right? You will be able to get it working again, won't you?'

'I think so.' Edward winced again.

'Here, let me see.' Lizzie pulled up Edward's shirt as he leaned forward gingerly and she looked at the huge red welt that lay across his back. 'It looks nasty.' She gave it a poke and Edward jerked involuntarily, crying out in pain.

'That hurts, does it?'

'A little,' said Edward through gritted teeth.

'It looks like you'll have a really nasty bruise and it's bleeding a bit. I'll clean it if you like. I'll be gentle.' Lizzie fetched some water and a rag from the sink and gently began to dab the blood away. While she did this, Edward explained the problems he was having with Constable Hodges and with his father.

'So,' he concluded. 'What with broken machines, interfering policemen, angry fathers and relatives possibly disappearing, it doesn't look like we stand much chance of ever getting Will back.' Edward stood up slowly and pulled his shirt back down. 'I need to get back to mending my machine. At least that way I'll be able to send you back home. In the meantime you must stay out of sight. You can't come outside I'm afraid, but I'll bring the machine in to work on it. That way I can keep you company and you can tell me any bright ideas you might have.'

Edward went outside and moments later he was dragging the heavy box back into the laboratory. Lizzie rushed to help him from the door when she saw the expression of pain that passed across his face at each pull. When it was safely deposited on the floor next to the workbench, Edward stood up straight, slowly like an old man with arthritis. 'I've just found something extraordinary lying on the floor by the machine. Did you drop this?' Edward held up a brass cigarette lighter with the initials *T.H.* engraved on it. Lizzie's eyes opened wide when she saw it and she took it from Edward's hand. She flicked the mechanism and the fierce little flame shot out of the top, much to Edward's delight.

'That is ingenious. It's only a flint and I presume a flammable gas in the container. Simple, yet brilliant. Is it yours?'

'No. It's Tom Harris's.'

Mr Young, the manager, stood contentedly behind the reception desk in the lobby of The George Hotel. There was an open ledger on the desk in front of him, listing all the guests and next to it was a brass bell that could be rung if a visitor needed attention. Behind him were rows of keys on racks and each key had a large plastic fob with the room number on it. He was idly reading down the list of guests, leaning on one elbow and absently fiddling with the brass bell with the other hand. He noted with satisfaction the length of the visits and imagining all the money it was bringing in. There was one guest in particular who was proving particularly lucrative. Mr Rawlings had already stayed for weeks and showed no sign of leaving. He was over here researching his family history apparently. Mr Young hoped he had a lot more family to research.

The revolving door of the lobby started to turn and Mr Young stood up sharply to greet the visitor with a look of efficiency. Ah! It was Mr Rawlings himself with a young friend.

'Good afternoon, sir,' he said warmly. You could almost see the pound signs in his eager eyes.

'Good afternoon, Mr Young.'

'I trust you had a successful morning's research.'

'No research today. I've been visiting. In fact I've brought one of my relatives to stay for a while. Mr Young, this is Will Rawlings.'

'Indeed?' Mr Young turned his attention to Will and immediately recoiled at his eccentric outfit. A T-shirt that reached the knees and rolled-up jeans were not his idea of suitable attire. He quickly recovered himself. While it would be nice if the young man were a little more presentable, one could not turn guests away. Particularly not friends of Mr Rawlings. 'What are you then, young sir? A nephew perhaps?'

Will did not know what to say, but Edward quickly helped him out. 'It's a little more distant than that. Is the room next to mine vacant?'

Mr Young ran his eyes down the guest list. 'Yes, sir. Room thirty-seven is free. Shall I book the young gentleman in?' Edward agreed and Mr Young picked up a pen to write Will's name in.

Edward took the key from Mr Young's hand when he had finished and the two Rawlings turned away from the desk. Edward had not missed the momentary grimace from the hotel proprietor. 'I think we had better get you some different clothes, Will,' he said. 'You're going to get some funny looks if we don't, and it will make you less noticeable to Inspector Morgan – you'll blend in with the crowd. How would you like to go shopping?'

Will's face brightened. 'Yes, please,' he said.

Getting Will to the shops was more difficult than Edward had anticipated. He had not been outside much in the twenty-first century and he kept gazing about in wonder at what was around him. The noise of the traffic, the neon signs above the shop fronts, the buildings of chrome and glass all seemed alien to him and it was difficult for Edward to keep him moving. More than once he had to pull him out of the path of oncoming buses and he was tempted to hold his hand to keep him safe. That would have looked odd, though, and Edward wanted to remain as inconspicuous as possible. Eventually they reached the glass doors of a large department store and Edward dragged the boy inside.

'Right,' said Edward, consulting a sign on the wall. 'Let's see where we need to go. Here it is, boyswear, third floor. Come on then.' Will did not move. He was blushing and looking distinctly uncomfortable. 'What is it, Will? What's wrong?' Edward looked around at their surroundings and noticed for the first time that they were in the ladies' department, more particularly, the underwear section. Not only were there women browsing among the racks of little, lacy garments, but there were also large photographs everywhere of smiling women wearing nothing but their bras and knickers. Will did not know which way to look. Edward smiled as he realized Will's predicament. From what he remembered of Victorian history, no woman would ever dream of being seen in public except in a dress that reached from her neck to her ankles. 'Bit of a shock, eh, Will? Never mind, keep your eyes down and follow me.' Edward took Will by the elbow and led him quickly to the escalator. 'Careful how you tread on this, Will. Once you're on, it will carry you upstairs. You'll be safe there.'

Will loved the moving staircase. In fact he liked it so much he did not want to get off at the third floor and so Edward let him go all the way up to the sixth floor and then back down again. He wanted to keep on going down past the third floor again and Edward had to remind him that if

he did not stop soon he would find himself back in the
ladies' department. Will suddenly decided he would stay on
the third floor after all, and soon they were looking among
the rows of jeans and sweatshirts. Will was not really interested in any of it, so Edward ended up choosing for him.
Before long Will was standing in front of the mirror looking
at his new appearance. Wearing a T-shirt and jeans that fitted,
and with trainers on his feet, Will immediately became less
noticeable.

'There,' said Edward. 'Inspector Morgan will never recognize you now.' Something was not quite right, though.
Edward struggled to locate what the problem was and then
he hit on it. His hair. It was too long. Looking around he saw
that most boys had it cut short and gelled. Will, with his
loose flowing locks, still looked like Little Lord Fauntleroy.
'We might have to get your hair cut later to finish the trans-
formation, but for the time being this will help.' Edward
leaned over to a nearby display, picked up a baseball cap and
planted it firmly on Will's head. Will grinned at his twenty-
first century image in the mirror as Edward went to pay for
the outfit.

Five minutes later he was back with Will. 'That's settled
then. Is there anything else you want to do while we're out?
No one will recognize you now and we might as well enjoy
ourselves rather than go back and sit in the hotel room.'

'Yes,' said Will. Something had been on his mind and it
now seemed like a good time to try. 'I want to go to a shop
where you can buy medicine.' This seemed like a strange
request.

'Why? Are you feeling ill?'

'I feel fine, but I wanted to get some medicine that Mrs
Stokes told me about. She said it was very good.' Will reddened as he realized this was a very strange thing to ask. He

was grateful for the brim of his new cap as it meant he did not have to look Edward in the eye.

'Well,' said the South African doubtfully. 'We could go to a chemist's, if you really want to. What was the medicine called?'

'I don't remember exactly. Anti-something-or-other.'

'Antibiotics?'

'Yes, that's it.' Will sounded excited and Edward looked at him, puzzled.

'I'm sorry, Will. You can't just buy antibiotics. They're what's called a prescription drug. That means a doctor has to write a letter telling the chemist that you need them.'

'Oh!' Will sounded terribly disappointed. 'Could we get a doctor to write us a letter then?' he pleaded.

'No, Will.' Edward's voice was gentle. 'Doctors only write prescriptions for people who are ill. We don't need the medicine so we can't get any. Will, what's all this about?'

'It's nothing.' Will's voice was sullen and he refused to look up. Edward decided not to press him any further.

'Come on then. While we're here, I'll show you what computers can do. If you liked television you'll love them.'

Edward walked back down to his laboratory feeling much more cheerful. He had had a wash and a change of clothes before lunch and thankfully his father had chosen to eat his meal alone in the library, so he was spared his scowls and silence while he ate. He was carrying some cold pie on a plate for Lizzie. She would have to rough it a bit while she stayed but hopefully that would not be for too long.

Edward wondered what his father's next move would be.

He could spoil everything, but as long as he gave him a day or so, Edward had every hope of finally sorting the problem out. He had taken the cover off the machine and there did not seem to be too much damage. Certainly he hoped to get it working again that afternoon. He had one power drum charged so he could send Lizzie back that evening. She could take a message to Will to tell him when the machine would be switched on and then tomorrow morning when the drums were recharged he would be able to bring Will safely back. What could possibly go wrong this time?

'Hello Lizzie,' he greeted the girl as he entered his laboratory. 'Here's some food. Sorry it's not much.'

Lizzie looked up and smiled as he entered. She was holding a red book in her hands. 'Thanks,' she said and got up to take the plate.

Edward frowned. 'That's my journal you've got there. There's not much that's private in it but it's not polite to read other people's diaries, you know.'

Lizzie blushed slightly. 'Sorry. I didn't mean to be rude. I promise I haven't been reading it. I only picked it up because I recognized it.'

Edward's brow creased with puzzlement. 'How could you recognize it? You've only just arrived.'

'Ah!' said Lizzie mysteriously. 'That is a mystery, isn't it? I'll give you another clue. I haven't opened it today but I do know what's in it.'

Edward was completely baffled. 'Well, what is in it then?'

'Some diagrams, some equations, some notes and a diary.'

Edward's face darkened again. 'You have been looking in it. What do you mean by telling me you haven't?'

'Because I haven't, honestly. I'll prove it to you. Here, write today's entry and I'll tell you what you wrote.'

Still suspicious, Edward took the journal from the girl's

outstretched hand and sat at his desk. He opened the book to the right page, dipped his pen in a pot of ink and made a few brief notes. As soon as he had finished he placed some blotting paper over the wet ink to stop it smudging and closed the book before Lizzie could see what he had written. 'Right, tell me what it says then.'

Lizzie screwed up her eyes in concentration as she tried to remember what she had read a couple of weeks before. Edward thought she might be attempting some sort of mind-reading trick. He shook his head sadly. He had quite liked Lizzie but now he thought her silly.

Lizzie was ready to make her prediction. 'You wrote,' she said slowly, 'something like "July 4th. Disaster. Father suspicious. Machine broken. Stokes child. Father must not find out."' She opened her eyes and looked at him expectantly. 'Well? Am I right?'

Edward stared at the girl and opened his journal again to check what he already knew. 'Almost word perfect,' he said disbelievingly. 'How did you do it?'

Lizzie thought it was time to put him out of his misery. 'I said I hadn't read your book today, but I did read it a few weeks ago. It was with some other papers in the records office and we looked at it while we were searching for clues about Will.'

'What? My private journal is in a public archive where anyone can simply wander in and start reading it? Is there no privacy in the year 2000?'

'Well, it's not as bad as all that,' Lizzie tried to comfort Edward. 'For one thing you've been dead a long time and dead people aren't worried about privacy.'

'You're making me feel much better. Really you are,' Edward scowled.

'And another thing,' Lizzie added with a mischievous grin.

'What?' asked Edward grumpily.

'Your handwriting is so bad no one can understand it even if they do look at it.'

Edward looked at Lizzie not knowing whether to be angry or amused. Lizzie smiled back and before long Edward felt the sides of his mouth twitching. He tried, but he could not manage to look offended any longer. 'Maybe you're right,' he laughed. 'I'll be more careful about what I write from now on, though. Right, that's enough talk. Pass me that spanner, please.'

'OK,' said Lizzie, her mouth full of pie.

Sarah Hodges pushed open the door of the little cottage and called out to announce her arrival.

'Hello, Mum. It's only me.'

She had the afternoon off once a fortnight and she always went home to visit her mother. Mrs Hodges loved to see her daughter and catch up on all the news from the big house.

'Come in, Sarah. Come in,' said the grey-haired lady, who was at the sink holding a teapot. 'Shan't be a minute, dear. We've got another visitor.'

'Frank!' cried Sarah as her brother got up to greet her. She gave him a hug and kiss, then started to untie her bonnet and shawl as her mother swilled the old tea-leaves out of the pot and placed it on the range to warm.

'There,' the old lady said. 'Kettle's on to boil. We'll have a cup of tea presently but first give your old mum a kiss.' Sarah hung her things over a hook on the back of the door and turned to give her mum the kiss she asked for. When the three were settled in their seats, Mrs Hodges spoke again. 'Now tell me all the news. All of it, mind. I want to know everything.'

'Well,' said Sarah with a wicked sparkle in her eye, 'there's a lot to tell. The news is that Mr Josiah and Mr Edward have been arguing again.' Mrs Hodges looked intrigued and Frank's eyes narrowed. He did not normally enjoy his mother's and sister's gossip but this might be worth some attention.

'Oh, it's a shame,' said Mrs Hodges, not sounding at all sorry. 'Things haven't been the same since Mrs Sophia died.'

'Don't be daft, Mum,' Sarah reproached her mother. 'Those two have always had hot tempers.'

'Maybe they have, but I still say things were better when the lady was alive. She could keep the peace.'

'Oh, yes. Things were certainly better, but the two could still argue.'

'Not like that nice Master Will. He's not like his father and brother. He takes after her more. He's a sweet child.'

'Yes and it's over Master Will that they've been fighting. And I really mean fighting.' Mrs Hodges leaned forward eagerly for the story but then had to get up to attend to the boiling kettle.

'Carry on,' she said impatiently as she poured the bubbling water into the pot. 'I can listen and make tea.'

'Well,' the daughter continued, 'it's like this. Apparently Master Will has disappeared.' Frank Hodges sat up sharply at this news and the helmet which had been balanced on his knees fell to the floor with a loud thud.

'What did you say? Master Will disappeared?' The two women looked at him in surprise. They had never known Frank to take such an interest before. 'Sarah, why did you not tell me this? I asked you to tell me if anything unusual happened.' His voice was reproachful, but Sarah waved his criticism aside.

'I'm telling you now, aren't I? Stop interrupting if you want to hear the rest.'

'Yes, Frank, be quiet,' said Mrs Hodges, fetching three cups and saucers from a cupboard and pouring a little milk from a jug into each.

'It seems as though Master Will has gone missing,' Sarah continued. 'Mr Edward made up some story to explain his going away and when Mr Josiah found out the lie, he was like a mad thing. He marched off down to Mr Edward's laboratory and started telling him what he thought. You could hear his shouts even up at the house. And then it got even worse. They started fighting and Mr Josiah was saying things like "unhand me" and "do you dare to assault me".' Here Sarah impersonated her employer's voice and broke off into giggles. 'When Mr Josiah came back to the house, he was in a terrible state,' she continued. 'His clothes were a mess and there was blood on his face, and the look of anger in his eyes – you never saw anything like it.'

Mrs Hodges listened to the tale enthralled. Her eyes were fixed on Sarah's face and her mouth was slightly open. She was pouring the tea without concentrating on what she was doing, and the steaming liquid brimmed over the first cup, into the saucer and then on to the table in a puddle.

'Mother! Pay attention to what you're doing.'

Mrs Hodges was suddenly brought back to earth by her son's shout and she quickly tipped the teapot back upright.

'Oh Lor! Look at the mess I've made. Sarah, you shouldn't distract me when I'm pouring the tea. You and your stories.'

'But you told me to, Mother,' said Sarah indignantly. 'Didn't she, Frank? She told me to carry on.'

Frank Hodges was not interested in whose fault the spilt tea was. 'Of all the silly girls,' he said sternly.

'What?' said Sarah defensively.

'You seem to take great delight in the fact that the

Rawlings have been fighting and you pay no attention to the most serious matter. What about Master Will? He's gone missing and you don't seem to worry.'

'Yes, the poor lad,' agreed Mrs Hodges. 'What could have happened to him?'

'Oh, he'll be all right, surely.' Sarah did not seem too concerned about Will. 'Mr Edward must know he's all right else he wouldn't have covered up for him.'

'Is that right?' said Frank ominously. 'That's all you know. I happen to think differently.'

'What do you mean?' asked Sarah.

'I told you Mr Edward was up to no good down in his, laboratory and I happen to know he has a very dangerous machine there. I'm very worried about Master Will's welfare indeed.' Sarah went pale at her brother's seriousness and Mrs Hodges sat down as if her legs would not support her. 'Yes. I'm off up to the house now, having heard this. I have something very interesting that Mr Josiah needs to hear.'

'What, Frank?' Sarah sounded panicky. 'What is it? You won't tell him what I told you, will you? Don't get me into any trouble Frank, please.'

'Don't worry, Sarah,' said the constable, standing and putting his helmet on. 'I won't get *you* into any trouble, but I cannot promise the same for Mr Edward.'

'There,' said Edward. 'That should just about do it. I've just got to reconnect these last few wires and screw the lid back down and she should be good as new.' Edward gave the machine an affectionate stroke as he spoke. He had grown to hate his creation in the past few days, but now that the end of their problems was in sight some of his old feelings for the machine were returning. Lizzie came and stood by his side and peered into the workings of the machine. To her it was just a jumble of wires and oddly shaped components, but Edward understood every detail.

'That looks complicated,' she said. 'How does it all work?'

'Well,' Edward replied, 'you're right. It *is* pretty complicated, but if you really want to know, it's like this. The antenna on top of the machine intercepts the time particles and they are relayed to this section here.' Edward pointed with his screwdriver. 'That filters and separates the different times and I adjust the dials to focus on just one time. Then that signal is routed through the copper coils and strengthened and when enough power is generated I engage the time destabilizer. That's that little metal box there. And that weakens the structure of time so that the area isolated by the time-boundary is released from its own location and jumps to the time the machine is focused on. A bit like an iron nail being attracted to a magnet.'

'Oh, I see,' said Lizzie, nodding.

'Do you?' asked Edward. His eyebrows shot up in surprise.

'No,' laughed Lizzie. 'Not really.'

Edward laughed too. He was liking Lizzie more and more. 'Well, you did ask,' he said.

'It's an amazing machine. We can tell when it's working in the year 2000 because the grass is all short here, but in 2000 it's all long and weedy with rubbish dumped in it.'

'So you see a small patch of neat lawn in the middle of the long grass?'

'Yes. What do you see?'

'Not much different really. The grass always looks the same, but once it was raining inside the time-field but not outside it. That was strange.' Edward suddenly remembered the coin in his pocket that he had found in the time-field. He drew it out. 'Here, look at this,' he said. 'I found this in the time-field this morning, just before you arrived.' Lizzie took the coin and studied it.

'1756,' she said thoughtfully. 'If it's 1879 now, that means this coin is 123 years old. Does that mean when you switch the machine on and send your time somewhere else, that 123 years ago appears in the time-field to take its place?'

'Something like that, yes,' agreed Edward. 'It may not be exactly 123 years, of course: the coin might be a few years old. I've not been able to work out why that time appears yet.'

Lizzie pondered for a moment longer. 'I'll bet that the coin was two years old when it was dropped.'

Edward looked intrigued. He was learning to take her observations seriously; she was a bright girl. 'You're an expert at dating coins now, are you?' he asked.

'Maybe,' she answered slyly. She did not say any more so in the end Edward had to ask.

'Go on then, tell me why it's two years old. I can't work it out.'

'Well,' she said, 'if the coin was dropped when it was two years old then it was dropped in 1758, which is 121 years ago. When the time-machine is switched, on this bit of 1879 moves forward to the year 2000 which is 121 years away as well, but in the other direction.'

Edward's jaw dropped with surprise. He was right to take this girl seriously. 'Lizzie, that is incredible. I've been puzzling over that one for weeks and you have worked it out in minutes.' Edward began to pace up and down as he tried to work out the implications of what Lizzie had just said. 'It must work like a mirror, or perhaps a balance would be a better way of putting it,' he said after a while. 'It's so simple. If I was to set the machine for only one year in the future, then last year would appear. Or if ten years then 1869 would appear.'

'Have you been using the machine much?' Lizzie asked.

'Yes. Quite a bit. Why?'

'You've been lucky not to bring anyone from the past here. If they happened to be standing in the right place in 1758 when the machine was switched on, they'd be brought here, wouldn't they?'

Edward groaned at this new line of thought. 'That's yet another risk I entirely failed to recognize,' he said dolefully. 'I think this land was pasture for sheep before the house was built so there's not much chance of catching anyone. We might get a sheep, though. Or even worse – half a sheep, if it was standing half in the time-field and half out.'

Lizzie was still thinking about the effects of the time-field. 'What happens to the bit of 2000 when 1879 moves there to take its place? I'll bet that jumps forward 121 years as well. That means if someone had been standing there when the machine was switched on they'd be taken to . . .' She paused while she did the sum. '. . . the year 2121.'

It was all getting a bit much for Edward. 'I think as soon as I've got you and Will safely back in your own times I had better stop using this machine. The risks are just too big.' He brooded on his mistakes for a moment longer before speaking again. 'Oh well. I had better finish rebuilding the machine, then I can send you home.'

Edward crossed over to his workbench to collect a smaller screwdriver. He was only there for a second but when he turned back there was no sign of Lizzie. He gaped in surprise. 'Lizzie? Are you there?'

'Shh!' came a hiss from the floor. Lizzie was crouched behind the workbench.

'What is it?' Edward asked in a quieter voice.

'Some men are coming. I've just seen them through the window. One of them is your father, I think. One of them looks like a policeman. I didn't recognize the other.'

Edward looked out of the window too. She was right. The third man was Stokes the servant. If Hodges had been speaking to his father then this did not look good. 'Quick,' he said to Lizzie. 'Hide in this cupboard. Do not be seen.' Lizzie was no sooner in there when Josiah's voice was heard, cold and menacing.

'Edward. I would speak with you. Come out here.' Edward did as he was bid.

'Yes, Father,' he said as he stood in the doorway.

Josiah was no longer in an uncontrolled rage, but there was a quiet, chilling fury in his eyes and in his voice which was even more unnerving. 'Hodges has just told me what that machine can do. He assures me he clearly witnessed a dog disappear when it was activated. Now having heard that William is missing he has very sensibly come to inform me, although he might have done this sooner.' Hodges shuffled a little uncomfortably as Josiah glanced severely at him. 'Tell me, Edward, and do not think of deceiving me again, what does that machine do and where is William now?'

Edward knew he could not hide it anymore. He had to tell his father the truth but even now he hesitated. He knew he wasn't going to be believed. 'It's a time-machine, Father. It can send people to the future and Will is now in the year 2000.'

Josiah's jaw tightened and his eyes burned dangerously. 'What?' he said. 'I told you to tell me the truth. What is the meaning of this fairy tale?'

'It's no fairy tale, Father, I assure you . . .' He got no further.

'Stand aside.' Edward did not move. 'I said stand aside, damn you. Are you going to add gross disobedience to your list of sins?' Josiah pushed Edward roughly out of the doorway and he had to stagger to avoid falling. 'Follow me, Stokes.' Josiah strode into the laboratory and Stokes hesitated before following. He kept his head down so as not to catch Edward's eye. 'There it is. That box and those two metal drums. Take them up to the house. You can use that trolley.'

Edward tried to reason with his father. 'Please. Don't take it. Trust me, Father.'

Josiah turned on him. 'Trust you? That is out of the question. I told you, you were dabbling with things you don't understand. I will get Travis to look at this machine and see what his opinion is.'

'Travis? Oh no, Father . . .'

Josiah cut him short. 'He is my finest engineer.'

'Yes, he's very good with steam engines, but this is something completely different.'

'That is my final word.'

And it was. All Edward could do was stand by and watch as Stokes and Constable Hodges made three trips up to the house with his precious machine. Josiah stood and oversaw the whole procedure without speaking. As the last drum was moved he walked away, still in silence. When it was safe, Lizzie crept to Edward's side as he gazed dumbstruck in the direction of the house. She realized her only link with the year 2000 had just been taken away. 'What will happen now?' she asked in a small voice.

'I don't know,' answered Edward. 'I really do not know.'

'What?' Dad looked aghast at Jed. 'You are not serious.' Jed squirmed in his seat at the kitchen table. He knew this wasn't going to be easy but it had to be said. Mum looked anxiously from her son to her husband. 'You don't expect me to believe that.'

Dad was right. Jed didn't expect him to believe it, but it was true, so what could he say? He sat in silence while Dad continued. 'Come on, Jed. Good story but I'm not buying it. Now tell me where Lizzie is.'

'Yes, please, Jed,' Mum pleaded. 'Where is she?'

'I've told you,' said Jed dully. 'It's not *where* is she, it's *when*.'

Dad snorted impatiently. 'And while we're on the subject, where's your friend? Has he gone home? Is Lizzie with him?'

'No,' said Jed. 'We've been trying to get him home all week and now he's gone to stay with a friend because Inspector Morgan is after him.'

Dad frowned at the policeman's name. 'What's Morgan got to do with this? Why should he be interested in your friend?'

'Because he's Will Rawlings.'

'Who?'

'Will Rawlings. The boy who disappeared over a hundred years ago. The boy in the photograph that Mr Harris showed you.'

Dad opened his mouth to make an angry retort but it never came. Instead he stopped with his mouth still open and paled slightly as this idea penetrated his mind. He sat down at the table. 'Will Rawlings,' he said quietly to himself and then fell silent for a while. He seemed to be struggling with conflicting thoughts. His main impulse was to reject the idea outright. That sort of thing just didn't happen, did it? But a small part of him couldn't help admitting that this outrageous idea was in fact entirely plausible.

Firstly, there was the boy's appearance. Dad knew he had seen Will somewhere before and now he remembered where. It had been the modern clothes that had distracted him. That and the subconscious desire not to believe the evidence in front of him. Then there was the kid's behaviour. He was weird. He had just thought him dim, but on second thoughts a lot of Will's oddness could be explained if you accepted the idea that all modern technology was completely new and unfamiliar to him. In fact it all made perfect sense. Why else would his mother have died of TB? Dad shook his head as he reflected, still not willing to accept the impossible. Jed saw he was weakening and decided a bit more proof would do it. He got up and ran to his room. Thirty seconds later he was back with a bundle of clothes under his arm.

'These are the clothes he was wearing when we first found him.'

Dad took them and straightened them out on the table. Still baffled he turned them over, examining the hand-stitched garments that wouldn't have been out of place in a museum.

'So what you're saying,' he said at last, 'is the machine that Morgan is so interested in is a time-machine. Will is a Victorian stranded in the future and Lizzie is currently trapped in the past.'

Jed nodded and Mum gave a little cry as she clutched her hand to her mouth. 'No. That can't be true. It can't.' Mum was sounding panicky, and Dad reached out and held her hand.

'How do you know all this?' he said, suspending his disbelief. 'How do you know Lizzie's where you say she is?' Jed explained as briefly as he could all that had been going on in the past few weeks. Dad listened intently, interrupting occasionally to ask for more detail. 'And did you see Lizzie go into the time-machine? Do you know why she might have done it?'

Jed had to admit he didn't. 'I didn't see her go, but

Morgan said she just disappeared in front of him and that's exactly what happens. I don't know why she did it though.'

'And are we to believe Morgan?'

Jed shrugged. 'Where's Lizzie if he's lying?'

'I think we need to speak to the inspector now,' said Mum forcefully. She was gripping Dad's hand tightly and she was clenching and unclenching her other hand. Her voice was a little shrill.

'What?' said Jed.

'We need his help,' Mum insisted. 'Lizzie's in real trouble and he *is* a policeman. We should never have hidden anything from him. We should have helped him from the start.' Mum was looking almost fierce in her determination and for a moment Jed was worried that his parents might have one of their rare arguments. But surprisingly, Dad seemed to agree.

'I think you're right, dear. This is way over our heads and if Lizzie really is missing, we have to report it. As much as I hate to do it, I'm going to have to go and grovel to Morgan. I'll phone him,' he said, getting up and looking around. 'What's his number? He left his card, didn't he?'

No one could find the inspector's card so in the end Dad phoned the police and asked to be put through to the right department. Five minutes later he came back into the kitchen holding the handset and looking serious.

'Well, that could have gone better,' he said, frowning.

'What?' cried Mum. 'What's the problem? Was Inspector Morgan angry?'

'No,' said Dad. 'I couldn't speak to him. They had never heard of him.' The looks of confusion grew on Jed's and Mum's faces. 'There's no such thing as U Division either. That's the branch he said he worked in. And when I mentioned the time-machine they told me that wasting police time was a serious offence and that if I didn't hang up I could be arrested. I hung up.'

'What's going on then?' asked Jed.

'It would appear,' said Dad, 'that Inspector Morgan isn't a policeman at all.'

Mum's eyes opened wide with astonishment. 'But what is he then?'

'A very good question. And one which I mean to find the answer to.'

Lizzie had no other choice but to spend the night in Edward's laboratory. Getting home seemed impossible, at least for a while, and she could not go up to the house because her presence had to remain a secret. She was not uncomfortable though. It was summer and the rays of the late evening sun shone in through the doorway giving the whole room a pleasantly warm, red feel. Edward brought her down some bread and cold meat for her evening meal and using a Bunsen burner they managed to make a reasonably good cup of tea. Edward stayed as late as he dared without rousing further suspicion. Before he left he strung a hammock from the beams in the roof and found some blankets and a cushion so that she would be warm as well as comfortable.

There was not much to do once Edward had gone back to the house. What did people do for fun in Victorian times? She began to look around for something to keep her amused until it was time to go to sleep. There were some books in the laboratory – a few of them were not about science – so she glanced along the spines hoping to come across a book that didn't look too dull. The only name she recognized was Charles Dickens and so, selecting the shortest, *A Christmas Carol*, she tucked the volume under her arm and wandered over to the hammock.

Getting into the hammock was not as easy as she thought it was going to be, though. It was hung quite high off the ground, and when she tried to pull herself up, the hammock would swing and twist about so that most of the blankets fell out. In the end she managed to get herself, the bedding and the book all into the hammock at the same time by using a nearby stool as a step. Once in the hammock she wrapped the blankets snugly around her and opened the book. She read for a while but couldn't concentrate. She found her eyes going over the same page again and again. In the end, she gave up and lay there thinking about their predicament. Would she ever get back home? She felt very, very alone and it was a long time before she fell asleep.

Josiah Rawlings sat at the desk in his library. William was gone and he was not coming back. Travis had been wary of the machine. Josiah had not asked him outright if it was a time-machine. He didn't want him to think there was madness in the family. But he had confirmed that it was dangerous. The high voltages could easily kill and he could not begin to imagine what the purpose of all the circuitry was. Could it completely vaporize a person? Is that what had happened to poor William?

The machine was standing against the wall, but he had covered it with an old tarpaulin so he didn't have to look at it. More than once that evening he had got up and, seizing the poker from beside the fireplace, had crossed over to the machine with a determined look on his face, only to change his mind again and throw the poker aside in frustration. It was, after all, a dangerous machine. He didn't want to get himself killed as well.

Little by little his anger ebbed away as he sat alone in his study, but as the anger died so his grief rose to the surface. Tears smarted in his eyes as he thought about his son. He had not cried since the night his wife had died and he felt his cheeks redden with shame as he remembered the way he had completely broken down that time. He was only grateful no one had witnessed him in his weakness. He blinked the tears back and rose to his feet in agitation. He would not humiliate himself again in that way. If anger drove the grief away, then anger it would have to be. He crossed over to the machine, tore off the tarpaulin and glared at it. His breathing was quick and his hands clenched and unclenched as his quiet fury slowly grew in his mind again. So determined was he that by force of will alone he shut down his softer emotions and, when he felt master of himself once more, he shook his head as if to forget his moment of frailty. He walked purposefully back to his desk.

His anger needed to be vented on something. Edward was the obvious target and grimly Josiah decided the fate of his eldest son. What to do about Will's disappearance posed more of a problem. He had resigned himself to never having Will back. He opened a drawer in his desk and pulled out a piece of paper. Unscrewing the top of his inkwell he took his pen, dipped it and began to compose a letter to his old friend Dr Wilkes. It was only a short note asking to see him the next day. When it was finished, he pulled the cord to summon Stokes who entered the room a few minutes later.

'Yes, sir.' The servant glanced nervously about the room and his gaze came to rest briefly on the machine. An angry noise in Josiah's throat made him snap his eyes away and back to his master.

'I have a note here for Dr Wilkes. Be so good as to see it is delivered this evening.'

Stokes cautiously took the note from Josiah's outstretched hand and with another yes sir and a bow he withdrew from the room as quickly as he could.

'Good morning.'

Lizzie woke as Edward opened the laboratory door. She slowly opened her eyes and lay there a while, confused and disorientated. The book was still in her hand and the surroundings were unfamiliar. Then the events of the previous day came flooding back and she sat up sharply. This was a mistake because while hammocks are safe enough when you are lying down, they become very unstable if you sit up. The hammock twisted wildly and pitched her sideways on to the floor. She shrieked and it was only by clutching frantically at the canvas that she managed to land feet first. She stood there, panting, for a moment, still holding on to the hammock.

'Well,' said Edward, when he had established she was not hurt. 'I've seen more graceful ways of getting out of a hammock, but never quicker. You must show me how you do that. It's quite a technique you have there.' He ducked as the cushion came sailing towards his head. 'All right. All right. I understand if you want to keep it a secret.'

'Be quiet, can't you?' Lizzie was still a little shaky from her fall and not quite ready to laugh about it. 'What have you got there?' she asked, to change the subject.

'What have I got here indeed?' said Edward, putting down his bundle on the workbench. 'Firstly, I have these to transform you into a nineteenth-century girl.' He held up a full-length dress made of dark grey cotton, a woollen shawl and a bonnet. Lizzie looked doubtful. She took the dress from Edward and held it up against herself.

'Do I have to?'

Edward smiled at the distasteful look on her face. 'I think it would be safer. If you're seen the way you are you'll definitely raise suspicions, but in that dress and with a bonnet over your hair, you won't look any different from any other girl.'

'All right then,' she reluctantly agreed. 'Where did you get them from? You haven't got a sister, have you?'

'No,' Edward laughed. 'I got these from one of the maids. If I had a sister she would wear something much nicer than that. I'm sorry but you'll definitely look like a servant in this.'

'What?'

'It's the best I could do.'

Lizzie grunted unappreciatively. 'Well as long as you don't expect me to do all the cooking and cleaning. It's only a disguise.'

'I was thinking the place could do with a tidy. Only joking.' He held up his hands defensively at the look on Lizzie's face. 'I'll go outside for five minutes while you change and then I'll come back and cook you some breakfast. It's about time you had a hot meal.' He showed her the second part of his bundle. It was a frying pan and some rashers of bacon wrapped in brown paper.

Half an hour later the two of them were enjoying their breakfast. Lizzie sat on a chair, feeling slightly self-conscious in her strange outfit. Fortunately she had been wearing leather, lace-up boots to walk the dog and while the soles were too thick and rubbery to pass as Victorian on close inspection, they certainly suited the time better than her trainers would have. Edward sat in the doorway, enjoying the early morning sun. They had finished their bacon and now they were drinking coffee out of tin cups. There was no milk, but it was made from freshly ground beans and Lizzie found she liked it.

'Have you found out what your father has done with the machine?' she asked as she sipped her drink.

'Yes,' Edward replied. 'I managed to get Stokes on his own and ask him. He was terrified of what Father might do to him, but he likes me and he told me as much as he dared.'

'What did Stokes say, then? Is the machine all right?'

'It's as good as could be hoped for. Stokes says it's locked in Father's library and he hasn't damaged it any further – yet. I think he's undecided about what to do.'

Lizzie's hopes were raised by this. 'Well, that's not too bad then.'

'No. Not too bad. But you have to remember I hadn't quite finished putting it back together and I haven't had a chance to test it since Father took a stick to it. On top of that, it is, for the time being, locked in Father's private room which he seldom leaves and for which he holds the only key.'

'Oh.' Lizzie's heart sank again as the enormity of their situation struck her once more.

'Yes,' Edward sighed. 'If only we could have had one more day I'm sure we could have sorted all this out. Now, who knows what will happen?'

'Could we get into the library somehow?'

'Maybe we could, but even that wouldn't be the end of our troubles. Only one of the drums is charged so there's only one chance of using the machine – if I can get it mended that is. I had hoped to send you back with a message and bring Will back on a second trip. We really need to get a message to Will and your family otherwise there's almost no chance of them finding the time-field when it's activated.' The two brooded on this problem for a while. Edward stood up in frustration and began to pace up and down. 'If only there was a way to get a message to them,' he said.

Lizzie finished her coffee and she placed the empty cup on Edward's desk. She idly ran her eyes over the cluttered surface and her gaze came to rest on Edward's red journal. A smile slowly spread across her face.

'Maybe there is,' she said. 'Edward, you need to find out how and when we can get into your father's library. I'll sort the message out.'

Jed led his parents into the foyer of The George Hotel. It was still the evening of the same day that Lizzie had disappeared. So much seemed to have happened already that day, but Dad had decided he wanted to meet Edward and have another look at Will. He was almost convinced of the truth of the story. Jed grinned when he saw Will and Edward waiting to meet them.

'You're looking good, Will. Nice hat.'

Will smiled briefly in return. 'Thank you, Jed.' Then he looked nervously at Dad who was staring at him closely and not saying anything. He had learned from the telephone call earlier that Mum and Dad now knew the truth, but Will still felt uncomfortable. Mum nudged Dad.

'Sorry, everybody. I was miles away. You're Ed Rawlings I presume.'

Edward admitted he was and they all moved to a quiet corner where they could talk without being overheard. Half an hour later they had heard Edward's version of the story, had a look at the letters from the other Edward and seen the Victorian photo of their house. Dad was at last convinced. He sat back in his chair before speaking.

'It's all true, then.' It wasn't a question; it was a statement of fact. There were a few moments of brooding silence before Mum spoke.

'What are we going to do?'

'I don't think there is much we can do, Mrs Stokes,' said Edward. 'I mean we haven't got a time-machine so we can't try and get Lizzie back. We'll just have to wait for Will's brother to send Lizzie back when he can.'

'But what about Will? We must get him home as well.'

'Er . . . Yeah, I suppose so.' Edward looked down as he spoke and the atmosphere grew noticeably tenser.

'What?' said Dad. 'What's it all gone quiet for?'

Jed caught his dad's eye and shook his head. Dad let the matter drop.

'I don't think Will's brother can send Lizzie back,' said Jed after a while.

'What?' There was no disguising the fear in Mum's voice.

'Well, if he was going to send her back, why hasn't he done it already? I mean it's a time-machine isn't it? He can send her back to any moment. He must realize we would be worrying about her so he would send her back to right after she disappeared. That way we wouldn't even miss her.'

Dad looked at Jed keenly. That was a very good point. 'He might be leaving it a while to make sure he doesn't send her back too early. He wouldn't want Lizzie to meet herself.'

'True,' admitted Jed, 'but I still think she'd be back by now.'

Dad nodded gloomily in agreement. 'So do I,' he said. 'What do you think's gone wrong?'

'I think Will's dad must have taken the machine away. That's what the letter says. That's what Edward's book said as well.'

'Book? What book?'

'Edward's diary. We read it in the records office. I can't remember everything but it definitely said something about his dad being suspicious and I think something about the machine getting broken as well.'

Dad was excited by this. 'You mean to say Edward's diary is in the records office giving us a day by day account of everything that went on in 1879? Why didn't you say? It must tell us what happens.'

Jed shook his head. 'No. He didn't write much each day and then it just stops. A lot of it was really weird as well and we didn't understand it. It makes a bit more sense now we know what happened, but there was one bit about merry moons and stuff that was just crazy.'

'What about Lizzie?'

Jed shook his head in exasperation. 'No! She didn't understand it either.' He was irritated that Dad assumed Lizzie would understand it better than he did. He knew she was the bright one, but he was a year older and he was not that dumb.

Dad tutted in irritation. 'Not did Lizzie *understand* the diary, but was Lizzie mentioned *in* the diary?'

'Oh!'

That idea had not even occurred to Jed. 'No, I don't think so. We would have noticed if Lizzie's name was in the book, wouldn't we?' Mum had been leaning forward eagerly as Jed was speaking, desperate to hear news of her daughter. Her face fell at Jed's answer. 'Wait a minute though.' Jed screwed up his eyes as he struggled to recall the entries. 'Yes,' he said excitedly. 'She is in the diary.'

'Make up your mind, Jed. Which is it?' Dad asked.

'Yes. Definitely yes, I think. There was a child mentioned but it only said "Stokes child". We thought it was one of the servants' children because we'd already read about a servant called John Stokes. But now we know that Lizzie went there, the book must be talking about her.' Jed grinned.

Mum beamed at him. She leaned across and held his hand. 'Oh, Jed, that's wonderful,' she whispered. 'What did it say about her?'

'I don't remember.'

'Oh Jed!' Mum was feeling one moment pleased with him, the next moment frustrated. 'It's important. We could find out what happens to Lizzie.'

'Do you want to?' Jed asked seriously. 'Even if it's bad news?'

Mum's lip trembled a little but she answered decisively. 'Yes,' she said. 'I want to know.'

'All right,' said Jed. 'I'll go back to the records office and read the book again.'

The three of them bid Edward and Will goodbye and left the hotel foyer in much better spirits than when they arrived. They still had no idea if they would ever get Lizzie and Will back home, but at least they had some positive course of action they could take. Moments later, Edward and Will got up to go to their rooms as well. When they were safely gone, Morgan stepped out of an alcove where he had been standing in the shadows. Following the Stokes here tonight had been very useful, he thought to himself with satisfaction. Very useful indeed. Now he knew where Edward was staying and who he was. Perhaps he should take another look at that diary too.

Lizzie sat in the chair swinging her legs idly as she read some more of *A Christmas Carol*. She was so absorbed by it that she did not seem to notice the figure standing in the doorway. The man's eyes narrowed and he quietly marched up behind her raising his arm to catch her off guard.

'Hello, Edward,' the girl said without looking up.

'What?' Edward stood there with his hand still poised and feeling rather foolish at being caught out. 'How did you know?'

'I could see your reflection in your stuffed animal cabinets,' she said, snapping the book shut and turning to face him. 'Well, what did you find out?'

'I'm not sure you deserve to know.' Edward perched himself on the edge of his bench as he spoke to her, his arms folded. 'You're a good deal too smart for your own good.'

'You have to tell me,' she teased, 'or I won't tell you how to get a message to Will.'

'All right then,' he conceded grudgingly. 'It's not impossible but it is going to be difficult. We're going to need a clear hour in the library I think. I have to finish mending the machine and with only one chance of using it I want to check it over completely before we do. Unfortunately Father spends most of his day there and although he does leave it sometimes, you never know when he might return, so . . .'

'What about at night?' Lizzie interrupted.

'As I was going to suggest,' he said meaningfully, 'night-time might be best. Father is usually in bed by eleven, but waiting until after midnight will be safer.'

'Good. How about getting in there? Shall we climb in through a window?'

'You're welcome to, if you really want to. I, however, shall unlock the door with the spare key and enter in a more conventional manner.' Edward looked smug and Lizzie protested.

'You told me that your father had the only key.'

'I was wrong. I cornered Stokes and questioned him and apparently there is a spare key which the servants use to get in to clean the room and light the fire in the mornings. Stokes wouldn't dare give it to me, of course, but he's told me where it hangs and I shall be able to pick it up without involving him. Poor fellow, all this plotting against the master is turning him into a nervous fidget.

'So then,' he finished. 'I've worked out my side of the plan. Now you tell me how to get a message to Will.'

'Easy,' said Lizzie, picking up a little red book and holding it out to Edward. 'We write it in your journal.'

A number of expressions passed over Edward's face as he digested this idea. First surprise at the simplicity of it, then concentration as he considered it more carefully, and finally disappointment as he realized the problems with the idea.

'That isn't going to work,' he said sadly.

'Why not?' she protested.

'For one thing, you've already read my journal. Did you see a message there for Will?' Lizzie shook her head. 'That means I didn't write one and that means I won't write one.'

'No, it doesn't. You can write one now. There's nothing to stop you. The diary in the future will just change, that's all.'

Edward did not look convinced. 'You think so? I'm not so sure, but let's just say you're right about that. What am I supposed to write, then? "Time travel will occur at this time on that date. Please do not be late"? My journal is a public document, for goodness' sake. We can't have everyone reading that sort of message, particularly if you say there are policemen investigating what's happening. We don't want your Inspector Morgan turning up because he's been notified of the appointment.'

This was a real problem and Lizzie had to think for a while. 'What we'll have to do,' she said at last, 'is write a message that will make sense to Will, but that others won't understand.'

'Oh, easy then,' said Edward bitterly. 'Which brings me on to my final objection. Your brother has already read my journal with you at the records office. Why should he go back and read it again to get the hidden message from the changed diary?'

Lizzie looked at Edward seriously. 'I really don't know if he will, but I'm pretty sure that now I've disappeared into the past, he'll remember the diary entry you wrote the day I arrived. When we read it first time we thought "Stokes child" meant your servant's kid, but once Jed realizes it means me, I think he'll want to go back and read it again for more clues.'

'It seems a pretty slim hope.'

'I know,' Lizzie agreed, 'but it's our only one.'

Edward sighed and stood up. 'All right. We've nothing to lose. If we can get into the library, we at least have an excellent chance of getting you back home. We'll just have to pray that Will gets the message and returns on the same trip.'

'OK,' said Lizzie, sitting forward eagerly now that they had decided on a course of action. 'Let's write the message. What needs to go in it?'

'First we need to decide a time and day to set the machine for. When would be the best time, do you think?'

Lizzie thought. 'I left on Wednesday the nineteenth of July, but Inspector Morgan saw me go so we can't make it the same time because he'll be there. He'll probably be chasing around all that day trying to get Jed to explain where I've gone.'

'Shall we say a day or two later then?'

'Yes, but not too long. My parents will be worrying about me, and it's getting more and more difficult to keep Will hidden.'

'Right. And the time of day?'

'Make it early in the morning. There's less chance of anyone else being about then.'

'Excellent,' said Edward. 'That's settled then. Now to devise a message that only those who need to will understand.' He sat down at his desk and picked up a pencil and notebook. 'Hmm. Could be difficult,' he said, chewing the pencil thoughtfully.

While Edward was thinking, a sickening thought came to Lizzie.

'Edward,' she said in a small voice. 'The time-machine isn't behind our house anymore, is it?'

Edward sat up sharply and the pencil fell out of his mouth. He reeled with shock at the thought of what he had been about to do. He had been going to send a message to Will telling him when the machine would be on, and then switch it on in a different place. Will would be patiently waiting at the back of the Stokes' house, while Lizzie materialized in the library of Rawlings House.

'My goodness, Lizzie. We nearly wasted our only chance of getting Will back.' The two sat in numbed silence for a moment before Lizzie broke even worse news.

'Your house is a nursing home now.'

'What?' Edward said incredulously. 'Do you mean a hospital?'

'Not quite. It's a place where old people go to live when they can't look after themselves anymore.'

'A workhouse! No!' Edward clutched his head in despair. 'This gets worse and worse. They're as bad as a prison.'

'Not quite as bad as that,' Lizzie disagreed. 'The people

aren't locked up or anything, but I don't think Will will be able to just wander in.'

'This spoils everything,' groaned Edward. 'What are we going to do?'

'Could we get the machine outside?' Lizzie suggested.

Edward looked thoughtful for a moment but shook his head. 'No. Good idea, but still no. The drums weigh a ton and it needed Stokes and Hodges to carry them up the steps. I'll bet they made a terrible row doing it as well.'

'We'll have to think of a time when the nursing home might be quiet enough for Will to sneak in, then,' said Lizzie. 'How about night-time again? Old people go to bed really early.'

'The place will be locked, surely.'

'Yes, but we know an old man who lives there. He might help. In fact I'm sure he'll be pleased to. It's Tom Harris.'

'Who? The man who owns that little brass gadget for burning things?'

Lizzie reached down into the pocket of her grey dress and pulled out Tom's lighter. She flicked the mechanism and the two of them watched the little flame burn between them. 'Yes, he likes your family. His granddad is a gardener here and he often talks about you. Well, what d'you think?'

'I think this will never work, but I don't see that we've got any choice.'

Edward bent over to pick up his pencil again and began racking his brains for a way of writing a message. An idea occurred to him and he began to scribble on his paper. He worked for a few minutes, occasionally reading it through, crossing bits out and correcting them. As he worked a smile spread across his face. 'I think I have it,' he said at last. 'I'll just write it in the journal and then you can try to decipher it.' Edward sat down at his desk, dipped his pen in the ink and wrote the message. When it was finished he sat back grinning and signalled for Lizzie to have a read. She leaned over his shoulder and read the still-glistening ink. Confusion spread over her face.

'Is that it, really?' she asked.

'Yes,' said Edward proudly.

'I'm sorry then. When I said I hadn't read a message in the records office, I was wrong. It just didn't sound like a message.'

'That, Lizzie,' said Edward, shutting the book with a flourish, 'is the beauty of a secret message.'

'Yes,' agreed Lizzie tentatively, 'but surely a message can be a bit too secret.'

'What?' Edward said in mock disbelief. He leaned back in his chair and placed his hands behind his head. 'Surely I haven't managed to outwit Lizzie. Are you telling me you don't know what my simple message means?'

'I haven't a clue,' she confessed.

At just past twelve o'clock Dad marched up to the records office and found his son leaning on the railings. 'Good. You're already here. Shall we go in?' Dad had insisted on coming with Jed to look at Edward's diary, but he only had his lunch hour to spare.

Once inside they had to wait for attention from the assistant because she was busy explaining something to a stout middle-aged woman. The explanation took a long time because the woman appeared to be deaf as well as stout. Dad clicked his tongue with impatience and Jed occupied himself by looking around the office. As usual there were seven or eight old people performing their bizarre rituals. Jed noticed one man who was trying to read from an old book that he was holding the wrong way up. Business as normal it seemed, but something was different. Jed racked his brains but could not place what the problem was. His thoughts were interrupted by the assistant who had finally managed to shake off the fat lady.

'Hello,' she beamed. 'Back again? Surely your project's finished now? The schools have broken up.'

'Er, yeah,' Jed said sheepishly. 'I sort of got interested and thought I'd come back and have another read.'

'Good. Good.' She seemed positively delighted to see him and for a moment Jed was worried she might give him a hug. 'You've not brought your sister though.'

Jed winced. 'No. She couldn't come. I've brought my dad instead.' Jed hoped he would be a suitable alternative, and after a brief inspection Dad seemed to meet her approval.

'Splendid.' She nodded to Mr Stokes who nodded back. He was seething with impatience but did his best not to show it. 'What would you like to see today?'

'Those Rawlings papers again. Particularly that red book that belonged to Edward.'

'How extraordinary. I don't suppose those papers have been looked at more than twice in ten years, but in the last couple of weeks I've hardly had time to put them away before someone asks for them out again.'

Dad started at these words and was about to ask questions but Jed laid a restraining hand on his arm. They were more likely to get an answer if he asked. 'Really?' he enquired innocently. 'Who else has been looking at them?'

'Well, let me think. Apart from you there's that silly foreign chap who's related to the family and some other fellow called Morgan who thinks I don't know he's a policeman.

He was in this morning, ridiculous man. Couldn't be more obvious if he had "copper" stamped on his forehead. Don't know what he wants with them. Right, shan't be long.'

She began to retreat to the store room to fetch the documents but as she did so, a low moan of dismay rose from the queue of elderly historians that had gathered behind the Stokes while they had been speaking. The woman turned back at once. 'All right,' she barked fiercely. 'I said I wouldn't be long. Now behave yourselves or I won't let you look at the documents.' The line of people immediately hung their heads and went silent. The woman winked at Jed as she turned away again. 'I've got 'em well trained,' she said. 'They're just like naughty puppies really.'

'Well,' Dad said as they sat at a desk waiting for the papers. 'She seems to have taken a shine to you.'

Jed grinned modestly. 'Natural charm, Dad. You could learn a thing or two from me.'

'I certainly could, son. If ever I need to impress a woman with a light moustache, a voice like a foghorn and who looks like she gets her clothes at jumble sales, then you're the man I'll see.'

The idea was ridiculous and Jed felt the urge to giggle. He tried to suppress it but a strange choking noise emerged as he went red with the effort. The disgruntled huddle at the desk turned and scowled. Nobody likes a teacher's pet.

'Seriously though,' said Dad, as Jed wiped his watering eyes. 'If Morgan's been reading that journal, there could be trouble. He'll know as much as we do and we need the advantage of knowing more than him.' He stopped talking as the woman deposited the box on the table.

'There you are.' She gave Jed another wink as she turned to go and Dad raised an eyebrow which set Jed off giggling again.

'Really Jed,' he said picking up the little red journal. 'Learn to control yourself, please. Now let's see what's in this.'

Father and son bent over the book together. They turned the yellowed pages one by one, looking at the diagrams and trying to decipher the notes. The earlier pages were fairly full and they reasoned that these must have been written before the time travel even began. There was not much use, then, in looking there for clues about Lizzie. They turned on to the section that was the diary and read through it.

'This makes much more sense now,' said Jed. 'That stuff about rabbits just seemed weird before but it must be about sending rabbits on time trips. And that dog he talks about must be Arthur because Arthur disappeared the same time Will appeared.'

'Yes,' agreed Dad. 'And this is the bit about Lizzie arriving. It says the machine got broken. That would explain why Lizzie hasn't come back. One thing I'd like to know is why she went in the first place. It doesn't tell us that. I'll just have to wait to ask Lizzie herself for enlightenment on that one.'

Jed looked at his dad as he read the book. Was he really that confident that Lizzie would return? If he had any doubts he hid them well.

'Damn!' Dad swore. 'It doesn't say any more about Lizzie. The rest of the book's empty. There's just this last bit which frankly I'm having trouble understanding.'

'Yeah,' Jed agreed. 'That's the really freaky bit. There's no way that makes sense to anyone in their right mind.'

Dad read the entry out loud, slowly and thoughtfully. '"*Nota Bene*. The moon of the Emperor Julius meets the merry god of agriculture on two crosses and two straights. At a solitary hour, meet in Minerva's lair. There the passage can occur."'

'See,' said Jed. 'Just plain weird.'

'Hmm. It certainly seems a bizarre thing to write. But I think those few lines might be the answer to all our problems.'

'What?' said Jed, incredulous.

'Well, maybe not *all* our problems. I don't know how you're going to stop that woman winking at you, but I think it will tell us something about what happens to Lizzie and maybe even how to get her back. You see, it starts with two words that I do understand. *Nota Bene.*'

'Are those real words then?' Jed asked. 'I thought they might just be made up.'

Dad sighed and looked pityingly at his son. 'It's not your fault, Jed. I'm sorry. I'm not a rich man. If I had money, I'd send you to a school where they still teach kids the important things in life.'

'What, like Randall's? No, thank you.'

'Don't knock it, Jed. They may have to wear fancy-dress to school, but at least they recognize the Latin language when they see it. *Nota Bene* is Latin and it means "note well" or "pay attention to this". Now tell me, Jed, why would Edward Rawlings write those two words at the beginning of this section?'

Jed thought. 'Because it's important?'

'Yes,' Dad agreed, 'because it's important, but why would he have to tell himself it was important?'

Jed frowned. 'I dunno. In case he forgot it was important?'

'Maybe. Or perhaps he was telling someone else it was important.'

Jed's look of confusion deepened and then the meaning of his dad's words sank in. 'Do you mean they might be a message meant for someone else?' Jed's eyes widened with excitement.

Dad smiled. 'Exactly.'

'But why? I mean, why would Edward write a message for someone in his private journal?'

'It was private in 1879, but Lizzie might have told him how you two had read it. That would make it a perfect place to write a message to us.'

Jed looked down in awe at the confusing little message. Had it really been written down over 120 years ago and been waiting there all that time for them to read it? 'If it is a message,' he said at last, 'it would help if we could understand what it's on about? I mean, why not just write us a plain message?'

'What, and have Morgan read it as well?'

'Good point. Well, have you any idea what it means?'

'I think, or rather I hope that the last bit is telling us about a time-trip. Passage can mean journey, can't it?'

'Yes!' Jed cried out in his excitement and people turned and scowled at him again. 'Yes!' he said again, more quietly. 'This is it. Brilliant, Dad. You've cracked it.'

'Why, thank you, Jed,' Dad said modestly. 'I'm overwhelmed by your appreciation.'

'What does the rest of it mean?'

'Haven't got the faintest idea,' Dad admitted.

'Oh.' Jed's face fell.

'But I'm hoping Will might. Perhaps it's something the two brothers both understand.' He picked up the book and looked at the entry again. 'Well, we'll need a copy so Will can look at it. I could write it down but it would be nice to have the original page. I wonder if they have a photocopier here.'

Just then the sound of the assistant's booming voice came across the room. She was talking to an obstinate-looking woman wearing an anorak and clutching an old book. 'No, I'm sorry. I've explained this before and there are notices on the wall to remind you. We do not photocopy pages out of the old volumes because it might damage them. These are precious historical documents and must be preserved for future generations.'

'But I want a copy of this page,' the woman demanded. She meant to get what she wanted but she had not reckoned on the greater stubbornness of the assistant.

'I'm afraid that's not possible.' The woman opened her mouth to argue but she was breezily dismissed by the assistant moving on to the person next in line.

Jed and his dad looked at each other. 'That settles that then,' said Jed. 'You'll have to copy it out. She'll never photocopy it for you.'

'No,' said Dad with a glint in his eye, 'but I imagine she will for you.' Dad held the book out to Jed.

'Dad!' Jed groaned.

'Go on. Use your "natural charm". Flutter your eyelids or something.'

Jed scowled at his dad, but took the little book from him nevertheless. He wandered up to the desk, embarrassed at what he was about to do. 'Er. We're really interested in this page and . . . er . . . we were wondering if you would photocopy it for us.' The assistant looked over her glasses at him, a little disapprovingly. 'Er . . . please.' He gave her a smile and her face softened.

'Oh, all right. But just the one.'

She took the book from Jed's fingers and turned away to the photocopier. Jed relaxed and turned to survey the room again. Carefully avoiding the glare of the woman who had just been refused a copy, his mind went back to his earlier thoughts on what was different about the office. That was it. No Mr Harris. Mr Jenkins was there sleeping gently with his head on the desk but Mr Harris was definitely absent. The assistant had returned with his copy. 'Thank you,' he said. 'Where's Mr Harris today? Has he gone home already?'

'Who? Tom Harris? I didn't know you knew him.'

'Yeah, sort of. He's always here, isn't he?'

'Yes. He's barely missed a day in all the time I've been here. Something serious must have happened.'

A nagging fear crept into Jed's mind. 'Do you think he's all right? I mean he's very old, isn't he?'

'Not as old as some of the punters who come in here,' the woman smiled. 'But yes he is old, and he has had a terrible cough.'

Thanking her again, Jed took the copy back to his dad, thinking seriously.

'What do you think?'

Edward smiled at Will as he sucked hard on the straw of his milk shake. Will did not answer until he had finished the last drop. He pulled the straw out and blew through it noisily. 'It's wonderful,' he said contentedly. 'Can I have another?'

'You could,' Edward answered, wiping the splatters of strawberry liquid off his face with a tissue, 'but you ought to eat your burger first. You might not feel like another shake when you're full.' Will looked down at the burger in a bun in front of him. He gave it a few prods before picking it up and biting into it. The layers slid around bewilderingly as he bit, and slices of onion dropped onto the table. When he pulled the mouthful off, a blob of ketchup was left on his chin. He chewed thoughtfully and then, deciding it was tasty, he swallowed and hungrily took another bite.

It had been a long and exciting day for Will. In the morning they had been ice-skating. Will had been sure Edward was joking when he suggested they went skating in the middle of summer, and when they arrived at the ice rink he had to bend down and touch the ice before he believed it was possible. Then he stepped out on his skates and shot off gracefully, gliding along and weaving in and out of the other skaters. Edward had stared in amazement at Will's ability while he shuffled along far more cautiously and clumsily. Will lapped Edward countless times in the next hour, laughing with glee each time. It was nice to be good at something for a change, rather than having to have everything explained. He was grateful for the hours he had spent skating on his lake at home each winter.

Afterwards Will had had his first experience of pizza. The strings of cheese had dangled from the corners of his mouth and danced around as he chewed, and he had washed his meal down with a fizzy drink that had made him cough and splutter. In the afternoon they had gone to the cinema which Will liked even better than television. He had sat in his seat peering over the top of a huge bucket of popcorn, absently eating while the huge, colourful images flashed across the screen and explosions of noise burst around his ears. When the lights went up and the curtain slid back across the screen he had sat back happily. He was even more excited when Edward told him they had not even seen the film yet; they had only watched the adverts and trailers.

Now it was teatime and Will was sitting in a fast-food restaurant surrounded by bits of polystyrene and cardboard. Edward sipped his coffee as Will finished his burger. After the pizza, cola, popcorn, and milkshake he had already had that day, Will decided he did not need another drink after all. He sat back feeling full.

'That was excellent, thank you,' Will said.

'So you're enjoying the twenty-first century then?'

Will saw the eager expression on Edward's face. 'Bits of it,' he said not wanting to sound too keen. 'Is every day as good as this?'

'Not every day,' the man admitted, 'but there is lots to enjoy and I haven't shown you half of it yet.' The two sat in silence for a moment. The question of what Will was going to do was still unresolved and neither knew how to raise the subject again.

'We ought to start getting things sorted out soon,' Edward said at last.

'What sort of things?' Will asked. He seemed to be concentrating on pulling the burger container apart and did not look at Edward.

'Well, there's your money for a start. We ought to get access to your bank account. There's no point being rich if you can't spend it.' Edward forced a laugh but Will did not join in. Edward struggled on. 'Then there are papers that need arranging. You don't officially exist in the twenty-first century. We'll need to get you registered and maybe get you a passport.' Will looked up. 'If you want to come to South Africa, that is,' Edward added hastily.

Will stood up. 'I think I'd like to go back to the hotel now,' he said. Edward looked hurt and Will felt guilty. 'Thank you for a lovely day, Edward. I really have enjoyed it.'

Edward smiled weakly. 'That's all right, Will. Any time.'

They did not say much as they walked back to the hotel.

Inside the lobby of The George the Stokes were waiting. Jed and Mum were quietly seated on one of the comfortable sofas that lined the walls, while Dad marched up and down impatiently. Every thirty seconds or so he would look at his watch or mutter 'Where are they?' to no one in particular. Finally the two arrived and the Stokes were so pleased to see them that any awkwardness between Edward and Will went unnoticed.

'Where have you two been?' Dad demanded.

'Where haven't we been?' Edward responded.

'That's right,' agreed Will. 'We've been skating and to the cinema and we've eaten something called pizza and drunk milk shakes and there was this thing called popcorn and . . .'

'What?' Dad was incredulous. 'You've been out in public all day? You might have been seen.'

'We couldn't sit in the hotel room all day, could we?' Edward defended their actions. 'Anyway, Will looks just like any other boy and the best place to not get noticed is in a crowd of people who look like you.'

Dad could see the sense of this but he was still irritated at having had to wait. 'Well, you might have told us. We've been here hours, going frantic not knowing where you were.'

Mum gently intervened. 'Not quite hours, darling. Nearer twenty minutes. Anyway the important thing is we're all here now. Why don't you explain what you've found?'

'Yes,' said Edward, giving Mrs Stokes a grateful glance. 'Shall we sit down? Or we could go up to my room.'

Dad looked around the hotel lobby. It was early evening and guests were milling around, some waiting for the evening meal to be served, some waiting to go out. There was enough general activity going on for the group to sit and talk unnoticed.

'Here will do,' he said and sat down on one of the sofas. 'Will, sit here and have a look at this.' Now that they were able to ask Will what he knew, Dad's excitement was rising again. Will took the paper and looked as instructed.

'Why, this is Edward's writing,' he said excitedly. 'Where did you get it from?'

'We had it copied out of his journal.'

'What, the little red book he's always writing in?'

'That's the one,' Dad confirmed. 'We've read through his diary entries and you see there?' Dad pointed. 'That's what he wrote when you failed to come back after the time-trip, and further down, that's what he wrote when Lizzie arrived there unexpectedly.' Will eagerly followed what he was saying and Dad had to wait again while the boy read every word.

'We think,' Dad continued, 'that the last paragraph might be really important.' He lowered his voice. 'It seems to be a message written in some sort of code and it might be to tell us how to get you back to 1879 and how to get Lizzie back here.'

'Really?' Will's eyes shone with excitement as he looked at Dad and eagerly he looked back down at the message.

'Well?' prompted Dad.

'Well what?' said Will.

'What does it mean of course?'

Will looked at Dad again. 'Don't you know?'

Dad clutched his head in impatience and spoke through gritted teeth. 'No, Will, we don't. That's why we're asking you. Please tell us. What does it mean?'

'I don't know.' Sighs of despair sounded from the Stokes. 'I mean it's just nonsense, isn't it?'

'No!' Dad almost shouted the word in his desperation and Will instinctively drew back, looking frightened. Mum laid a restraining hand on Dad's arm. 'I'm sorry. I didn't mean to frighten you, Will. I mean no, it's not just nonsense. We're sure it's a message and I thought you might be the one who could understand it.'

Will read the page again and shook his head. 'I'm sorry but it doesn't seem to make any sense at all. How do you know it's a message?'

'Yes,' interrupted Edward. He had not reacted yet to the

idea of a hidden message, but the family could see that he was tense. 'What makes you think it's so important?' he said, his accent becoming thicker with emotion.

'Well,' said Dad, 'for one thing I don't think your brother is the type of person to write nonsense, is he, Will?' Will shook his head. 'Another thing, I've worked out that the word "passage" probably refers to a time-trip.' Will's eyes darted to that part of the page.

'Yes, you might be right,' Will agreed excitedly.

'And lastly,' said Dad. 'He's started the message with the words *Nota Bene* which I'm sure Will will be able to translate for me.' Dad looked at Will, his eyebrows raised in expectation, but the boy looked blank. Dad groaned. 'Come on, Will, don't let me down. It's Latin.'

'Oh. I'm not very good at Latin, I'm afraid.' Will was downcast. 'But I do like the stories about the wars and the gods and things.'

'That's nice, but it won't help you translate the words. They mean "pay attention" which might be good advice for you in your Latin lessons, Will.'

The group sat quietly for a moment. 'That seems to be that then,' Edward said at last. He sounded relieved.

'Maybe not,' said Mum. Four pairs of eyes fixed on her keenly. 'I think we can work it out.'

'How?'

'I think Will knows more than he thinks. You said you liked the Roman stories, didn't you, Will, but couldn't translate the language well?' Will nodded in agreement. 'And Edward knows that I suppose.' Will nodded again. 'Then I think the Latin at the beginning is a clue that Roman things will help you understand the rest.'

Jed snatched at the paper Will was holding and gazed at it. 'Yes!' He spoke loudly in his excitement and many heads in the room turned to look at him. He shrank back into his seat, embarrassed. 'I think you must be right, Mum' he whispered. 'Look, it says "Emperor Julius". That's definitely Roman. And the "god of agriculture". That could be Roman as well. They had all sorts of gods, didn't they? Rome must be the clue.'

Dad's eyes were gleaming. 'Well done, darling.' He leaned over and gave Mum a kiss.

'Right, let's work it out,' said Jed. They huddled round the paper and began racking their brains, giving each other suggestions. Only Edward did not join them. He remained seated on a separate chair feeling very left out.

'OK,' started Dad, 'the god of agriculture should be easy for you, Will. Who is it? Neptune?'

'No,' laughed Will. 'He's god of the sea. It's Saturn, and he's called the jolly god because he's known for feasting and merrymaking as well.'

'Saturn. Good. Now we're getting somewhere.'

'Are we? I still don't get it,' said Jed. 'What's Saturn got to do with anything?'

'Patience, Jed,' said Dad. 'It should become clear when we understand the rest of it. Now then, Saturn meets the moon of the Emperor Julius on two crosses and two straights. What might that mean?' Blank looks all round.

'How about if we draw two crosses and two straights to see what it looks like,' Mum suggested.

'Another excellent idea,' Dad enthused. He pulled his pen out and turning the page over he drew two crosses like plus signs and two straight lines. Four pairs of eyes studied it closely.

'Nope. It's still got me.' Jed was not the only baffled one.

'Perhaps you drew them in the wrong order or wrong sizes,' Mum said.

'Maybe,' Dad agreed. 'I'll tell you what.' He tore off a strip of paper which he then ripped into four pieces. He drew a plus sign on two of them and straight lines on the other two and handed them to Jed. 'Here, Jed, you shuffle those around until you can work out what it's meant to look like.'

'Thanks a lot,' moaned Jed as he laid the pieces on a nearby table.

'OK,' Dad continued. 'Now for the Emperor Julius. What do you know about him, Will?'

'Julius Caesar? Easy, he wore laurel leaves on his head and he tried to conquer Britain in 55 BC.'

'Yes.' Dad's voice lacked enthusiasm. 'Anything else? Do you know about his moon?'

'I didn't know he had a moon. Does it mean the moon that comes out at night or something else?'

'Well, there is only one moon, I think,' Dad reasoned.

'How can Julius Caesar have one then?' Mum asked.

'Oh, I don't know,' said Dad, exasperated. 'How are you getting on, Jed?'

'I'm doing my best but the only thing I can make out of them is a television aerial.'

'Keep trying, son. Come on, the rest of you, what else do you know about Julius Caesar?' Silence. 'Or moons, for that matter?' Mum was wearing a frown of deep concentration, but gradually a smile spread across her face.

'I think I have an idea. I seem to remember that the word month comes from the word moon.'

'Yes, that's right,' Dad agreed, 'because the moon goes round the earth about once a month. Well?'

'Julius Caesar didn't have a moon but he does have a month.'

'Yes,' cried Will. 'July is named after Julius Caesar. The message must be telling us that something is going to happen in July.'

'Which is now, of course,' said Dad. 'A lot of things have already happened in July. Let's hope it gets more specific than that. How are you doing, Jed? No pressure, but we've nearly cracked our bit.'

'Two telegraph poles?' Jed hazarded.

'Hmm. Possibly not. Try again. Right, let's see what we've got. The god Saturn is going to do something in July with something we don't know what it is yet. OK. Let's try the next sentence. Minerva, Will?'

'The goddess of learning and wisdom and war,' Will said immediately.

'Wisdom *and* war? I wouldn't have put those two together. War and stupidity perhaps. Anyway where is her lair?'

'I don't know, I'm afraid.'

'You do surprise me.'

'But I think I might have worked the Saturn bit out.'

'Yes?' Dad's voice was eager.

'Yes. Julius Caesar has a month and Saturn has a day.' Will's smile showed his pleasure.

'Well done, Will,' said Mum. 'A Saturday in July. We're getting close now.'

'Brilliant,' agreed Dad. 'It looks as if the message is giving us a date, so it should be giving us a time and place as well. I'll bet "Minerva's lair", wherever that is, is the place and the time must be the "solitary hour".'

'Easy,' Mum interrupted. 'Solitary means "alone" or "lonely", doesn't it? The hour that's on its own is "one". So it's one o'clock.'

'Yes!' Dad's voice was rising with excitement again. 'We've nearly done it. One o'clock in Minerva's lair on a Saturday in July the passage will happen. Brilliant.' Dad, Mum and Will looked at each other, their eyes gleaming with pleasure. Only Edward in his gloom and Jed in his puzzlement did not share the excitement.

'It's all very well you getting excited about that,' Jed complained, 'but if we can't work out what these two crosses and two straights are, we might as well not understand any of it.' He spread the four bits of paper out in front of him again. 'The only other thing I can make them look like is a couple of deckchairs.'

'Don't you worry, Jed,' Dad said. 'We'll soon have it sorted.' The four of them bent over the little scraps of paper and thought hard. But Dad was wrong, they couldn't work it out at all. They were so badly stumped that even Edward began to cheer up. Perhaps they were never going to fathom these last bits of the clue.

As they had been talking, the busy hotel lobby had calmed down a little, with most guests either having their meal or having gone out, but now the door swung open again as one straggler made his way out. A breeze from the door wafted across the room and the little bits of paper fluttered. Exasperated, Dad clicked his tongue and put out a hand to straighten them, but Jed just as quickly stopped him.

'No, Dad. Leave them.'

'Why?' Dad asked irritably.

'Because I think we've been going about this the wrong way. Look at them now.' They all looked but still could not understand what Jed meant. The pieces of paper looked no different except that they were no longer lined up squarely. Jed straightened up the two lines, but the two crosses he rotated so that they were no longer upright. 'The crosses aren't plus signs, they're Xs.'

'Twenty-two!' Dad leapt to his feet again and punched the air like a footballer who has just scored. 'Jed, you've got it. XXII. It's so simple. Roman numerals for twenty-two. How could we have been so slow?'

There was a wide smile on Mum's face. 'Saturday, July the twenty-second at one o'clock. Well done, everybody.'

'That's the day after tomorrow,' Jed pointed out. 'Which means we haven't long to work out where Minerva's lair is.'

Dad was in a buoyant mood. 'No problem.' he waved his hand dismissively. 'We've cracked the rest of it in about half an hour. We'll get it.'

The sound of a scraping chair silenced their jubilation. They turned immediately but Edward was already halfway across the room. A second later the door slammed and he was gone.

Dad stared in amazement. 'What's up with him?'

Jed groaned. 'I think he's worried about his continued existence in this space-time continuum.'

There were raised eyebrows from Mum and Dad. 'Really? And your precise meaning of those words are?'

'It's all that *Star Trek* stuff you told Lizzie about,' said Jed gloomily and he explained the predicament they had with Edward not wanting Will to go home. All the elation they were feeling at cracking the coded message drained out of their faces as they understood.

'Oh no!' said Mum. 'What are we going to do? We must send Will home, surely.'

Dad shrugged. Will looked uncertainly at the family.

'Are you going to keep me here?' he asked in a small voice.

Mum put her arm around the anxious boy. 'We all need time to think about that one, Will.'

'Shall I go and see Ed?' Dad asked.

'Better not now.' Mum shook her head. 'It's getting late. He might be a bit calmer in the morning.'

'What shall we do about Will, then?'

'He can come home with us.'

Dad nodded and gathering up the bits of paper he and the others made their way out of the hotel.

Ed Rawlings sat alone at a table in the bar of the hotel. It had been over an hour since the family left and he had drunk five whiskeys in that time. He drained the last drop from his glass and was about to order another when a voice prevented him.

'Good evening, Mr Rawlings.'

'What do you want?' he asked moodily and looked up to see who he was talking to. The man Edward knew as Inspector Morgan looked back at him smiling grimly.

'Not Mr Smith any more then?' Edward was not thinking clearly after drinking so much but he realized what he had just done. He struggled momentarily to extract himself but then gave in. He probably wasn't going to exist in two days' time so what was the point?

'No, Inspector,' he said. 'I'm not Mr Smith and I never was.'

'Now someone is talking sense at last.' Morgan called for two more whiskeys and sat down with Edward. 'As far as I can make out, Mr Rawlings, you've got nothing to lose and everything to gain if young Will doesn't go home.' Edward looked dully at the man and said nothing. The whiskeys arrived. Morgan swirled his around the glass, the ice clinking, before taking a sip. Edward just took a gulp of his and set the glass down again.

'Now then,' Morgan continued. 'I have here a somewhat cryptic message, which I believe might be important but I cannot for the life of me work it out. Do you know anything about it?' He held up his pocket computer. There was a scanned image of the page from the diary, glowing on the screen.

'Yes, officer.' His voice was slurred.

'I think it might be to your advantage if I knew what it meant. Don't you?'

Edward struggled inwardly, his alcohol-numbed brain doing its best to decide what to do. He saw fleeting images in his mind of Will, of himself, of his home, of the photographs in his album. What should he do? It was unreasonable for everyone to expect him to make decisions like this. He took another gulp of his drink and made up his mind.

'Yes, officer,' he said again.

'Aren't you going to tell me then?' Lizzie looked expectantly at Edward as he leaned back in his chair, holding his journal with the mysterious message.

'I might later,' he smiled infuriatingly. 'In the meantime, we have a whole day to waste before we can make our attempt tonight.'

'Only one day?' Lizzie was confused. 'I thought we were giving them a few days to throw Inspector Morgan off the scent.'

'We have,' said Edward. 'I've told them to be at the rendez-vous at one o'clock on Saturday morning in the message.'

'Have you?' Lizzie still looked blank.

'Yes. We don't have to wait that long though. It's a time-machine.' The confusion in Lizzie's face cleared as this sank in. 'Don't worry,' Edward smiled. 'It took me a long time to get used to the implications as well. What would you like to do today?'

'What is there to do?'

'Well . . .' Edward puffed out his cheeks as he tailed off. He did not have much experience of entertaining children from the future. 'I don't know really. I think we ought to get away for the day though. If we can avoid Father altogether today that would be best, I think. He was seeing Dr Wilkes in his library when I was up at the house. I don't know what they were scheming, but it can't last all day. I think we should go now while we can.' Lizzie was keen to see some more of Victorian England so after a careful look outside the two of them slipped through the door and into the woods.

'These are the woods where our dog found Tom Harris's lighter the first time,' Lizzie observed as they walked along the path together. Occasional shafts of sunlight broke through the canopy of leaves, otherwise the light was green and cool and pleasant. She pulled the lighter out and handed it to Edward. 'If you still have your time-machine after all this is over, could you try and give it back to him in 1940. It means a lot to him.' Edward took the lighter from her as she explained the story of Tom Harris's lost love.

'Another life I've ruined with my meddling,' he said rue-fully as he slipped the lighter into his pocket. 'I'll try and get it back to him, I promise.'

The walk through the woods was pleasant but short. It soon brought them out on the far side near the tow path of the canal and having nothing better to do they set off towards the cotton mill. There was no traffic on the water-way and so the water lay still and quiet. Only the occasional fish rising to surface caused a ripple and once a kingfisher skimmed over the surface. It snapped at a fish which flicked its tail in a flash of silver and was gone. Edward quizzed Lizzie about life in her time as they walked along.

'The canal is still there,' she said in answer to his question, 'but people don't use it for moving things any more. People go fishing there and have holidays on the barges.'

'Holidays on a barge?' Edward could not believe it. 'Why would anyone want a holiday on a barge? It's dull and hard work.'

'Yeah, but it's different in the twenty-first century,' Lizzie said. 'People are really busy and so they like a holiday that's really slow. And a lot of people work inside at desks all the time, so it's nice to get outside and do something active for a change.'

'Strange,' said Edward. 'If they don't use barges for transport how do they move things? Railways I expect.'

'There are railways, but most of the stuff goes on lorries.'

'Lorries?'

'Yeah, you know big vehicles that drive around on the roads.'

Edward did not know but he wanted to. 'Really, on the roads? I saw pictures of something like that in the newspaper. What powers them?'

'Petrol.'

'A sort of oil, eh? I expect the oil's burned to make steam and that drives them.'

'No,' Lizzie laughed.

'Well, how then?'

'I dunno. You just put the petrol in and start the engine and away it goes.'

'Lizzie! This is the most exciting idea I've ever heard and you don't even know how it works. Oh, this is so frustrating. What else can you tell me? What's that thing I read about in the paper? Begins with an *r*. Radio! That's it. What does that do?'

The conversation continued like this for the next hour: Edward desperate to find out about future technology and

Lizzie describing what it did but not having a clue how it worked. In the end Edward gave up.

'It's no good, Lizzie. You have given me a tantalizing glimpse of the future and haven't been able to tell me a thing.' He shook his head sorrowfully.

'Sorry. I didn't know you were interested else I'd have brought a science encyclopaedia with me. Hey!' Lizzie broke off as they rounded the last corner that brought the mill into view. The machines must have been as busy as ever because the great engine houses were belching out their thick black smoke and even at a distance the noise could be heard. 'It's working,' she cried and broke into a run to take a closer look.

'Stop! Where are you going?' Edward shouted and started to run after her. 'Lizzie come back. My father might be there.' That brought Lizzie to a halt and Edward caught up with her. 'What do you mean anyway, "it's working"?'

'That big chimney is smoking and the engines are running.'

'Of course,' said Edward laughing. 'They never stop. That's my father's mill where he makes his cotton and his money.'

'Well, they've stopped by our time.'

'Really?'

'Yeah. That big building's a boat house now and the rest is all falling down.'

'What, it doesn't make cotton any more?'

'No.'

'So much for my father's commercial empire,' Edward laughed. 'Where do you get your cotton from then?'

'I dunno. India I think.'

'India? We sell cotton to India.'

'Well, I don't know.'

'Wherever it comes from, I wonder what Father would say if he knew.'

222

'Can we go and have a look at the machines working?'

Edward smiled at her curiosity. 'All right,' he said. 'Let's just hope Father isn't about.'

Edward took Lizzie to the engine house first. The huge furnaces were glowing white-hot as men with no shirts and dirty faces shovelled coal into the cavernous opening. Sweat was running down their backs, streaking the grime on their bodies. Over the furnace, the water boilers of great, riveted copper plates were boiling the water to make the steam, but most impressive of all was the engine itself. Its massive flywheel, twice the height of a man and made from tons of steel, was thundering around in a blur, and the great pistons that drove it were hammering in and out too fast for the eye to follow. Lizzie stood mesmerized by the motion and the pounding rhythm and the puffs of steam that hissed out each time a valve opened. Her eyes flicked from side to side as they instinctively tried to follow the motion of the pistons. The great drive belt disappeared through an opening in the far wall and Lizzie wanted to know what went on through there. The noise was too loud to allow her to ask Edward, except by signs, and when he understood what she wanted to know he signalled her to follow him.

Outside they could talk again. 'That was amazing,' said Lizzie, breathlessly. 'Where does that big spinning chain thing go?'

'That drives the machinery in the workshop. I'll take you there if you like.'

The two of them set off along the edge of the building and as they rounded the corner they met a familiar figure.

'Stokes!' cried Edward.

'Afternoon, sir.' He looked nervous.

'What's the matter, Stokes? You're squirming uncomfortably.' A look of worry suddenly flashed across Edward's face. 'Is Father about?' The unfortunate servant nodded. 'I won't keep you then. It wouldn't do your reputation any good if you were seen fraternizing with me, would it?'

Stokes looked pained. 'Don't be like that, sir. You know I'd do anything for you and the young master. It's just . . .' He tailed off, not knowing how to finish.

'I know, Stokes. You've got a good job and you don't want to lose it. I didn't mean to suggest anything.'

'Thank you, sir.'

'I too have good reason for not wanting to see Father, so if you'll excuse us . . .'

It was too late.

'Edward! Where the devil have you been?'

Reluctantly the three turned and saw Josiah Rawlings approaching, his face dark and frightening. Stokes hung his head and moved back a little and Lizzie, not wanting to be seen either, stood with him.

'Edward, I came to find you this morning in your laboratory. You were not there.'

'Er . . . no, Father, I was er . . . here.'

Josiah's eyes were suspicious. 'It is the first interest you have shown in this place for some years. Why now?' Edward made vague gestures as he tried to think of an answer and Josiah lost patience with him. 'I will talk with you now.' Josiah turned to take Edward to one side but then noticed Lizzie for the first time.

'What is the meaning of this? Why isn't this girl at work?'

Lizzie looked indignant and had she got a chance to open her mouth, she might have spoiled everything but Edward interrupted just in time.

'She doesn't work here, Father.'

'You seem to know an uncommon amount about the

business all of a sudden.' Josiah glared at Edward. 'If she doesn't work here, then what is she doing here? You girl, come here. What's your name?'

Lizzie decided politeness was the best course and kept her eyes down as she spoke. 'Lizzie sir, Lizzie Stokes.'

'Oh, I see. You're with Stokes here then.' Stokes looked confused but catching Edward's eye he did not disagree. He did not look comfortable though. Deceiving Josiah in any way at all seemed to unnerve him. 'Well, Edward,' Josiah continued, 'I'm waiting. Come this way.'

The father and son withdrew until they were out of hearing, leaving Lizzie and John Stokes together. The servant let out a deep sigh of anguish.

'Oh dear,' he groaned. 'This is all too much, it really is.'

Lizzie gave his hand a squeeze. 'Don't worry. You haven't done anything wrong. You were only talking with Edward.'

'That's Mr Edward if you don't mind.' Even in times of anxiety Stokes liked to maintain a proper sense of respect.

'Is your name really Stokes, or was that some lie you dreamed up?'

'It really is.'

'Well, I'll be blowed. I didn't know there were any other Stokes round here. Where do you live? Who are your parents?'

'I live near here. It's a little hard to explain really. Mum and Dad are called Robert and Jane.'

Stokes shook his head to show he had never heard of them and Lizzie was saved any further interrogation by the return of Edward. He looked very grave.

'We have to succeed tonight,' he said in a low voice, his face pale. 'If we don't then on Monday morning I'll be attending Will's funeral and catching the next boat to South Africa.'

Will sat at the kitchen table next morning after breakfast. Cereal boxes were piled around him and he had half a mug of coffee left to drink, but he was absorbed by Edward's old photograph album. Jed was walking Arthur, while Dad washed the dishes and Mum had decided to give Lizzie's room a clean in anticipation of her coming home. Page by page, Will turned over the photographs of his family, from one Edward, through the generations to the last Edward. He was so immersed in what he was doing that Dad had to speak twice to him.

'I said have you finished your coffee, Will?'

Will looked up. 'Sorry. No.' He picked up the mug and began drinking as Mum came back into the room. She was holding a medicine bottle half full of yellow liquid.

'Aren't you going to be late for work, dear?'

'I've phoned in to say I'm taking a day's leave,' Dad explained. 'I haven't got time to go to work. We've got a lot to sort out before tomorrow and I've just had a nasty thought.'

'What?' Mum sounded worried. She had begun to have hope that Lizzie would return and could not face any more disappointments.

'There are two one o'clocks each day.'

Mum put her hand to her mouth in horror. 'Oh, my goodness. Just think if we had got everything worked out perfectly only to turn up twelve hours late.'

'Exactly,' said Dad. 'Which means we have to be there at one o'clock in the morning as well which gives us even less time. Still I'm sure we'll manage. What have you got there?' Dad was looking at the medicine bottle.

'Lizzie's antibiotics for her chest infection. The silly girl only took half the course. No wonder it took her so long to shake it off.' She put the bottle down on the work surface and Will stared at it in amazement. So that was the medicine. He could not believe his luck. Edward had told him you could only get it with a doctor's permission and here was half a bottle full. He was wondering what Mum was going to do with it and if he should ask for it, when Jed returned from his walk.

'Excellent,' said Dad. 'We're all here. We can continue our planning.' He sat down at the table and pushed all the cereal packets up one end. Mum and Jed joined them. 'Firstly we need to work out where Minerva's lair is.'

'No,' Will disagreed. 'We need to decide what to do about Ed.' The family looked at him uncomfortably.

'I know it's awkward . . .' Dad began, but Will interrupted him.

'It's more than awkward. I've been looking through his album again and I'm not sure I should go back now.'

'What?' The Stokes all spoke together.

'But yesterday you were scared we were going to keep you here,' said Dad. 'I don't understand.'

'Of course I still want to go back but I'm not sure I should. Look at all these people.' He flicked through the pages of the album. 'If I go back home then none of them will exist any more.'

'They're nearly all dead anyway,' Jed pointed out. 'They won't mind.'

'Edward's not dead.'

'Well, what do you want to do then?' Dad was a little exasperated at Will's change of heart.

'I want to go back, but I'm not going to unless Edward agrees.'

227

'But he'll never agree.'

'Then I won't go back,' said Will quietly

They were interrupted by a noise coming from the back garden. Dad leapt up to see what it was.

'Now's your chance to ask him. What on earth is he climbing over our back fence for?'

'To avoid the camera.'

Dad had forgotten about that. 'Oh, is that why you lot were scrambling over the fence on Sunday? I'll bet you've been doing that all week, haven't you? If you've trodden on my rhubarb there'll be trouble.'

'Dad! Your only daughter is trapped in the year 1879. Is this the time to talk about rhubarb?'

Dad grunted as he unlocked the back door. Edward walked in looking very much the worse for wear. His hair was unkempt and his skin was pale and glistening with a thin sheen of sweat. His shirt was crumpled and stained where it had been dragged over the fence.

'Ed! Whatever's the matter?' said Mum, concerned. Dad was more frank.

'Good grief! You look awful.'

Edward managed a weak smile. 'I don't feel so good either. Drank a bit too much last night and then I didn't sleep much.'

'Can I get you something?' Mum offered. 'Do you want breakfast?'

Edward's face became a paler tinge of grey at the mention of food. 'No, thank you. A glass of water will be fine, and perhaps some aspirin.' Mum got him what he asked for while he sat down.

'I've got a confession to make,' he said as he gently cradled his head in his hands.

'I've got something to say first,' Will put in quickly before he could change his mind. 'I won't go back unless you say it's all right.'

'What?' Edward looked up sharply at the boy.

'I mean it. I don't think it's fair on you.'

'Oh Will. That's kind.' Edward reached over and gripped his shoulder. They looked each other straight in the eye without any of the awkwardness they had felt yesterday. 'Thank you, Will. Thank you so much.' Will smiled. 'But I want you to go back,' Edward continued. Will's eyes widened in surprise.

'What? But you kept trying to make me stay.'

'I know. Of course I wanted you to stay, but I was being thoughtless.' He let go of Will and looked down at the table as he continued. 'I did something I'm not proud of yesterday – I'll tell you in a minute – and after I'd done it I felt really bad. I realized that if I made you stay I'd feel that terrible for the rest of my life. If you go, I'll probably disappear but then I won't know anything about it. Really Will, it's better if you go. Better for you and for me.'

Will sat still for a moment and then got up and threw his arms around Edward's neck. 'Thank you, Ed,' was all he could manage to say.

'Ed, this is really good of you,' said Dad.

'Yes,' agreed Mum. 'I think that's the kindest and bravest thing I've ever heard anybody say.'

Edward laughed and then regretted it as pain shot through his temples. He put a hand to his head to soothe it. 'Well,' he said, 'I'll enjoy the compliments for a moment because in a minute you're going to hate me. It's time for that confession.'

'What have you done?' asked Dad. 'It can't be that bad.'

Edward looked down at the table again. 'I told Morgan everything you had worked out about the clue.'

Dad sat back looking stunned. 'It *is* that bad,' he croaked.

There was numbed silence for a minute before Mum spoke. 'Oh dear, Ed. What were you thinking of?'

'I wasn't thinking clearly at all,' he said, throwing his hands up in frustration. 'I'd had a lot to drink. And I was angry with you all, and he came and found me and started suggesting that if he knew when the machine was next going to work then he could stop Will returning and . . .' Edward tailed off. 'I'm sorry,' he finished.

The Stokes and Will were shocked but no one had the heart to be angry with Edward because he had just been so generous to Will.

'This makes things more complicated,' Dad said diplomatically. 'He's not a policeman, you know.'

Edward didn't know and was surprised to hear it. 'But I thought . . .'

'Yes, we all did.' Dad explained about the telephone call of the night before.

'Impersonating a police officer is a serious offence,' Edward said when Dad had finished. 'Why don't we report him and get him arrested. That will get him off our backs.'

'We can't,' said Jed. 'The story is too far-fetched and when Dad phoned yesterday, they threatened to arrest him.'

'Could we at least get rid of that camera at the front of the house?' Edward looked distastefully at the stains on his shirt from scrambling over the fence. 'I mean now we know it's not interfering with police procedures or anything.'

'We could,' said Dad eagerly, thinking about his rhubarb again. Then he changed his mind. 'No. We don't have to. If he doesn't know we know about it, we might be able to use it to our advantage.'

'Yeah, but what I want to know is if he isn't a policeman, where does he get his stuff from?' Jed asked.

'Stuff?' Dad raised an eyebrow. 'Really, Jed, I take everything I said about your schooling back. Your range of vocabulary is quite extraordinary. Which particular "stuff" are you referring to?'

Jed scowled. 'All right, his surveillance equipment.'

Dad fell silent for a moment. 'I don't know,' he said at last. 'If he's a crook, he has access to some pretty hi-tech "stuff". There's more to Morgan than meets the eye.'

'I think it's a good thing we hadn't worked out the place last night,' said Mum. 'At least we still have that advantage over him.'

Edward looked up intrigued. 'Have you worked it out now then?'

'Well, no,' Dad admitted. 'We were just going to as a matter of fact.'

'It might be all right,' said Mum. 'If we can work out the place and keep it from him then it won't matter about him knowing the time and day.'

'Except that he'll follow us,' said Dad gloomily.

'I don't understand why the place has moved anyway,' said Jed. 'I mean it's always come on in exactly the same spot before and I thought if it comes on in a different place now, it means Edward must have moved it to that place in 1879. Am I right?'

Will nodded. 'I don't know why Edward has moved it either. He never moved it before.'

'I think your father may have been the cause of that,' said Dad. 'We know he was beginning to interfere so maybe your brother moved it somewhere more secret.'

'Maybe.'

'Well,' said Edward. 'We need to work out where Minerva's lair is then.' Everyone looked at him a little uncomfortably. 'What?' he said. Nobody answered. 'Oh I see.'

His voice betrayed his hurt feelings. 'I'll understand if you don't want me to know. I suppose I deserve that. Shall I go?'

'No,' said Will decisively. 'I trust you, Ed.' The rest of the family did not look so sure but didn't say anything.

'Thank you, Will.'

'OK,' said Dad. 'Minerva is the goddess of wisdom and war, which means her lair must have something to do with either or both of those. Suggestions please.'

'A school,' said Mum. 'Or a university.'

'An army camp,' volunteered Jed.

'Any good, Will?' Dad asked.

Will shook his head. 'My school is miles from home and the nearest university is Oxford where Edward went. I don't know where any military camps are and I don't see why Edward would move his machine there anyway. He would have to choose somewhere very near because it's big and heavy and he charges the power supply up at the water mill.'

'He'd have to keep it in or near your home then,' Dad agreed.

'How about a library?' This was Edward's suggestion.

'There is the Institute down in the town but . . . Oh no!' Will broke off and the others all looked at him in alarm.

'What?'

'My father has a library up at the house and he has a statue of some Roman goddess in the corner. It might be Minerva. It's his study really and he spends all his time there. If he's taken the machine there, then how is Edward going to get to use it?'

This was bad news and as it sank in Jed had an even worse thought.

'Never mind how Edward's going to manage at his end. Your house is now a nursing home so how are *we* ever going to get in there at one in the morning?'

There was a stunned silence before Dad spoke again. 'I think it's time to visit Tom Harris.'

Jed and Will stood at the gates of Rawlings House Nursing Home later that morning. Dad had been intending to come but Jed knew this would be a mistake.

'No offence, Dad, but Mr Harris really doesn't like you and you'd spoil everything,' Jed had said honestly.

They were nearly there and Jed could not help worrying about what they would find. He had not forgotten about Mr Harris's unheard-of absence from the records office and he hoped that they would not find him seriously ill, or worse.

'Well, Will, is it good to be home?' The two boys were walking up the gravel drive together and Will was staring around at his once familiar home. Only subtle changes existed outside: some trees missing, others grown much bigger; the fountain crumbling and not working; the summer house in ruins. Inside the change was much more apparent: there were chair lifts and hand rails everywhere; green uniformed staff bustled around; elderly residents shuffled around much more slowly. Will wrinkled his nose.

'It smells . . . unusual,' he finished tactfully.

Jed laughed. 'That's putting it politely. C'mon, let's ask that lady where to go.'

The two boys crossed the hall to the reception desk.

'Please,' said Jed. 'We'd like to see Mr Harris.' The woman's smile faltered at his words. 'He is all right, isn't he?' Jed's voice was anxious.

'Oh yes,' the woman sought to reassure them. 'Sort of.'

'What do you mean?'

'He's not ill, but he's been acting very strange. He hasn't been out at all these last three days and he usually goes out regular every morning.'

'I know,' said Jed. 'That's why we're worried about him.'

'And he's not eating much and talking to no one, except himself. He keeps muttering and crying and saying "Sally" over and over and saying sorry for something he's done.'

'Oh dear.' Jed was really concerned. 'Will he see us?'

The woman looked doubtful but said they could try and she led them up to his room. There was no answer when she knocked, so she knocked again and spoke through the door.

'Visitors, Mr Harris.' There was still no answer so rolling her eyes in exasperation the woman turned the handle and opened the door. Mr Harris was sitting in his chair clutching a letter and a photograph. He refused to look up.

'Mr Harris,' the woman said, 'I've brought some young visitors for you, now please be nice enough to speak to them.'

Mr Harris looked up briefly and when he saw Jed his eyes lit up a little. 'Your sister here?' he asked.

'No,' Jed replied. 'She couldn't come.' Mr Harris's eyes sank down again. 'I've brought someone else to see you though.'

Jed pushed Will into the middle of the room and Mr Harris looked up again. He was not impressed.

'Don't know this one,' he grumbled. 'Wanted to see your sister.'

Jed pulled Will's cap off and let his long hair dangle freely. Immediately the old man's expression changed. He leaned forward and grabbed Will's arm in his trembling old fingers as if to see if he were real.

'I think you do know him, don't you, Mr Harris?' smiled Jed.

''Tis Will Rawlings,' he whispered.

'Well,' said the woman. 'That's the most I've heard him say for three days. You two seem to be good for him. I'll leave you to it.' She smiled and left.

234

Mr Harris sat staring at Will. 'It can't be,' he said. 'I seen your grave. You didn't ought to be here.'

'There's a long story behind that, Mr Harris.' Jed told the old man as quickly as he could everything that had been happening in the last few weeks, including the problem that faced them now. Mr Harris listened quietly until Jed finished.

'That explains a lot,' he said matter-of-factly. ''Tis a shame about your sister. I wanted to see her.'

'What about?'

'Never you mind.' Mr Harris had opened his box of precious things on Wednesday morning only to find his lighter had strangely disappeared again. Edward discovering it in 1879 meant that it never got the chance to lie there undetected for Arthur to dig it up in the year 2000. The shock of losing it again had almost been too much for the old man, but this visit from Jed and Will seemed to restore some of his former resilience.

'I 'spect you want my help,' he said.

'Yes, please,' said Jed. 'The time-machine is going to come on again tonight, but not by your old hut like before. It'll be inside the house this time, in Josiah's library. We need someone to let us in tonight if we're going to send Will home.'

'Let's go and see then.' The old man teetered to his feet. 'Where's your dad's library, Will?'

Will led the way back downstairs and into the reception hall. The receptionist looked in amazement at Mr Harris.

'It's along that corridor,' Will said. 'Can we go that way?'

'Yes. That's where I have me dinner.'

Will continued to lead them along the corridor, past a big room filled with tables and chairs and smelling faintly of cabbage, to another smaller room that had armchairs in it.

'Here,' he said.

The three of them went in and looked around.

'This should be fairly easy,' said Jed. 'Look, there's a fire exit so you can let us in here and we won't have to go through the front door. I hope there isn't an alarm on it.' Jed peered at the door and there did seem to be wires around the door but he could not tell what they were for. 'How about it, Mr Harris? Do you think you can let us in?'

'Well,' the old man said ponderously, 'if I don't take my pill I might be able to stay awake and then I'll have to sneak past reception. There's always someone on duty in that little room behind the desk.' Jed looked worried. 'I reckon I might,' Mr Harris finished.

'Good,' said Jed hesitantly. 'We'll see you here tonight then at quarter to one. Please do your best.'

'Don't worry, son.' Mr Harris laughed at Jed's anxious face – a laugh that quickly turned into a coughing fit.

The three walked back to reception together. The woman at the desk smiled at the sight of them.

'Well, Mr Harris, I am glad to see you're feeling better.'

'Shut up, you silly woman,' growled the old man as he shuffled off back upstairs.

'He's quite his old self again,' she said affectionately when he had gone. 'I don't know what you two did, but you've worked wonders. You can visit again *any* time.'

'Thank you,' Jed smiled. 'We will.'

At home Dad opened the kitchen door to let them in. His eyes scanned the back garden for any sign of rhubarb damage before he spoke to the pair. 'Well? Any luck?'

'Should be fine,' said Jed. 'As long as we can shake Morgan off.'

Dad held up his hand. 'Say no more. Great minds have been at work on that one and the perfect decoy has been found. Darling?' Dad shouted. 'Come here a minute.'

The door from the hallway opened and in came Mum looking slightly self-conscious wearing Will's old clothes.

Jed and Will stared at Jane Stokes as she stood in the kitchen doorway. At first glance it was a pretty convincing disguise. Mum at just over five feet was not much taller than Will and she had shoulder-length fair hair. It would never pass a close inspection though.

'What do you think?'

'She looks a bit like Will, I s'pose,' Jed admitted. 'How's that going to help though?'

'Simple,' explained Dad. 'Morgan knows when the machine is going on so he's bound to be watching the house closely. I don't know where he'll be but probably in a car nearby so that he can follow quickly if we move. At half-past twelve I'll park the car outside the front door, bang in front of his surveillance camera, leave the engine running and the passenger door open. I'll hang around looking suspicious for a minute.' There was a wild glint in Dad's eyes as he spoke. 'I might even wear my balaclava.'

'Don't get too carried away,' said Mum. 'Or you *will* get yourself arrested.'

The fire in Dad's eyes dimmed. 'OK, I'll just give Morgan time to get excited and then I'll usher Mum out quickly with her head down and bundle her into the car and drive off. Morgan'll never know it's not Will and he'll follow. Then you two can wait five minutes for us to get away and walk down to the nursing home entirely free of interference.' Dad beamed proudly as he finished and Jed had to admit the plan seemed pretty good. In fact the more he thought about it, the better it got. It was watertight. Nothing, it seemed, could go wrong.

'Pretty good, Dad.'

'Thank you, Jed. High praise indeed for that work of genius.'

'Can I change now?' Mum was wriggling uncomfortably. Will's clothes were a little tight around the hips.

'Yes, certainly.' Mum disappeared upstairs and Dad turned to Will. 'It looks like you're going home, Will. We shall miss you.'

Will nodded. 'I'll miss you all too. I'll take some things to remind me of you.'

'Good idea,' Dad agreed. 'What would you like?'

'I've got my new clothes for one thing, and I'd like a picture of you if I can. And I'll take Ed's photograph album if he says it's all right. I'd like something to remember him by. Where is he?'

'He's lying down upstairs at the moment. He'll feel better later and you can ask him. I'm sure he won't mind. After all,' he added under his breath, 'he probably won't be needing it.'

Dad left to find Will some photographs of the family and Jed turned to the sink to make himself a drink. Will carefully picked up the half-empty bottle of medicine that Mrs Stokes had left on the work surface and slipped it into his pocket. That was another memento of the twenty-first century he would like to take with him.

At midnight things were getting tense in the Stokes' house. Mum was standing nervously in her disguise and Dad paced up and down, anxious to get started. Jed and Will were sitting on the sofa, Will with a bag on his knees that contained all the things he wanted to take with him. Only Arthur seemed relaxed as he dozed on the carpet.

Edward had not gone back to the hotel. He had not been good company that evening as he brooded quietly on his fate and the rest of them had been relieved when he said he was going to bed at ten o'clock. They had tried to make it sound as if they were wishing him an ordinary good night, but he left the room more like a condemned criminal than someone getting an early night. No one said anything about Edward when he had gone, but each of them wondered what they would find in the morning. Would he still be there by some miracle? If not, would he have vanished without trace or would there be some grim memory of him such as a pile of crumpled clothes fallen as his body left them. The thought made them shiver.

At half-past twelve Dad looked at his watch for the thousandth time and said quietly, 'Right, it's time to go. Everybody ready?' Each of them nodded. 'Goodbye, Will,' Dad said gravely, 'and good luck.' Mum did not say anything but gave Will a tight squeeze and there were tears in both their eyes as they parted. Jed would have to say goodbye later at the nursing home.

Dad went to the front door and looked out. It was a beautiful summer night, mild and well lit by the moon. He unlocked the garage and started the car, which he then manoeuvred into the road in clear sight of the camera. He left the engine running as planned and then, making lots of furtive glances this way and that he locked the garage again and opened the passenger door of the car. He headed back to the house and was pleased to see a car slowly pulling up to the corner of the street as he did.

'I think Morgan's on to us,' he said excitedly. 'Ready, love?' Mum nodded and lowering her head so that her hair fell forward and obscured her face she hurried out to the car and jumped into the front seat. Dad was right behind her and in a moment he was at the wheel. Then with a squeal of tyres the car shot off up the street. Seconds later another car followed.

'Right,' said Dad happily. 'Morgan's on our tail. Let's take him for a ride. I suggest we get on to the ring road, go round the town a few times and then head out into the country somewhere. Agreed?' Mum said nothing which Dad took as a yes.

'It's working!' Jed cried in excitement. 'Now it's our turn, Will. Ready to go?' Will nodded and picking up his bag the two boys left the house.

They made their way quickly and quietly up the street, their hearts beating faster in anticipation of what lay ahead. They did not think to turn around to check behind them, but if they had they might have seen the quiet figure of a man lurking in the shadows, following them at a safe distance.

At midnight the figures of Edward and Lizzie could be seen creeping noiselessly along the outside wall of Rawlings House. Edward was clutching a leather bag of tools and Lizzie had changed back into her modern clothes. They kept well back into the shadows because they did not want to risk being seen. At the side door Edward carefully undid the lock and the two slipped inside. Edward signalled to Lizzie to wait while he went and found the library key. Within a few minutes he was back and they crept along the corridor to Josiah's private study.

Once in the library, Edward closed the door and lit a candle so he could assess the situation. The machine was over by the wall, next to the French windows that opened on to the gravel drive. Both power drums were stacked next to it so there would be no problem in connecting them up, but where were the cables and metal spikes? There was a frantic five minutes as they both hunted around the room by candle light looking for the vital missing components.

Eventually they were found, bundled into a sack and placed behind an armchair in the corner. Edward breathed a sigh of relief as he finally turned his attention to the machine itself. He had not had time to secure the cover when it was confiscated so now it simply lifted off. With Lizzie holding a candle for him to see by, he snapped open his leather bag and pulled out a screwdriver.

At a quarter to one Jed and Will were waiting outside the fire exit at the old people's home. Jed had his nose pressed up against the glass and his hands cupped around his eyes to prevent the security light glaring on the window. He could see the dimly lit corridor opposite but could make out nothing in the darkened room itself.

'What can you see?' Will asked.

'Nothing,' grumbled Jed. 'Hang on though, I think this is . . .' Jed broke off and grabbing Will roughly, he dragged the boy off to one side and flattened himself against the wall. Will began to ask Jed what the matter was but Jed hissed at him to be quiet. 'There are lots of people running about in the corridor,' he whispered. 'I don't know what's going on, but Mr Harris will never be able to creep past that lot.'

The two boys waited anxiously for almost five minutes until without warning the fire door clicked and swung open. They pushed themselves further back into the shadows, not knowing who had opened the door and for another minute they waited tensely, hardly daring to breathe.

'Well,' said a familiar wheezy voice at last. 'Do you want to come in or not?'

Mr Harris had somehow managed it. The two boys gratefully tumbled into the room to see Mr Harris grinning at them in his pyjamas and dressing gown. It was not a particularly attractive grin as he had not bothered to put his teeth in, but Jed was so pleased to see him he could have kissed him.

'How did you manage it, Mr Harris?' he asked. 'There were people running all over the place. How did you get past them?' His eyes darted to the doorway and noticed thankfully that the door was now shut.

'Course they was running about. I made 'em run about. I pulled the red cord in Jenkins's room and they all upped and run there thinking he was having a heart attack. Soon as they was gone I come down here with no one to see me.' The old man was looking very pleased with himself, and Jed grinned as he heard the story.

'You're brilliant, Mr Harris,' he said warmly. He looked at his watch which said nearly five to one. 'Now all we have to do is wait five minutes and the machine should come on.'

'That's right Jed,' said a new voice.

The three of them spun round and faced the fire exit. Morgan stood there silhouetted in the doorway. 'Thank you for showing me the way, boys,' he said. There was menace in his voice. 'Pleased to meet you at last, Will. I knew you were about but somehow our paths never seemed to cross. In five minutes the time-machine will come on and I will be going back to 1879 in order to learn the secret of it. Until then, you three will wait here and watch. Don't think about making a sound. Against the far wall, please.' He waved them over to the side of the room. As he moved his hand, they noticed he was holding a gun.

By ten to one Dad and Mum had driven right round Milford. Dad had enjoyed himself enormously. He had changed lanes, slowed right down to thirty miles an hour and then raced away at seventy miles an hour. Whatever he did the car behind matched him exactly. The headlights shone in his rear-view mirror to show his pursuer was still doggedly following him.

'I think we might turn off here, don't you?' he said at last. 'It will be a bit of variation for Morgan.' Dad indicated left and slowing down he manoeuvred into the slip lane. At the roundabout he went round twice, just for fun, before picking a random exit that led off into the countryside. At every move the twin lights of the car behind stayed with him.

Dad drove on, gently humming the theme from *The Italian Job* to himself. This road was much quieter and the car behind hung back a little as if not wanting to alert Dad to the fact that he was being followed. Suburban housing gradually gave way to open fields and street lighting disappeared. Five minutes later an enormous brick building came into view on the left – Randall's school. Another few minutes and Mum suddenly spoke for the first time on the journey.

'Turn off here.'

Dad indicated right and turned down a particularly winding lane. 'Fancy seeing the old place again?' he asked quietly, looking across at his wife. Mum nodded. Dad drove on and before long he pulled up in front of a big old farmhouse. 'Little Moor' was written on a sign on the big five-barred gate that was closed across the driveway. Dad looked at the glowing clock display on the dashboard.

'Just past one o'clock,' he said, full of satisfaction. 'Lizzie should be back by now, and if I'm not mistaken this will be Morgan.' A crunch of tyres on gravel and the beam of headlights showed that the following car had arrived. 'I am going to enjoy this little chat.' He wound the window down and turned to greet the false inspector. The smile froze on his face as he saw that the figure that was now holding up an ID card was not Morgan at all. It was a genuine policeman, and he was looking very grave.

It was one of those rare occasions when Dad was lost for words.

'I . . .' he began but could say no more.

'Indeed, sir. I've been following you for quite a while.' Dad gaped foolishly at the policeman who continued. 'I must say, sir, that your driving is a little eccentric, I might even say erratic.'

'I . . .' Dad tried to articulate again without success.

'Your speed fluctuated wildly, and you did not choose a particularly direct route coming here.' Dad was silent. 'Which leads me on to the obvious question. What are you doing here, sir? It's not strictly illegal of course, but we are suspicious in the force about people like yourself, sir. People who drive out to isolated houses in the dead of night. We wonder what their motives might be.' The policeman's voice became more threatening. 'I'll ask you one more time, sir. What are you doing here?'

Edward worked slowly and methodically over the whole of the machine's inside for the next half an hour. Lizzie was terribly impatient and kept fidgeting. Besides which, her arm ached from holding the candle up and so she would swap arms every few minutes. Edward ignored her agitation and very carefully checked every part and every connection until he was as sure as he could be that the machine would work. Only then did he lean back and allow himself to smile.

'That's the best I can do. If she doesn't work now, then she never will.'

'Don't say that,' said Lizzie anxiously. 'It must work. Say it will work, Edward.'

'It will work, Lizzie,' he said. 'Don't worry.'

The girl smiled weakly. 'Let's try it then. How do you know which of the drums is still charged?'

'Easy,' said Edward, reaching into his bag. He brought out a leather glove and a large spanner. He pulled on the glove and grasping the spanner firmly he laid it across the two terminals on top of the first drum. Nothing happened. He pulled the spanner off and laid it across the terminals of the second drum. This time a huge blue spark cracked out as the iron tool made the connection. An acrid smell of electrical smoke hung in the air. Lizzie was not ready for that and she cried out sharply before she could stop herself. She immediately put her hand to her mouth and froze where she stood. She and Edward looked at each other anxiously for perhaps thirty seconds, not daring to move or speak. Nothing seemed to be stirring in the house so eventually Edward spoke.

'I think perhaps the second drum is the live one.'

'You might have warned me you were going to do that,' Lizzie hissed angrily.

'Sorry,' said Edward. 'Shall we get the rest set up?'

Lizzie nodded and for the next few moments they were busy again. Edward connected the heavy cables from the drum to the machine while Lizzie laid the metal spikes out in a circle on the floor. She could not push them into the ground upright but Edward assured her that would not matter. Soon they were ready to try. Edward carefully set the gauges for the right time and date. Lizzie gingerly stepped over the wires into the time-field and stood there waiting.

'This is it, Lizzie,' said Edward. 'In a few minutes you should be safely back in your own time. I just pray that Will will be back here.' The two looked at each other for a moment.

'Thank you, Edward.'

'For what?'

'For helping me get home.'

Edward smiled. 'If it wasn't for my meddling you wouldn't be here in the first place.'

'Well, thank you anyway. Don't forget Mr Harris's lighter, will you?'

Edward patted his pocket. 'I won't. Are you ready?' Lizzie nodded and Edward carefully pulled the lever and the familiar electrical hum began. Edward looked up excitedly.

'It's working,' he cried. His hand hovered over the switch as he watched the needle rising on the gauge. 'About ten seconds to go.'

Lizzie began to count down in her mind but did not get any further than nine for, as soon as Edward spoke, the door to the library flung open and Josiah entered the room. It took him only a second to register what was happening and with an inarticulate snarl of rage he crossed the room. Edward's hand was still poised over the switch, but it was too soon; the needle had not yet reached red. He tried to keep an eye on the needle and on his father at the same time. Josiah had gone to the fireplace, taken up the heavy iron poker and was now turning back towards Edward and the machine.

'Father no, please!'

'Out of my way, boy. I mean to smash that machine once and for all and if you are in the way then that is no concern of mine.'

Josiah was now halfway towards the machine. Edward looked one last time at the needle. It still showed the machine was not ready and so in desperation he turned and launched himself at the approaching man. The old bruise from his last tussle with his father stabbed with pain as, once again, Edward flung his arms around Josiah's upper body and the two men crashed to the library floor.

Jed, Will and Mr Harris stood reluctantly against the wall in the nursing home. Morgan stood in the centre, his eyes constantly surveying the room in search of the active time-field, but never letting his gun waver as it covered the three of them. It was not the Morgan they had grown accustomed to. Gone was the shabby brown overcoat and in its place there was a strange-looking knee-length black jacket which was done up to the neck. Jed could not tell how it was fastened, whether by buttons or zip or some other method. It hugged his figure and Jed was surprised at how muscular the man appeared. He seemed taller too. He must have been deliberately walking with a stoop until now to draw less attention to himself. The overall effect was one of a younger, more athletic man. His hair was still iron grey but Jed could not confidently guess his age. He had with him a black case, the size of a small suitcase, which was resting on the floor by his feet.

'I don't understand,' Jed said.

The man glanced briefly his way but then resumed his search of the room. He answered nevertheless.

'What don't you understand, boy?'

'How you're here. I mean we thought you were following Dad. We saw a car go after him.'

Morgan now turned and gave Jed his full attention. 'Did

you?' he asked with icy calm. 'Your father thinks I'm stupid, doesn't he?' Jed did not disagree and the man gave a laugh as he continued. 'Well, that's not a bad reputation to have. It lets the enemy underestimate your true ability. You may have conspired to outwit me so far but it doesn't appear to have done you much good, does it?' Morgan's face had a slightly mocking sneer about it.

'Yes, your father was followed,' he continued. 'I couldn't tell exactly what was going to happen tonight but I knew you would try and distract me so I simply made an anonymous phone call to the police station. Told them I suspected your father was about to commit a burglary. They've been watching your house since lunch-time and as soon as your father had finished his little pantomime and shot off into the night thinking he was James Bond, the police followed straight after him. I wonder who's feeling stupid now?' He grinned with grim satisfaction.

'Who are you?' Jed asked frowning.

The man smiled again. He was firmly in control of the situation and seemed to be in the mood to indulge all this questioning. 'Why, I'm Inspector Morgan,' he said. 'You know me.'

'You're not an inspector at all,' said Jed fiercely. 'We phoned the police and they had never heard of you.'

'No, I don't suppose they had. Nevertheless, I am called Morgan, and where I come from I am what you might call a police officer.'

'Where's that?' asked Jed, but Morgan was not willing to give that much away.

Will now spoke up for the first time. 'Please, Mr Morgan,' he asked in a small voice. 'Will you let me go home?'

The man's eyes softened a little but his face remained firm. 'Sorry, Will, I can't let that happen.'

'Why not?' pleaded Will. He was so close to finally getting home that the desperation could be heard in his voice.

'Two reasons. One, I promised Ed Rawlings that if he helped me with the clue I'd stop you going home.'

'But that's different now,' Jed broke in. 'Ed wants Will to go home. He told us this morning.'

'A likely story,' said the man. 'But even if that were true I wouldn't take you. I mean to have this machine and I imagine I will meet some resistance from your brother. The last thing I need is you there to help him.' Morgan's face hardened and there was a chilling threat in his voice. 'I warn you, Will, if you attempt to come with me I will not hesitate to use this.' He brandished his gun.

'What do you want the machine so badly for?' Jed had asked this question once before but now he hoped for a truthful answer.

'Again I have two reasons. Firstly, the people I work for want it. Secondly . . .' he paused for a moment and his voice dropped. 'I need it to get home too.'

There was a moment's shocked silence at these words before Mr Harris's weedy voice broke in.

'Don't look much like anybody's going to 1879, does it?' The three others turned and looked at him and he nodded at the clock on the wall. 'It's already ten past one.'

The hum of the machine rose higher and higher until the library buzzed with its high-pitched whine. It was surely ready now and only needed the flick of a switch to activate the time-field and send Lizzie home. Josiah struggled viciously as his son pinned him to the carpet. The poker was still clutched in his hand and as they struggled it beat against the floor, sending clouds of dust out of the carpet. Edward dared not loosen his grip on his father for a second for fear of what damage he might do with the iron bar. He frantically tried to reason with him but the old man was in such a rage that nothing would make him listen.

Lizzie stood helplessly inside the time-field, looking on in desperation. One simple flick of a switch was all that was needed and there was no one to do it. She did not suppose the power in the drum would last for ever. In fact it looked as if the machine was already beginning to overheat as it remained on full charge longer than usual. It was vibrating slightly and Lizzie could not be sure but there appeared to be a faint waft of smoke rising from under the cover. She wondered if she could flick the switch herself. She leaned over as far as she could and found she could just about reach. But which switch was it? There were so many. Her hand hovered indecisively over the panel, but a moment later Edward shouted at her in warning.

'Don't touch it!' His voice was almost a strangled scream as he wrestled with his father and tried to talk at the same time. 'If you turn it on,' he managed to gasp out between dodging the swinging poker. 'Then half of you will be transported but I don't know about the half that's leaning outside the field.'

Lizzie pulled her hand back sharply.

Just then, a group a servants burst through the doorway and stood peering nervously into the room. John Stokes was at the front of the little huddle holding a candle and looking extremely worried.

'Mr Stokes! Please come and help,' Lizzie cried.

The servant edged into the room, not knowing what to do. He looked in horror as his master and son appeared to be trying to kill each other.

'Master, I don't think . . .' he began nervously but was immediately interrupted by Josiah.

'Stokes,' he roared and the servant winced at the sound of his name. 'Pull this . . .' He struggled to find a word bad enough to describe Edward. '. . . this unholy son of mine off me at once.'

'Yes sir, at once, sir.' Stokes answered quickly but moved more slowly. The two men were still thrashing around violently and Stokes seemed reluctant to interfere. He edged forward carefully and made tentative moves to intervene, always keeping his eye on the poker. Edward managed to pin his father's arm down momentarily and this gave him a chance to speak.

'Stokes, please don't,' he panted. 'I need your help. We need your help. Will and I.'

Stokes stopped and looked questioningly at Edward but Josiah shouted again. 'Don't listen to him.' Edward continued over the shouts of his father.

'Stokes, if you ever want to see Will again I need you to do something.'

'For Master Will? What, sir?'

Josiah bellowed with rage. His face was crimson and he looked in danger of bursting a vein in his head. 'Stokes, how dare you question me,' he eventually managed to say. 'I've given you an order, haven't I? If you disobey me you will never work here again.'

Anguished indecision was all over the servant's face. He reluctantly began to edge forward again. Edward continued. 'I need you to flick a switch on my machine. If somebody doesn't soon, Will will never come back.'

'Never, sir?' The servant's voice was hoarse and Edward could barely make out what he said.

'Never, Stokes,' said Edward urgently. 'Never. Do you

hear? Please do it. It's the small brass switch next to the red dial. Please!' He would have continued but Josiah suddenly broke one arm free. It might have been because Edward had relaxed his hold or possibly Josiah's rage at Stokes' disobedience had given him new strength. Josiah now managed to push himself up and half throw Edward off. The sudden move from Josiah strengthened Stokes' resolve. Closing his ears to his master's continued threats he marched decisively over to the machine and before he could change his mind he flicked the little brass switch. The piercing whine died instantly and with a shimmer Lizzie disappeared, leaving a small patch of grass in the middle of the carpet.

Morgan glared at Mr Harris as if it were the old man's fault.

'Well,' he said at last, 'either something has gone wrong in 1879, or your brother meant one o'clock in the afternoon, Will. This is unfortunate as it means I will have to return in twelve hours at a much less convenient time. In the meantime, what do I do with you three?' He broke off as he noticed he had lost the attention of his three captives. They were staring, astonished, past his left elbow. Turning quickly to follow their gaze, Morgan saw Lizzie standing by the open fire-exit on a little patch of differently coloured carpet. The air around her was shimmering slightly. Her mouth was open in astonishment as she returned the man's stare, and she gave a little gasp as she noticed his gun. Morgan's face broke into a wide smile.

'So Edward was successful after all. Welcome home, Lizzie.' The girl did not speak but continued to stand there in dismay. The man's voice hardened. 'Now join your brother over there. It should be quite a reunion.' He waved his gun towards the wall. Lizzie still did not move so he strode over to her. He reached her in two paces and pulled her out of the time-field. 'I said move.' Lizzie dejectedly joined Jed and the others as Morgan stooped to pick up his case. He stepped into the time-field and turned round with a look of triumph on his face. Four sullen faces stared back.

'What a sorry lot you are. Cheer up. You may have lost, but at least the best man won.' For the first time since he entered the room he allowed his gun to drop slightly. 'It won't be long now. What is it, nearly a minute since your arrival, Lizzie?' The girl did not answer. Morgan glanced at his watch impatiently and opened his mouth to speak. But he never got the chance.

With a piercing cry which made them all jump, another man leapt through the open doorway. The startled inspector's gun instantly jerked back up and he turned to meet the new arrival. Ed Rawlings hit him full in the chest and the momentum carried them both across the room and well clear of the time-field. They staggered into a table and toppled right over it with an enormous crash. A second later there was the sound of a gun going off. Then there were further scuffles and quiet swearing as the tangled men continued to wrestle under the table. Morgan seemed to be struggling to heave Edward off but not managing it in the confined space. Edward did not seem to be putting up much of a fight at all. The four spectators stood there frozen in astonishment until Lizzie had the presence of mind to speak.

'Will, the time-field. Quickly! We don't know how long it will last.'

Will tore his eyes from the fight and raced over to the time-field. He turned to face his friends with a look of intense excitement on his face.

'I'm going home,' he cried.

'Don't forget this,' grinned Jed. He picked up Will's bag and threw it to him. Will caught it and clutched it tight to his chest.

'Goodbye and thank . . .'

They never heard the end of his sentence. It was finished in 1879.

Jed and Lizzie hugged each other in delight.

'We did it,' cried Jed. Lizzie grinned.

'Yes we did. Did you miss me?'

'A little,' Jed admitted. 'I'd have coped, though.' He broke off as he noticed the strange expression that had come over Lizzie's face. She had turned deathly pale and looked as if she might be sick. 'Are you all right?' he asked.

Lizzie staggered a little as he spoke. 'I don't know,' she mumbled. 'I feel a bit weird.' She stepped back from her brother, swayed slightly and then keeled over, unconscious. Jed stared in surprise at his sister before he too stumbled and fell to the ground.

Stokes cried out in terror at the sight of the disappearing girl.

'That girl, sir!' There was panic in his voice. 'She's gone.'

'Don't worry, Stokes,' Edward gasped. 'That's part of the plan.' Josiah had stopped struggling as he watched in disbelief.

'You've killed her!'

'No, I haven't, Father. Just watch.' The old man seemed to co-operate but Edward did not dare let go of him. There was no knowing when his rage might return. The two of them lay on the floor, their hair ruffled and clothing displaced, neither loosening their grip while Edward continued to give instructions to Stokes.

'Count to sixty, Stokes, and then flick the switch back again.'

A strange and unnatural calm descended over the room. The little huddle of servants frozen in their tableau at the doorway, their mouths all open. Edward and Josiah still like marble statues locked forever in a wrestling hold. Stokes stood at the machine, his trembling hand on the switch and his mouth moving silently as he counted slowly to sixty.

'Now, Master Edward?' he asked when he had finished.

'Yes. Now, Stokes.'

A flick of a switch, a shimmer in the air and Will Rawlings was with them.

' . . . you,' the boy said. He blinked, shook his head as he took in his surroundings and cried out in delight. 'Edward, Father, it's me. I'm home!'

Edward released his grip on his father and scrambled to his feet. Seconds later his arms were around his brother.

'It's good to have you back, Master Will,' Stokes said, a broad smile on his kind face as he watched the two brothers embrace. Will looked over Edward's shoulder and smiled back at him. Then he tapped his brother to let go. Josiah was approaching.

Edward stood back as the old man, limping slightly, crossed the room to greet Will. He laid a hand on his son's shoulder, his face twitching slightly with emotion.

'Welcome home, son,' he managed hoarsely. 'Welcome home.' Will reached up and gave his father's hand a squeeze and tears started into the old man's eyes. He blinked them back furiously and his grip on Will's shoulder tightened. He must not break down and cry. Not in front of the servants.

Will sensed his embarrassment and looked away. Josiah turned quickly and began to limp to the door. 'Edward, I will see you in the morning,' he muttered as he left, not daring to meet his elder son's eye. A moment later he was gone.

The very room seemed to breathe a sigh of relief as the master of the house left. Servants clustered round smiling and greeting Will and patting him on the back. He had kind words for everybody as he tried to answer the barrage of questions that hit him. It was not for another twenty minutes that the two brothers had the room to themselves.

'I'm glad you're home.' The relief that Edward was feeling was indescribable. For days he had felt as if a heavy weight had been pressing down on him and now it had been lifted. 'I'm so sorry, Will.'

'Sorry for what? It wasn't your fault.'

'Yes it was. I should never have risked your life with my foolish experiments. Still I've learned my lesson. No more time-travel for me.' Edward paused and slipped his hand into his pocket. He pulled out the little brass lighter. 'Apart from one more necessary journey. This needs restoring to its rightful owner.'

Will was digging around in his bag and he pulled out the bottle of medicine. 'Make that two trips, Edward,' he said triumphantly. 'This is medicine that can cure Mother.' Edward stopped in amazement at his brother's words.

'Are you sure?'

'That's what Jed and Lizzie's mother said.'

Edward took the bottle of yellow liquid, deep in thought. Then he put the bottle down and crossed over to his machine. Putting on the leather glove again, he laid the spanner across the terminals on the power drum. A much smaller blue spark crackled and he quickly removed the connection. He turned back to Will.

'There's barely enough charge left for one more trip. We can't do both, Will. What's it going to be?'

Slowly, Jed regained consciousness. He felt as if he were floating in blackness, but as his senses returned he sensed light above him and he began to rise towards it as if he were underwater drifting towards the surface. But it was not quite like water; it was a bit like a tunnel as well – a tunnel that branched off in different directions. Jed somehow knew the way he would go, although he had no control over his direction. That is he knew his way until he reached one particular junction. He felt himself drifting towards the familiar branch of the tunnel but then at the last moment he jerked across to the other with a sickening lurch. His mind screamed out in protest. He kicked and struggled but to no avail. He continued to float onwards towards his destination and within moments he was awake.

He opened his eyes but remained lying face down on the carpet, disorientated. It was only after some seconds that he realized the carpet had changed colour since he last saw it. Before it had certainly been green, but now it was dark red with a pattern. It was a deeper pile too and the fibres were tickling his nose. He pushed himself up and glanced feverishly around the room. The carpet was not the only change. Gone were the armchairs of the old people's home and in their place were a leather-inlaid writing desk, bookcases, portraits on the walls and, in one corner, a marble statue of a Roman goddess. His mind raced as he tried to take in all these changes and only when Lizzie groaned at his feet did he remember the others in the room. He looked round to check on them. Lizzie seemed to be coming to. There was Mr Harris perched on the edge of a chair with a vacant, almost wistful look on his old face. He looked different, although Jed could not place how. No sign of Inspector Morgan anywhere. That only left Edward.

Jed felt a sense of dread as he scanned the room for Edward. He did not think he would find him. Then his spirits leaped as he saw Edward's shoes sticking out from behind the desk.

'Ed!' he cried out in joy as he raced over to his friend. But then his joy turned to horror as he saw that, although Edward was still with them, his face was deathly white and there was a slowly spreading slick of crimson blood seeping across the chest of his white shirt. 'Ed,' he groaned. Lizzie joined him at his side and together they looked down at their friend, not knowing what to do.

They did not have to wait long as that moment the door burst open and a man ran into the room.

'What is it? What's going on?' He was dressed in pyjamas and carrying a shotgun which he waved about the room. 'Who goes there?' he said and then he stopped as he saw the children. 'Oh it's you Jed, Lizzie. What are you two doing here at this time? What was that bang? It sounded like a gun.'

Jed was confused. This man seemed to know them, but Jed had no idea who he was, or what he was doing in Rawlings House in the middle of the night. He was about to open his mouth when Lizzie cut in.

'It's Ed. He's wounded.'

The man followed her pointing finger and within seconds he was kneeling at Edward's side.

'Mister Rawlings?' No response. He tore Edward's shirt back to better see the wound. 'It's a bullet wound. It's in his shoulder. Not too bad I think.'

'Not too bad?' Lizzie was wincing at the sight of the raw wound, the flesh scorched and gaping where the bullet had torn through it.

'No. It's only in the flesh and I don't think an artery has been hit. Quick, Jed. Dial 999 and call an ambulance. Better get the police here as well.' The man tore off a strip of his own pyjama top and twisting it up, he thrust it into the wound to stem the flow of blood. Edward's face twisted with pain but he did not regain consciousness. Jed grabbed the phone from the desk and was soon talking to the emergency services. Mr Harris now spoke for the first time.

'Is Sally about?' he asked wistfully

The man looked up sharply, noticing the old man for the first time. 'What?'

'Is my Sally here?' repeated the old man.

The young man held the old man's gaze for a moment before returning his attention to the unconscious Edward. 'You do ask some stupid questions, Granddad,' he said as he tightened another strip of torn pyjama around the shoulder. 'Where do you suppose she is?'

'What's it going to be then, Will?'

Edward had explained the whole story of Tom Harris to Will and now they had to decide what to do with their last trip in the time-machine. Will hung his head and fiddled idly with the bottle of medicine. Edward gently took it from him and laid it on the desk. Next to it he placed the lighter and together they looked at the two items that symbolized the fates of their mother and an old man from the future. 'Mother or Tom Harris. Who shall we visit? What do you think?'

Will's voice was barely a whisper when he spoke. 'Mother,' he said.

Edward sighed deeply. 'I think Tom Harris,' he said at length. Will looked up sharply, tears in his eyes. He said nothing but Edward knew what he was thinking. 'Will, you know I loved Mother more than anyone,' he protested. 'You know it's true.' Will nodded.

'Why, then?' the boy asked.

'I'll tell you why.' Edward spoke urgently as if he did not trust himself to be master of his own feelings; he needed to say it quickly before he changed his mind. 'One reason. I'm scared of going back in time to change things. I've explained why and meddling in time has proved nothing but disastrous so far. Reason number two.' He counted them off on his fingers. 'I've ruined Tom Harris's life and I need to put that right if I can. Number three. We don't even know if this medicine will work.' He spoke more loudly to drown Will's protests. 'And four.' His voiced lowered again and he paused before giving his final reason. 'I promised Lizzie I would.' He was looking at his brother as he spoke. 'Now tell me your reasons,' he asked softly. Will dropped his eyes again.

'I want Mother back,' he said.

Edward struggled to keep his voice steady. 'I know you do.'

'Can we, then?'

Edward did not answer for a moment. 'I think it's much too risky. It could all go horribly wrong, but if you insist, we'll do it. Even though it means breaking a promise.' Will looked up at his brother. 'The choice is yours, Will.' He opened his mouth to answer immediately but Edward held a hand up and continued. 'But please, when you decide, try and do what you think is right which isn't necessarily the same as doing what you want.' Edward turned and walked to the French windows, leaving Will with his mouth still opened.

Edward swung the doors open on to the night and took a deep breath. The moon was still bright and the garden shone with the mysterious beauty of night. The shadows were blue and soft and a breeze wafted into the room tinged with the scent of lavender that grew in the bed near the doorway. Edward closed his eyes and let the turmoil in his mind seep away. It was not for a while that he noticed Will was standing next to him. They stood side by side sharing the scene together. Will spoke at length.

'That smell reminds me of her.'

Edward nodded. 'Yes, she used to keep lavender bags in her clothes drawers, didn't she, so her clothes smelled sweetly. I always think of her when I smell it.'

'So do I,' Will agreed. There was another long silence and then Will spoke again.

'There'll always be lavender, won't there?'

Edward could not help smiling at this observation. 'Of course there will.'

'Good. What happened to Mother's things?'

'I don't know. I think Father has kept her room exactly as it was.'

'What do you think happened to her ring? The diamond one she used to wear. I used to love it when it sparkled in the light.'

'I really don't know, Will. I suppose it's still in her room. Why do you ask?'

'I was just thinking.'

'What?'

'When we give Tom Harris his lighter back, he might have use for a nice ring, mightn't he?'

Edward spun and looked at his brother. 'Are you sure?'

Will nodded and there was a gleam in his eyes.

'Right, let's get to work then,' said Edward, turning back to the machine. 'We'll have to move the machine back down to my laboratory again. I don't think there'll be enough power for more than thirty seconds of time-travel so you'll need to be right next to the hut. I'll go and wake Stokes again to help me move it. You go and find Mother's ring.'

Will turned and ran lightly to the door, but Edward called out again just before he left the room.

'Will?' The boy turned and looked expectantly. 'I think you've grown since I saw you last.' Will grinned and left.

Tom Harris stood despondently outside his hut. He had changed out of his wet things but he was still chilled to the bone. The kettle was taking a long time to boil and while it was heating he hunted around on the ground outside in search of his elusive cigarette lighter. Every minute or so he would glance up at the house where John Sullivan had gone to tell Sally about the lost gift. His troubled emotions stirred again – anger, grief and frustration jostling for first place, but all of them trailing behind despair. This was surely the end of him and Sal. There was no way he could wriggle out of this one. His eyes dropped back to the dewy grass again and he continued his search.

'Hey, Tom.' A child's voice sounded behind him. He spun and for the second time he was confronted by Will Rawlings. He recoiled in fear and tried to speak, his nervous eyes twitching this way and that.

'Wh . . . What are . . .' He could not continue.

'Can't stop long, Tom. You'll understand one day. Got something for you.' He tossed a little brown paper package at Tom who moved to catch it but missed, his fingers trembling from fear and cold. 'It's two things, Tom. One is something that belongs to you. The other's a little present to make up for all the trouble we've caused you. Use it well.'

With that the boy was gone and Tom was left blinking in amazement. Questions were crowding into his mind. What is going on? And why was Will's ghost wearing such strange clothes? Only a minute or two later did the question of what was in the package come into his head. He stooped and grabbed the bundle, tearing off the paper as he examined the contents. A big smile spread slowly across his face.

'Tom?' A female voice sounded sharply behind him. 'Tom, is it true?' Tom turned to face Sally and saw ugly John Sullivan standing far too close to her, looking smug. Tom would soon change that, but there was no hurry. He would do it in style.

'Hello dear,' Tom smiled sweetly. 'What's that ugly slug doing here?'

Sally frowned. 'He's not ugly, Tom, so don't you be so cruel. He's been good enough to tell me how much you care about my presents, Tom Harris. Is it true?' There was anger in her voice but the tears in her eyes showed sadness, as if she were longing for it not to be true. Tom said nothing but patted his coat pockets as if searching for something. John Sullivan grinned. Tom pulled out an old pipe and a leather pouch of tobacco and slowly and methodically he filled the bowl, pressing the dark brown tobacco into it with a dirty thumbnail. When the pipe was full he gripped the stem between his teeth and began absently patting his pockets again. John Sullivan smirked and stepping forward he pulled out his matches.

'I expect you'll need a light, Tom,' he began. Then his jaw dropped and he stared silently as Tom pulled out a brass cigarette lighter. With a flick of the mechanism the fierce little flame burst into life and after a couple of puffs Tom's pipe was lit.

'Is what true, my love?' Sally said nothing but her face shone with happiness. Tom continued. 'Is it true that John Sullivan is an ugly liar? Yep, that's true all right.'

Sally turned angrily on John who backed off uncertainly. He was confused but one thing was clear – he had lost the lead in the race for Sally.

'I . . .' he began but was instantly silenced by a resounding slap across his face. Anger burned in his eyes to match the smarting red hand-print that was fast appearing on his cheek. 'Why you little . . .' He would have said more but Tom was already between them.

'I've had enough of your company today, John Sullivan,' he growled. 'Why don't you clear off?' He puffed a cloud of smoke into John Sullivan's face.

John's hand clenched into a fist but he mastered himself and scowling fiercely he turned and strode off.

A moment later Sally was in Tom's arms. Her head was buried in his neck and she cried as she spoke. 'I'm sorry, Tom. I'm so sorry. I don't know what I ever saw in him. You're the man for me, Tom Harris.'

Tom could not remember ever being happier and he let her carry on saying nice things for a little longer while he stroked her hair. Presently her crying and talking subsided and Tom looked Sally in the face.

'I've got something for you, Sal.' He took her hand and, telling her to shut her eyes, he slipped the diamond ring on to her left hand. Her eyes sparkled as she opened them and she threw her arms around him again.

'Oh, Tom, it's beautiful!'

'It's for you to remember me by when I'm gone to war, Sal.'

'I'll remember you every moment of every day, Tom,' she murmured, 'and I'll be here waiting when you come home.'

Tom smiled contentedly and he knew that she would.

Jed and Lizzie slipped out through the French windows and began to make their way home. They were glad to get away and no one seemed to be paying much attention to them now. The ambulance had come and taken Edward to hospital and the man had been right; his wound was not that serious. He had woken briefly as he was moved on to the stretcher and he had caught their anxious expressions as they watched him. He managed a smile. There was a lot to talk about but that would have to wait. The man in the pyjamas had turned out to be Tom Harris's grandson somehow. The police had come and interviewed the children and old Tom Harris. Their stories seemed to agree that a man in a black jacket had broken into the library of Rawlings House and had shot Edward during a struggle. The children were allowed home on the understanding that they report to the police station the next day to make an official statement. They left the police taking photographs, dusting the room for fingerprints and embarking on a search of the grounds. Morgan seemed to be long gone though.

The brother and sister walked down the drive of Rawlings House and out on to the street.

'Well, that seemed to turn out all right,' Jed observed. 'What was it like in 1879?'

'Great,' said Lizzie. 'Edward was really nice, but their dad was scary. What's going on, Jed?'

'Huh?'

'What's going on? Why's everything different?'

Jed spoke slowly. 'I'm not sure but I suppose the past has been changed and so things are different now. I seem to be remembering things I didn't know before. How about you?'

Lizzie nodded. 'It's all a bit muddled at the moment. I hope it gets clearer.'

'I hope it's all changed for the better. It would be terrible if we found out really bad things were happening now because of what we'd done.'

'It all seems good so far. Ed's still here, for one thing,' Lizzie observed.

Jed agreed. 'And that man seems to be Mr Harris's grandson which means he must have got married. Do you think it was to Sally?'

'I hope so. I asked Edward to return the lighter if he could. Mr Harris still lives at the house even though it's not a nursing home any more.'

'Yeah, that is strange. I wonder what it is now. There's a lot to find out.'

The two of them walked on together in silence before Jed spoke again. He sounded confused.

'Lizzie, d'you remember where we live?'

'Of course . . .' Lizzie began but then tailed off, confused like her brother. 'That is I think I do. Why?'

'Well, I thought we turned off here.'

Lizzie put her head on one side as she grappled with her shifting memories. 'Yes, you're right. We do turn off here,' she said at last.

'Where has the road gone, then?'

Jed and Lizzie turned to face their street and saw nothing but trees and grassland.

Rob Stokes had his eyes shut and he was not sure why. He felt as if he had just been picked up, spun around a few times and put back down again. Where was he? That was right. He was in the car in the middle of the night being interviewed by a policeman because of suspicious behaviour. He groaned as he opened his eyes. There were better situations to wake up to. The policeman was still talking.

'I asked you what you are doing here, sir.'

'Yes, officer, you did.' He cast his mind about trying to remember what he actually had been doing. He did not have to tell the policeman of course but it would be comforting if he himself knew. That way he could tell a lie and be sure it really was a lie. He massaged his temples gently as he thought, but it was no good, he did not have a clue.

'I . . .' he began vaguely but just then a little clear thought popped into his head. He concentrated and bit by bit the thought grew like a beacon casting its light on to confused darkness. So that was what he was doing here. Of course. On reflection it seemed as if honesty might be the best policy after all.

'Why am I here, officer?' he said lightly. 'I'm here because I live here.' Now it was the policeman's turn to be confused.

'Do you?' Dad fished out his driving licence which showed his address. 'I see, sir,' the policeman said at last. 'Well that seems to be all in order then. Sorry to have troubled you. Good night, sir.'

'Good night, officer,' cried Dad jubilantly from the car window as he watched the retreating figure. 'And thank you for your concern. One can never be too careful about suspicious characters and you have been a credit to your force. Fear not, loyal officer,' Dad exclaimed, really going over the top. 'Many have criticized the police force for over-officious interference and I myself have been guilty of that slur. But rest assured, you defenders of justice, you will get a glowing report in my next column in the . . .' Dad stopped himself, startled at what he was about to say. '. . . in *The Times.*'

He turned to his wife as the policeman's car roared into life and disappeared down the country lane. 'How long have I worked for *The Times*, dear?'

There were tears running down Mum's cheeks as she leaned over and hugged her husband. 'Can we go inside now?' she said.

'We certainly can, darling,' he said and putting his hand into his pocket he pulled out the key to the front door of Little Moor.

Breakfast was late at the Stokes's that morning. Mum and Dad, after the initial joy of finding out where they lived, had realized that Jed and Lizzie were miles from home and were probably trying to get into the wrong house. A quick car journey had found the two children looking lost at the place where they thought their road was. Then after emotional reunions the family had stayed up late into the night swapping stories and experiences.

The eleven o'clock news bulletin was playing on the radio as the family ate their toast and drank their coffee:

. . . Mr Edward Rawlings, heir to the rawlite fortune, is today recovering in hospital from a gun wound received while challenging an intruder late last night at his home, Rawlings House, in Milford. His condition is described as stable. The intruder has not yet been apprehended. He is described as a man in his forties with grey hair wearing a black jacket. The

public are advised not to approach him as he is armed and dangerous. And now the shipping forecast . . .

Dad reached over and switched the radio off. 'So they haven't caught Morgan yet. I wonder if they ever will. He's a bit of a mystery, that man.'

'Yeah,' agreed Lizzie. 'We still don't know where he comes from.'

'Or when,' added Jed. 'Do you think we should tell the police what we know?'

'Well,' Dad considered, 'you could, but having to visit you in your padded cell afterwards might prove tiresome eventually.'

'So we're sticking by our story then. We saw a man in a black jacket in the library and Ed tackled him.'

'Spot on, son.'

'Dear Ed,' said Mum. 'I'm so happy for him. After thinking he wouldn't even be here we find him not only alive and well but apparently one of the richest men in England too.'

'Yeah, what happened?' asked Jed. 'Where did all his money come from? And what is rawlite? It seems like a word I know really well, like I hear it ten times a day, but I don't know what it is.'

Nobody could shed any light on the matter so the conversation turned to their own changed lives.

'Won't you get into trouble for not being at work, Dad?' Lizzie asked.

'Well, Lizzie, I might be, were it not for two things. One, it's Saturday.'

'Is it?' Lizzie seemed genuinely surprised. 'I think it was Thursday when I left 1879.'

'And two,' continued Dad. 'I don't go to work. Haven't done for years.' Three pairs of eyes fixed on Dad in amazement. 'That's right,' he said. 'Although my memory isn't quite sorted out yet I've managed to work out what's been going on in our lives with the aid of my diary.'

'Do you keep a diary, Dad?'

'I do indeed, Jed. I have plans one day to publish my memoirs so it's useful to keep a day by day account to act as an *aide-mémoire* to help me write my life story.'

Jed looked confused. 'Are you talking English, Dad?

'No, French.'

Jed nodded. 'That's why I can't understand you. Anyway, what does your diary say?'

'It says that about ten years ago, we received a legacy from an unknown benefactor.'

'That's someone who left us some money without telling us who they were,' Mum translated.

'I'll bet I can guess who,' Lizzie smiled.

'Yes,' said Dad. 'I think it's pretty clear who was responsible. About a hundred years before the money came to us, someone had invested £10,000 for us at six per cent a year.'

'How much was it worth when we got it?'

'Nearly three-and-a-half million,' grinned Dad. There was a stunned silence as this news sunk in. Then Dad continued. 'Which is why I don't go to work anymore and neither does your Mum, come to that.'

'Don't I?' Mum wrestled with her memory for a while. 'No, you're right, I don't.'

'All I do,' said Dad, 'is write a weekly column for *The Times* and the odd novel here and there. Otherwise I am a man of leisure who has enough money to send his kids to a decent school.'

A look of dread passed over Jed's face and he clutched his head in despair. 'Oh no! I've just had a really nasty memory,' he groaned. 'I go to Randall's, don't I?'

Edward stood nervously outside his father's library, fidgeting restlessly. It had been a long time since he had had to stand outside his headmaster's study at Randall's but the old feelings seemed very familiar again. He clutched a few items in his hands. His conversation throughout the night with Will had told him many things and he knew now what he had to do. Knowing he had to do it did not make it any easier though. Will's last words to him had not helped. 'Remember,' he had said, 'try and do what you think is right which isn't necessarily the same as doing what you want.' Edward laughed hollowly as his own advice came back to haunt him.

Josiah called for Edward to enter. He gave his son a cold look when he stood before him and then he opened the interrogation. 'You look dreadful. Did you sleep in those clothes?'

'No, Father.' Edward did not lie. He had not slept in them as he had not slept at all. He had not changed though.

Josiah grunted and Edward shuffled his feet awkwardly. Josiah eventually spoke again. 'Edward, you have defied me outright and plotted to deceive me times beyond counting in the past few weeks. Am I right?'

'Yes Father, but . . .'

'No "buts",' the old man glared. 'Yes is a sufficient answer. Not only have you disobeyed me but your defiance is spreading. In full view of other members of the staff yesterday you persuaded Stokes, a senior servant here, to disobey my explicit order. I shall have to deal with Stokes, be it ever so severely, if this . . . this malaise of disobedience is to be stopped.'

'But Father . . .'

Josiah thumped the table. 'What did I say about "buts"?' Edward lapsed into silence. 'Now I am ready to confess that I might have been too hasty in preventing you from using your machine in order to recover Will. Hodges had told me that it made people disappear, but if it was not for the evidence of my own eyes I would have never believed such a thing was possible. I don't know what devilry you used to do it but it was truly remarkable.'

'Not the devil, Father, science. Although I'm beginning to wonder what the difference is.'

'Quite,' agreed Josiah. 'Now I recognize that a certain amount of subterfuge was necessary for you to retrieve your brother and the happy conclusion is that he is now back safe and well. You know what the consequences would have been had he not. Thankfully I can cancel the funeral arrangements. Who was that girl by the way?'

'That was Lizzie Stokes. You met her at the mill.'

'I remember I met her at the mill,' said Josiah irritably. 'I thought she was with Stokes. What did you do with her this morning? Where did she go when the machine was switched on?'

'Back to the twenty-first century, where she came from.'

'Indeed? And that is where Will was?'

'Yes, Father.'

'You have proof I suppose of this time travel?'

'Yes, indeed, Father.' Here some of Edward's old eagerness returned. He put down the items he had been clutching all through the conversation. 'This is a newspaper from 1940.' Josiah picked up the now grubby paper and looked at it in wonder. 'And this is a bottle of medicine from the twenty-first century.' Josiah turned his attention to it and twiddling the top he clicked the cap around and around.

'Seems a dashed silly bottle if you cannot get the top off the damned thing,' he growled.

'That's the ingenious thing about it, Father. You see the medicine is apparently quite potent and if you look at the cap it has the words "child safety cap" marked on it. It's to stop infants from drinking the medicine by mistake.'

'Ingenious? Doesn't seem ingenious to me if nobody can get the top off.'

'Ah, but adults can because they know how. There's a little ratchet mechanism in the cap which makes that clicking noise. Now if you push the top down as you twist then the ratchet is passed by and the top will unscrew.'

Josiah did as instructed. He pushed down hard and began to twist, his face tense with concentration. After a few more clicks the top suddenly slid round, flew off and spilled the sticky yellow liquid all over Josiah's black morning coat. Edward winced as Josiah quickly pulled out his large white handkerchief and began dabbing the liquid out of his clothes, muttering and grumbling as he did so.

'God help us,' he said, when he had regained his composure, 'if this is where the nation is heading.' He eyed the bottle with loathing in his eyes. Edward hurried to make amends.

'I wasn't interested in the bottle as much as what the bottle is made of.'

Josiah picked the bottle up again and studied it.

'What is it made of?'

'Apparently it's something called plastic. Will says everything is made of it in the twenty-first century.'

'Really,' said Josiah distastefully.

'Yes. Even this.' Edward offered the final item he was holding to Josiah, who seized it, looking more interested.

'This is the strange shirt Will was wearing, is it not?' He

examined the cloth carefully and took out a magnifying glass for a better look. Textiles were his business. 'Strange fabric. It's not cotton, or wool or linen. What else is there?'

'I told you, Father. It's made of plastic, like the bottle.'

'Don't be absurd. The bottle's a solid object and this is a cloth.'

'Yes, but the fibres are made out of the same substance, only stretched out fine.'

Josiah sat back in his chair deep in thought. Edward looked on anxiously. 'Is nobody wearing cotton then?' he asked at last.

'Apparently they are.' Josiah smiled with contentment before Edward continued. 'But they buy it all from India.'

'What?' Josiah was incredulous. 'But India's one of my best markets. They ought to be buying it, not selling it.'

'Lizzie did tell me that the mill is in ruins in her time and this house has been sold to become some sort of rest house for the old and diseased.'

Josiah rested his head in his hands in despair and Edward knew it was time to strike.

'Father, I think we need to get in on this plastic idea early. That way we'll be ahead of the game when the cotton industry collapses.'

'What are you suggesting?' groaned Josiah through his hands.

'I think I ought to be the man to invent it.'

Josiah looked up sharply. 'Do you know how to make it?'

'No,' Edward admitted. 'Not yet but I know I could find out. I have a suspicion it's an oil-based substance. It can't be that difficult.'

Josiah sat back in his chair, the tips of his fingers touching as he considered this idea for some time. 'The fact is, Edward,' he said at last, 'I called you in here this morning to discuss your outrageous conduct of late, and we have not even begun to talk about the tremendous risks you exposed your innocent brother to, and here I am being persuaded to reward you with more money for you to continue your researches.'

Edward lowered his eyes. 'I understand, Father, and I confess that my conduct with Will has been inexcusable. If it's any comfort I've suffered more than anyone these last few days, not knowing where Will was and feeling the responsibility of bringing him home.' Josiah grunted as if he was not much impressed with Edward's level of suffering. 'And,' he continued, 'I am decided that I must continue with your plans to send me to South Africa.'

Josiah's eyebrows shot up in surprise. 'Are you?'

'Yes, Father,' said Edward decidedly. 'Not only would it be fitting for me to go away for a while, but Will has shown me a photograph album of our descendants and apparently I am to meet my wife there.'

'Really? Your wife?' Josiah smiled mysteriously. 'What is the young lady like?'

'According to the family album, she is called Elizabeth and she is a very pretty girl.'

'Indeed. This punishment sounds more and more attractive, does it not?'

Edward tried to keep his mouth from smiling. 'It will be hard but I will do my level best to endure it with fortitude worthy of the name Rawlings.'

Josiah laughed out loud. 'Very well. You have beaten me. You shall have your trip to South Africa and an allowance of five hundred a year, but I shall expect good results.'

'You will have them, Father. I promise you. And Father?'

'Yes?'

'Don't be too hard on Stokes.'

Josiah's eyes narrowed. 'Stokes disobeyed my direct order and that cannot go unnoticed, Edward.'

'No, Father.'

'He shall be punished. I think extra responsibilities might make him recognize the serious nature of authority. When he has to give orders then he will soon grow to recognize the importance of obeying them.' Josiah's face twitched a little as if he were trying not to laugh. 'He will of course need a corresponding rise in pay to match his increased responsibility.'

'Thank you, Father,' said Edward.

DECEMBER 24TH, 1882

Will Rawlings lay on the sofa in front of the roaring log fire with a book propped open on his chest. Josiah paced up and down anxiously, stopping occasionally to nervously adjust a decoration on the tree or speak irritably to Will.

'William, for goodness' sake get your feet off the furniture. You've still got your boots on.'

'Yes, Father,' the boy said absently. He moved his feet perhaps an inch and continued to read. Josiah continued to pace.

'Why don't they come?' he asked a minute later, not for the first time.

Will snapped his book shut and sat up. 'They only said they would try to be here by Christmas, Father.' Stokes entered the room.

'Yes, yes?' cried the old man eagerly.

'I was wondering if you needed anything, sir.'

'Yes I do. I need to be told that my son has come home.'

Stokes smiled indulgently at his employer. 'Very good, sir. I will do my best to give satisfaction in that quarter when the situation arises. Is there anything else?'

'No,' said Josiah wearily. 'You may go.'

'Very good, sir.' The servant withdrew.

'He's getting very good, isn't he?' said Will.

'Who?'

'Stokes. I mean he really sounds like a butler now, and he's getting fat enough to be one.'

Josiah was about to tell Will a thing or two about respect for elders when there was a sharp rap at the door. Not even waiting for a servant to answer Josiah himself left the room at top speed and opened the door on to the wet night. Two figures muffled in oilskins stood there.

'Edward?' There was a tremble in the old man's voice. The taller figure threw back his raincoat and Edward's curly hair and piercing eyes confronted them. 'Edward!' cried Josiah again. Disregarding the rain and wind, he threw his arm around Edward's shoulder and gripped him hard. He held him for a moment before speaking. 'It's good to have you home, son.'

'It's good to be here, Father.'

'But what am I doing? How could I be so rude? We've left the young lady standing on the doorstep. Come in, my dear, come in.'

The smaller figure entered and began removing her oilskins. Her black hair dripped water and her dark eyes looked up nervously at her father-in-law.

'Father,' said Edward proudly. 'I would like to introduce my wife, Elizabeth. Elizabeth, this is my father.'

'I'm very pleased to meet you, sir,' said Elizabeth. 'Edward speaks so much about you and Will that I feel I know you both already.'

'And I am delighted to meet you.' He took the young lady's hand. 'This house has been without the civilizing presence of a lady for too long. You are most welcome indeed.' Elizabeth smiled at the old man's warmth and squeezed his hand in return. 'This is capital! Let us go in and get you both warm. Edward, tell me how your research is coming along? Any nearer the elusive formula? When can I expect to see this plastic?'

'Plastic, Father?' grinned Edward. 'We're going to call it rawlite.'